But what was that! Daphne saw a quick sharp light like a single beam cutting the darkness in the cellar! Instantly it was gone, but then a dancing speck of light flashed around at the end of the house, low-flashing, then sweeping in a wide circle, showing quick glimpses of shrubs and bushes, glancing across the dark hood of a huge truck. Suddenly something heavy dropped and there was a movement in the bushes, a stealthy closing of the cellar door, and silence! Awful menacing silence!

A moment later Daphne heard the sound of feet in the grass hurrying along the end of the house—and three gun shots rang out in quick succession. Then she heard a moan . . .

Grace Livingston Hill

DAPHNE DEANE

Guideposts®

CARMEL • NEW YORK 10512

Printing History
J. B. Lippincott edition published 1937
Tyndale House edition/1991

This Guideposts edition is
published by special arrangement
with Tyndale House Publishers.

THE sky was very blue, yet there were tiny dabs of cotton clouds lingering in the offing for a glorious sunset which they understood was being staged that evening. The sun was golden and gracious, sifting down like fine powdered metal dust over the late afternoon, and glorifying even the grimy old sweatshirts of the ball players as they hurtled over the wide diamond, or poised with hands on bent knees, and intent gaze on the pitcher.

High up on the grandstand, a village-made affair of weatherbeaten boards, Keith Morrell sat outlined against the golden-blue of the sky. He was not especially interested in the ball game, but the grandstand offered the only attractive resting place while he waited for the five o'clock train, which was supposed to bring a local real estate agent who had charge of the old Morrell homestead. He had written the agent, William Knox, that he would be at his office that afternoon to consult with him about the sale or rental of the place, but Knox with the easy-going ways of the suburban agent, had gone to the nearby city to meet another man, and left word he would be back at five o'clock. Keith Morrell was thoroughly disgusted with him, and almost minded to go away without seeing him, only that he knew he would have to return another day, inevitably, and who knew but Knox would have another call to the city when he came the next time? So he strolled about the familiar streets a few minutes until he discovered the ball game going on at the old stand where he had often played himself in days gone by. He climbed to the top row and sat there looking about him, trying to bring back the picture of other days, trying to bridge the five years that had passed since he had been in town last.

A great many things had happened since then. The family had closed the house during his second year in college and gone to Europe, and he had spent his summers there with them, his briefer vacations with classmates at their homes. Then at the close of his college course he had met his parents in England and they had toured the orient together for several months. It was while he was taking a special course in architecture in England that his father had died, and a year later his mother. All the ties of his boyhood home wiped out! And now he was back in his native land and his native town!

He hadn't wanted to come here. His mother's death was too recent and he dreaded old familiar scenes. His grief was too new to bear going back to where his life had been so closely associated with hers. But the agent had insisted that he come and understand thoroughly the terms on which the prospective buyer would take the house, and finally he had come, running down from New York on the noon train, hoping to get the matter finished and get the four o'clock train back. This delay was most annoying.

He looked around at the people who were beginning to swarm up the little grandstand. It would soon be filled to cap-acity, for Rosedale was only a suburb, and this ball ground was just a village enterprise, a sort of community affair.

He looked down among the players, and marveled

that they all seemed so young to him, none over sixteen or seventeen. They seemed so much more immature than high school students had when he was one of them. And yet, he had been only seventeen himself when he was graduated from high school. Had he looked as youthful as some of those kids down there tearing around that diamond as if the fate of a universe depended upon winning that game?

Suddenly it came to him that he was thinking in terms of a very old man who was soured on life, and here he was barely twenty-three. Probably to some other eyes he looked even now as immature as those youngsters down there did to him.

And just then one of the fellows, tall, well-built, with springy brown hair that waved crisply, walked over from the bench below the grandstand to a girl sitting at the extreme end of the stand, in the third row up, and handed her a watch and a wallet. He was a nice-looking chap with big brown eyes and well-chiseled features. And he didn't look so immature after all, now when he raised his eyes and smiled. He was probably only about seventeen at the most, but already there was a set about his well-molded chin and his pleasant lips that showed determination and purpose.

Keith noticed the girl now for the first time. She must just have taken her seat for the place had been vacant a moment before, he was quite sure. She was a pretty girl. She had ripply brown hair like the boy's, yet where the sunlight touched it, it gleamed almost golden.

Then she lifted her eyes and turned about, looking up behind where Morrell sat, in answer to a motion of the boy. They were both looking up and waving to someone at the farther end of the seat, an older man with iron-gray hair and a plain business suit who smiled and waved back to them. The girl had brown eyes too. The boy and girl must be brother and sister. When they smiled they looked very much alike. The girl's features were delicate and lovely. There was a haunting familiarity in them. Could it be that she reminded him of his mother? It seemed to him that she looked as he imagined his mother might have looked at nineteen or twenty. Was she someone he should remember? No, surely not, for he never could have forgotten a face like that! He reviewed rapidly the local girls he used to know, girls who were in his social set before he went to college, but she was none of them. No, she must be some newcomer since he left.

And now the skirmishing on the field had stopped and the real game had begun. He could see the good-looking young giant who had just given his watch to the girl on the stand, stride out and take his place. Ah! He was pitcher! Morrell settled into a comfortable position, his hands clasped around one knee, and gave himself up to the beauty of the day, in retrospect imagining himself a boy again with a real interest in that game down there.

Then his gaze wandered back again to the girl as she sat watching. He noticed the sweetness of her face and studied it idly, letting it recall his mother's sweet expression. It interested him to watch her.

She did not seem to have come with anybody, she was sitting apart from the young people who were clamoring noisily to one another about the game. She had just dropped down at the end there among the younger children. They smiled at her now and then, and one little girl reached across two others, gave her a bunch of wilted violets to hold and received a radiant smile. Could that be her little sister? And why was he so much interested? Just because he was lonely, and afraid of thinking back into the past? Then there came a boy of twelve, all out of breath, bearing a bag from the grocery that looked as if it might contain a loaf of bread, and dumped it in the girl's lap. That must be another brother. He was asking for something. A clean handkerchief was handed out surreptitiously and he hurried around to the front to curl down on the grass with his knees drawn up to his chin. Yes, that must be her brother. But there was a different kind of understanding between this sister and her family from that of most girls with their younger brothers and sisters. At least, the girls he knew. There was no impatience in this girl's face, no protest at being made a dumping-ground for their various belongings. There seemed to be a comradery between them, as if they were all a part of a pleasant whole.

He studied the girl intently. More and more he admired the expression of her face. There was nothing sharp or self-centered or restless about it. It almost seemed as if the word peace would describe the look in her eyes as she turned to smile at the little girl.

She was wearing a simple white dress, cool and becoming, and a trig little white felt hat which showed her soft brown hair. To his eyes, her costume seemed to fit perfectly the day and the moment. It almost seemed as he studied her that she wore her garments with distinction. And yet there was a sweet quietness of refinement that set her apart from the crowd of smart young people who obviously felt themselves to be socially the elite of the town. Her garments lacked the bold sophistication that marked so many of her day. There was no lipstick and no rouge, he was sure, about that face. He hadn't thought about it before, but suddenly he knew he had an aversion to lipstick. There was a soft flush on this girl's cheek that he felt sure was real. He found himself glancing again and again in her direction. And when the young giant pitcher was doing his part she had on her face a breathless interest that made the soft color deepen. Yes, that was real!

Suddenly he realized that he had been staring at her, and she must have felt it, for she turned and let her glance go sweeping up over the seat back of her until it found his gaze, and her eyes went wide, and full of something almost like recognition. For an instant he thought she was going to nod to him as if she knew him. She didn't of course, but he wished she had. His glance lingered and suddenly there was withdrawing in hers, a kind of quick blankness and a hurrying on of her gaze, but the color had stolen up over her cheeks as she turned away. She had probably thought he was someone else and then discovered her mistake and was embarrassed by it. He felt a definite disappointment. He almost wished that he had been able in time to make his own glance a little more encouraging. He had never practiced the art of picking up strange girls, but here was a girl he felt he would distinctly like to know. Strangely familiar, too, yet he could not place her.

His thought traveled back to Anne Casper, the girl he had been trying to persuade himself he was interested in. She had been definitely the cause of irritation to him for the last week or two, because she insisted on taking a part in the fashion show that was being put on in a smart resort that month for the benefit of some charitable purpose; modeling, by her own choice, some exceedingly modern bathing suits. He thought of it now with a frown as he continued to study furtively the girl down at the end. Was he all wrong? Was it true as Anne Casper had tried to convince him that everybody, "simply *everybody*" wore such brief garments on the beach all day and nobody thought anything of it? Why was he so sure that this girl wouldn't appear in one of those obnoxious affairs? Was it just because she reminded him of his lady-mother, and he knew she would not have approved such apparel?

More and more as the game went on he became interested in watching the girl's reaction to the game, and her eagerness in her brother's good work. More and more he wished he had some way of meeting her. But she did not so much as glance around again.

Well, he would be gone back to New York in a short time now, and he would likely never know who she was. And that was too bad, for he would certainly like to test out his intuitions about her and see whether she was different from the girls he knew, or whether after all she was just a girl like any of them and would prove to be just as disappointing as they all were, if he once had a chance to meet her intimately.

He found himself taking a deep interest in the young pitcher. Good work he was doing, and the team was playing up to him well. When that chap got to college he would likely make a name for himself in the athletic world.

The sun was getting lower, and the lights on the girl's hair were beginning to take on a reddish tinge instead of the gold. The game had been a clean close one, and would soon be over now. It was almost time for the agent's train to come in, but Keith Morrell had forgotten about that train. He was trying to plan a way to get nearer to that girl, to see how she really looked face to face, to invent some excuse for speaking to her. Perhaps if he was nimble and got down to her vicinity before the game was quite finished, she might drop one of her parcels, or the wallet she was holding, and he might be fortunate enough to pick it up and restore it to her. It might give him a legitimate cause for looking into her eyes, even for speaking perhaps.

So much did this thought obsess him that when two men beside him rose and stepped over his feet to get down, he followed them stealthily, unobtrusively to the ground, making his way by a devious path over behind the grandstand, and mingled with a group at her end of the stand who were eagerly watching the finish of the game. He did not turn to look at her, but from the side of his eye a furtive glance could see her now and then.

When the game was over she did not drop one of her packages as he had hoped, but she lingered for a moment standing by her seat till the big pitcher came over with his sweater tied around his broad shoulders and claimed his wallet and watch. He grinned at her, said a hurried word and departed with his gang. She watched him go with a smile and came slowly away, still smiling, speaking to this one and that, but not mingling with the crowd.

The little girl came eagerly with a crowd of companions and explained something, then flew off with the girls, and the youngster from the grass came and restored a grimy handkerchief and was off with another boy. The girl turned across the field and walked away toward the street.

It was just then that Morrell's path crossed hers. She looked up and their eyes met. Then, suddenly he was sure that he had seen her before. He lifted his hat, his most courteous smile upon his lips, and spoke:

"I wonder if you aren't somebody I used to know," he said eagerly. And now he wasn't at all sure that she was, and there was a puzzled earnestness in his eyes as he looked into hers.

"Why, yes, I am," she said with a little twinkling smile playing almost mischievously about the lips, "but so very unimportantly that I doubt if you remember it."

He had a feeling that she was quietly laughing at him, though her voice was very gentle, but the color came into his face. She had seen that he did not know who she was. He felt suddenly mortified.

"It does not seem to me that anyone could have known you once and not have remembered you," he said. "I felt there was something familiar about you when I first saw you, but I'm ashamed to say I cannot place you. I decided perhaps it was just that you reminded me of someone. Do you mind telling me who you are? If there was any acquaintance at all I'd like to renew it."

"Oh, it wasn't an acquaintance," she said quickly. "I was only in your algebra class. You probably never knew I existed."

He turned and looked sharply into her face, trying to trace out a memory of her.

"You weren't that littlest girl of all, were you? The one with brown curls who was promoted into the class in the middle of the semester, and then beat us all in exams? The smartest one of the class?"

The girl laughed.

"I don't know about the smartness. I had the brown curls and I was small enough. I used to be very sensitive about that. My name is Daphne Deane."

There was a sweet dignity about her as she said it, and Keith Morrell's eyes lit up with interest as he watched her.

"Now I remember. Yes, you were smart. I remember being terribly mortified that you got a problem once that I couldn't master. I sat up half the next night till I'd worked every problem in the lesson perfectly. No more taking chances the way I had been doing, not with you in the class!"

Daphne laughed.

"And I remember being terribly afraid of you," she said. "I never studied so hard in my life as that winter, just because I didn't want you to get ahead of me."

He grinned.

"We must have been helping each other a lot, I should say, though neither of us was aware of it. But say! I still can't place you beyond algebra class. Where did you live? I surely must have met you elsewhere besides in school."

"I think not," said Daphne gravely. "I never moved in your social orbit at all. I lived just where I live now. In the house that used to be the gardener's house on your father's estate!"

She lifted pleasant amused eyes to watch his face. What would he think of that? And she saw a look of utter amazement come over his face.

"You don't mean it!" he said. "As near as that, and yet I didn't know you! I cannot understand."

"That's easy to explain," she said lightly. "While we were growing up Mother kept us very close at home. Always in our own yard, except when we went to school or church, and our way to those led around another block from the way you went. Besides, you were a little older than I was. We just never came into any other contact, that's all. Although I knew you a great deal better than you ever knew me." She laughed again dreamily.

"Oh, I say!" said the young man wistfully. "Was that quite fair? Please tell me about it."

"Well, I guess there wasn't anything underhanded about it," said Daphne, "it was all perfectly natural. You remember the gardener's house—which we rented for a while until father was able to buy it, after your garage was built with accommodations for your gardener over it?—it was in direct line with the western gable of your house. You know there was a rather high stone wall about our place and from downstairs we could see very little of what went on at 'the big house' as we always spoke of your home, but from our upstairs back windows we could look across straight into the windows of your end room there. I've never been in your home of course, but I know pretty well the layout of that room for it was my fairyland to watch when I was a little girl. It had a great fireplace at the other side of the room directly opposite the big wide windows, and sometimes when the fire was burning it was our delight to stand with our noses against our windowpanes and watch the flames leap and dance over in your room. I don't know whether it was your playroom or nursery or what, when you were a little boy, but I can remember seeing you sitting on the floor in front of the fire building blockhouses, and running your wonderful electric train when you were a little older. Mother used to use you as an example of perfection for us children. One night when we were whining at having to go to bed I remember mother saying, 'Come now, away with you to bed! The little boy at the great house is saying his prayers in front of the fire, and if you don't look out he'll beat you to bed!' And when we went to the window we could see you in pretty blue pajamas kneeling by your mother's knee in front of the fire, with your head in her lap. And after that we always ran to the window when we were sent to bed to see if the little boy in the big house was on his way to bed, too. But there! I shouldn't have told you that! You'll think we were very nosey little children, prying on your devotions that way."

"No, I won't think that!" said Keith gravely. "It's very touching to think you knew about those days—" His voice was husky with feeling. "I didn't know there was anybody left now that knew about those days since mother died. I think it's rather wonderful for you to tell me that."

Daphne's cheeks were scarlet now with embarrassment. She looked up keenly to see if he was sincere.

"I was just thinking aloud," she apologized. "You see, it was the only excitement we children had when we were little, to watch the big house, and we wove it all into a sort of fairy tale. Mother had only to say, 'The little boy at the big house is going in from play now to do his lessons, and you must hurry in too and get your spelling, or he will get his homework done before you do,' and we would hustle in breathlessly and settle down to our tasks. You see you really were a means of grace in our household."

Daphne looked up and smiled, trying to cover her confusion with frankness.

He looked down at her wistfully.

"Well, I'm sure I wish I had known about it. Such rivalry might have been a means of grace to me, too. I'm quite sure I wasn't the angel-child you would make it appear. I guess I was taught to say my prayers all right, but I'm quite sure I *un*said them many a time when I wasn't being staged before a fireplace for an unknown and admiring public. But please tell me, if I was so well known to you, how was it that the only memory I have of you is that brief session of school when you were in my algebra class? How was it that I didn't meet you out places as we grew up? How was it that we didn't play together as children if our yards joined?"

Daphne smiled a bit distantly.

"Oh, we weren't in the same class with you socially at all, of course. My father had lost his modest fortune in a bank failure and we were living in the gardener's house. And your father was a wealthy bank president living in a great beautiful old house with everything that money could buy. We had absolutely no contacts at all. Even that six months we were together in algebra we scarcely knew one another to speak to."

"But why was that? My mother had no feeling of pride of that sort, pride of wealth or house or family. She only questioned whether my companions were decently behaved."

Daphne's eyes were downcast, but then she lifted them and raised her firm young chin with a little smile.

"I'm afraid my mother had," she said wistfully. "She did not want to force her way to the notice of people who might well consider her beneath them. She kept us very closely in the confines of our own yard. She was very careful who came to play with us, and she gave us our social contacts through make-believe. That was how you came to be our hero, you know, and how it came about that you never saw us enough to remember us."

The young man studied her face.

"It seems to have been a charmed way of bringing children up," he said. "But when you grew older, when your father bought the house and it was no longer our gardener's place, surely you went out among the other young people of the town? How was it that I did not meet you?"

Daphne shook her head.

"No, we didn't go out much then, either. Father was paying for the house, and saving to send us to college. We didn't have money for dressing the way others did who went out socially, and besides Mother had ideas about a lot of things, especially about girls' recreations when they were in school. And then afterward, you went away to college, you know."

"Yes, I know, but there were things before that. The high school affairs, picnics and parties and the like. There were a lot of functions, I remember. Did you never come to those?"

Daphne gravely shook her head.

"No, I had no time. Mother was sick all my senior year. I had to hurry home to work. I was housekeeper. She was very sick for a long time. We were afraid we were going to lose her." Her voice trembled a little.

"Oh!" he said, "I didn't know. But I do remember I voted that your essay was the best of all. I was sorry that they did not make you valedictorian of the class instead of me. I told the principal so."

"That was nice of you," said Daphne. "I should have been terribly set up if I had known that. But of course I was only in that class on grace, having been promoted so late in the semester. It wouldn't have been right at all."

"Well, I think it would have been right. But of course the faculty didn't see it that way so I couldn't do anything about it. But I think true merit should always be recognized even if it does establish a precedent. Your essay was very original, and mine was merely technical."

She lifted her eyes to his.

"I thought yours was original," she said earnestly, "I never heard anybody get together a lot of statistics like those and make them really interesting, and then go to work and draw conclusions from them that held a vital truth."

"Did you think I did that?" he asked studying her face. "I tried to, but I didn't think it got across. Not with the professor anyway. He wanted me to leave that part out. I never thought he quite understood it, or else he didn't approve it. I used to suspect him of being a communist at heart. But of course, I was very young."

"You had very keen thoughts though," said the girl. "I used to enjoy hearing your essays read because there was always something worth while in them. I didn't always agree with them. I was young, too, you know, and had ideas. But your essays were always interesting, and I loved the way you never fenced with an issue, but always faced it and clarified it."

"Say, that's great praise! Did I really ever do that?"

"You certainly did. That time when you were discussing the foreign policies, you made it so simple that the very dumbest of us could understand. And the one on the gold standard. I thought that ought to be published. As I think back to it I still think it should. You know you were ahead of your times in anticipating some things that I haven't noticed anywhere else."

"But I was only a kid," he mused. "I guess likely I had absorbed some of my father's ideas. You know, I had a wonderful father."

"And a wonderful mother," breathed the girl softly. "Oh, I didn't know her face to face, but a girl can't watch a woman from a little distance daily, as I did your mother, and not know what she's like. And I guess my mother helped on my image of her, for she admired her very much, too. She had a lovely face and a charming, gracious way. You could see it in every movement as she walked about the grounds sometimes with her arm across your shoulder, looking down into your face when you were just a child. But there! I'm revealing again what a shameless onlooker I was."

"I think we should be very much honored that anyone had such unbiased interest in us," he said smiling. "I only regret that my mother couldn't have known you as you seem to have known her. I am sure the interest would have been mutual. Do you know what I thought of when I saw you sitting down on the grandstand below me? I wonder if I dare tell you? I thought you looked somehow familiar, and couldn't think who you reminded me of, and then it came over me that you reminded me of my mother. Somehow your expression made me think of her, the light in your eyes. I always felt that my mother was the dearest thing on earth."

"Oh!" said Daphne a little breathlessly, "that is the very nicest compliment I ever received. Of course I know I attain to being like her, but I shall treasure that thought at least. For she was very lovely. Mother feels that way, too."

They were almost to the Deane gate now, a white picket affair with an old-fashioned latch, set in the arch of a thick hedge, and Daphne paused and wondered whether she should ask him in. But before she had the opportunity, a flashy yellow sports car which neither of them had noticed coming toward them, drew up with a flourish at the curb, and a rich assured voice called out:

"Well of all things, if there isn't Keith Morrell! Where have you been keeping yourself, darling? I hadn't heard you were in town."

2

THE girl in the yellow sports car leaned over and addressed herself to Keith Morrell. "If this isn't the best luck! If anyone was heaven-sent it is you. Do you know what you are going to do? You are going to hop right in with me and go home to my dinner party. I've just had a telegram from one of the men I'd depended on that he's met with an accident and can't come, and what to do I didn't know. I was on my way out into the highways and hedges to compel someone to come in to make even couples, and who should I happen on but you?"

She had gushed on giving no space for greeting, and she smiled into Keith Morrell's face, utterly ignoring Daphne Deane.

Young Morrell turned a bewildered gaze toward the young woman and tried to think quickly, back five years.

"Why, it's Evelyn Avery, isn't it?" he said politely, lifting his hat, searching out a possible classmate from a face almost utterly changed by rouge and lipstick and absence of eyebrows. "You know I've been away so long I'm afraid to make any rash statements, lest I might mistake a granddaughter for her grandmother. You certainly look young enough to be your own grand-daughter."

"Well, now, I like that!" pouted the young woman. "You always did say things no one could quite understand, and left a person in doubt as to whether you meant a compliment or a slam."

"I assure you I was complimenting you," smiled the young man. "You know Miss Deane, don't you? Daphne Deane? She's another classmate. Since you're still living here I suppose you see her often."

The Avery girl thus adjured turned a cold stare on Daphne.

"Really?" she said with an almost insolent inflection. "Daphne Deane? It seems as though I remembered hearing that name before. You aren't that child that crashed into our class a little while before commencement and tried to grab all the honors, are you?" she asked with a disagreeable lift of her chin, measuring Daphne with a cold appraising look.

Daphne grinned.

"That's my description exactly!" she said as if she enjoyed it. "I didn't think you'd remember me!"

Evelyn took the parry contemptuously.

"There are some things one can't forget even if one tries," she laughed, and then turning to the young man:

"Honestly, Keith, I never was more in need of a friend than I am now, and I beg you will get in and go home with me at once."

Keith answered a little haughtily.

"I'm sorry. I'm meeting my agent who is supposed to arrive very soon now, and then I must hurry away and catch my train to New York."

"Agent?" said Evelyn. "What for? You aren't going to sell the house, are you? I hope that doesn't mean you are leaving town permanently, does it?"

"I am not just sure," answered Keith coldly. "The agent wrote he had a possible purchaser, or tenant. I have not decided what the outcome will be."

By his side Daphne caught her breath and put her hand up to her throat with a little quick movement and then down again. He felt the gesture rather than saw it, and he turned and looked at her:

"Should you care?" he asked.

But it was Evelyn who answered.

"Care?" said Evelyn. "I don't know that I should. This isn't such a desirable site any more, and you could probably build something more up to date over near the park, say on Latches Lane or along Winding Way. There are some lovely sites over that way, quite near the golf links. But you certainly ought not to leave town. We've missed you terribly since you went away. However, I can't stay here and gossip. I've got to get back to my highways and hedges. Come, get in and I'll take you to wherever you have to go, and then you'll have to come home with me to my dinner party. Come on, be a good sport! You can't do any business in New York until Monday, and I'll guarantee to get you to the midnight train if you'll stay and help me out."

Keith cast a worried look at his watch.

"If you'll just drop me at the corner of Maple Street I'll be grateful," he said. "I'm late for my appointment already!"

Then he turned suddenly back to Daphne.

"I'll be seeing you," he said in a low tone. "I'd like your answer to that question."

Then just as he was getting into the car there loomed a stalwart youth beside him with a white sweater tied across his shoulders, and a mop of crisp bronze curls over a pair of keen hazel eyes.

"Oh, hello!" said Keith Morrell putting out a quick hand and grasping the big strong hand of the erstwhile pitcher. "Congratulations! That was a good game! I enjoyed it, and you had the star part. You certainly have grown out of all recognition since I saw you last, but I hope I have another chance soon to watch you pitch. Some college is going to be proud of you soon, I can see."

"No chance!" said the youth frowning almost haughtily. "I'm going to work!"

"Say, that's an idea!" said Morrell looking at him with interest. "I'd like to talk that over with you some time soon and get your point of view. Just now I've got to hurry to a business appointment, but I'll see you again. Perhaps you don't remember me, but your sister will tell you who I am."

He waved his hand, for Evelyn had started her engine and drowned out further conversation, and they shot away from the curb.

"Who is the perfectly stunning looking kid?" asked Evelyn Avery languidly. "One of your former caddies?"

And back on the sidewalk Donald Deane, known among his compatriots as "Donnie" Deane, stood glaring after the fast disappearing car.

"Now what the dickens was that hand-painted girl doing down our respectable street? That was Keith Morrell, wasn't it? Beats all how quick she can hunt 'em out the minute they land in town. Like molasses to the fly! What was he doing here?" He turned and gave his sister a searching look. "Come to borrow a key to get into his house or something?"

"No," said Daphne, watching the distance with a puzzled look in her eyes, "I gathered that he came down to meet his agent, something about a tenant or a possible buyer for the property."

"Good night!" said her brother with dismay in his voice. "Seems sort of awful, doesn't it, after all the way mother made up fairy stories about the place, to have it pass out of the family that way. Still, I suppose it's what we've got to expect."

"Yes," said Daphne. "It probably looks old-fashioned and uninteresting to one who has spent several years abroad. But of course, if he had really been the radiant loyal youth we pictured him to be—or rather mother pictured, and we believed—he couldn't do it! He'd have to keep the place for old association's sake."

"Well, he probably isn't what we thought he was!" said Don frowning heavily, with a sigh of disillusionment. "I wish he'd stayed away. I hate like the dickens to lose a hero. There aren't so many these days! Mother made him out a sort of Sir Galahad, and I've about found out there aren't any more of them, so I hate to see him go."

Daphne laughed.

"It doesn't necessarily mean that he hasn't a fine character, you know, if he has to sell his property. Besides, it may be awfully hard for him to come back to the old home now his father and mother are gone."

Don shook his head.

"I couldn't do it!" he said firmly. "Not if I had to starve to keep it. Look at those lines! Look at those great columns, look at the curve of the porch and the arch of that mullioned window!"

Daphne laughed.

"There's more to it than lines," she said. "You've got architecture on the brain just now, but there's a certain character to that old house that makes it lovely, even if the lines weren't right. There's a family life that was lived there, that I feel somehow will live on in memories. I know it will in mine. Of course, mother idealized it for us. I've been realizing that for some time. Yet there was something real about it that has grown into our lives, yours and mine, and perhaps the other children's, too, that can never die. Come on, Donnie, let's forget it. We can't do anything about it and it's not for us to worry about. But I'm glad he liked your playing. Wasn't it nice of him to say so?"

She caught her brother's big hand and nestled her fingers into it affectionately, and together they went into the gate and up the steps of the pleasant white house behind the high hedge that was their home.

3

KEITH Morrell, as he stepped into the car and took his seat beside Evelyn Avery, had a distinct sense of loss, as if something pleasant that he was about to grasp had been ruthlessly torn from him. He hadn't time to analyze this impression and understand just what it meant. He didn't exactly connect it with Daphne Deane, this almost unknown girl out of a past that had not been conscious of her at all. He simply felt that something sweet and tender connected with his boyhood had touched him and given him a longing for things that were no more, made him almost wonder if such an atmosphere was still upon the earth somewhere.

But there was not time to reason about it. Evelyn Avery was very much in the present, and most insistent.

"Honestly, Keith," she said, as earnestly as a girl with such red lips was able to speak, "I'm in a horrible jam and I'm appealing to you to help me out. It's a matter of life and death so to speak, and I know you won't fail me. You were always so gallant toward anyone in trouble!"

She looked at him with daring black eyes into which she could, on occasion, put an essence of wistfulness that seemed almost real.

"You see, it's this way." She lowered her voice till her words took on the nature of a confidence. "Cousin Nada is staying with us. You remember Nada Beach who spent a winter once with us and went to school with me? Sort of a highflier, you know. Mother quite disapproves of her now, she's so much worse than she used to be. And she has a friend staying in the city whom she's crazy about, and as soon as she finds out that one of the men can't come to the dinner she'll do her best to get him asked. She's already suggested it to mother in case someone fails. And it happens he used to be engaged to one of my guests and jilted her, treated her scandalously, and I simply couldn't bring them together at my house! You can see that. And I can't explain either. I promised I would never tell anyone. I'm sure you will see what a jam I'm in and come to the rescue."

Keith Morrell tried to explain how necessary it was that he get back to New York at once, but Evelyn overcame all his arguments. He simply must help her out, and she would see that he got the midnight train from the city if that was absolutely necessary.

They had reached the agent's house by this time and the young man, made to feel exceeding selfish if he did not yield, gave reluctant consent.

"I'm not dressed for a formal dinner," he said as he got out, brightening at the thought of a real excuse at last. "You know I didn't bring a suitcase with me."

"Oh, we're not formal," laughed Evelyn. "Anything goes in this town this time of year. Besides, I'll tell them I grabbed you from the train and compelled you to come in. Or, if you don't like that, my brother Bronson will lend you something. He has dinner coats galore. Though you're quite all right as you are."

"All right, I'll come!" he said as gracefully as he could.

"I'll wait for you" beamed Evelyn. "A bird in the hand is worth two in the bush!"

And no protest could stir her from this decision.

He went into the agent's house feeling that he was caught in a trap, and it was all his own fault.

The agent had a buyer and he was anxious to consummate the sale at once, but strangely enough, although he had come down from New York expecting to sell, and anxious to finish the matter up as soon as possible, Keith found a sudden reluctance upon him. A dim vision of a little boy in pajamas and bare feet kneeling at his mother's knee beside an open fire, seemed to come between himself and any possible buyer. It was as if the old house had suddenly become a holy place with which he had no right to part lightly.

The agent painted the sale in glowing terms. The buyer wanted to take possession at once, and was willing to pay cash. He was planning to pull down a portion of the present house and make radical changes, modernize the whole thing, make an apartment house out of it, and then cut up the rest of the land into small building lots and make snappy little bungalow homes out of them. He might even go a thousand or two higher if Mr. Morrell didn't feel he was getting enough.

Keith Morrell thought of the little white house behind the hedge where the white picket gate hung, with an old-fashioned latch. He thought of children at its back window watching out toward the old house to see a little boy who was their hero and a lovely mother walking in the garden at evening with her arm around her boy. Something clutched his heart!

What was the matter with him? Modernize the house? Break up the lovely grounds into an operation of cheap little houses? Well, what was the matter with that? It was the sensible thing for the new owner to do if he could put it over. Why should he care? If he sold it—and he had expected to sell it, of course—why should he care what became of it?

He sat there staring at the agent, a cool mask upon his face, while he struggled with emotions he did not quite understand. Why was it that something stood in his way when he thought of assenting to a program like this?

At last he arose and faced the agent:

"I will give you my answer day after tomorrow," he said. "I shall have to think it over."

"Well, but I understood you were anxious to sell!" said the agent anxiously following him toward the door, and seeing his fat commission vanishing into dim uncertainty.

"Yes, I was," said Keith Morrell thoughtfully, "but something has—come up—" He hesitated for the right word and ended lamely, "I shall have to think it over."

"You mean the price is not enough?" asked the agent eagerly. "I'm quite sure the man would pay more if he had to."

"No, it is not a matter of money," said the young man, more as if he were arguing with himself.

"You mean you are considering coming back to live there?"

The agent's mouth drooped with anticipated disappointment.

"No, I hadn't thought of that, exactly."

"Well, you mean you might withdraw the house from the market?"

"I don't know really what I mean," said Keith. "I shall have to think it over. Perhaps I shall have to go over the house again."

And suddenly it came to him that that was just what he must do. He would have to go over the house and find it bleak and empty, in order to wipe out that vision of the little boy praying at his mother's knee beside the fire, before he could ever hand over that house to be metamorphosed, and obliterated from life and history.

The agent followed him almost out to the car, talking eagerly, suggesting the buyer might take another place instead if he kept him waiting, persuading him that it was a great offer, cash, in these hard times. But Keith only looked down gravely at the path as he walked and reiterated pleasantly, "I will give you my answer day after tomorrow. Possibly I will telephone you from New York."

He had not really been listening to what the agent said. He had been wondering why he was suddenly so unsettled about selling the house.

The agent watched the car drive away with a disappointed sag to his shoulders. He had been planning what he would do with that nice fat commission that had seemed so surely coming his way. And Evelyn Avery gushed noisily in her triumph as she drove her quarry home, openly exulting in her success. But Keith Morrell was silent, almost absent-minded, suffering her conversation, but giving little heed to the news she was pouring forth. He was still wondering why he was so undecided. What would he do with the house, supposing he should keep it? He had no intention of coming back alone to live in it, even supposing he could arrange his business connections to make that possible. And certainly Anne Casper, provided the breach in their friendship should be healed, would never be willing to live there. She would call it an old-fashioned barracks, perhaps, or maybe even a dump. It seemed ridiculous to allow himself even for an instant to think of such a thing as keeping the house. It would only fall into ruin if it were left standing idle, an expense for caretakers and taxes. Why couldn't he make up his mind to sell it and have it over with at once?

Yet somehow it seemed as if the spirit of his mother were softly protesting. The idea of making the lovely old rooms into apartments was abhorrent to him, and the influx of noisy common people that the building of cheap houses would surely bring, a disrespect to the lovely old estate where his childhood had been spent.

On the other hand, equally unpleasant was the thought of a tenant, that is some tenants, going about familiarly in his mother's home! It was unthinkable! Almost he would rather see it torn down than that! A fool he was, of course, and probably only very tired from the heat of the day. Perhaps tomorrow would bring clearer thoughts and a firmer determination. It had been a mistake to come down amid the old associations again. It had upset him, brought back his sorrow and loss. Better to have stayed in New York and had it out with Anne Casper. After all, she belonged to the modern age and he had to live his life in the present, not the past. He must shake off this strange sentimentality that had him in its grasp. It must be that girl, Daphne, who had reminded him so much of his mother! The girl, and her talk of other days!

He was almost glad to get out of the car and enter the ornate Avery mansion, with its air of sophistication, its ostentatious luxury, and rouse to the immediate present.

Back he was at once in the world he was learning to know as his life now—cocktails and free careless converse, daring attire and startling make-up.

They welcomed him noisily, the guests who had already arrived; they claimed an intimacy he had never felt with any of them, and plied him with jokes that were not to his taste. He had been out in the modern world for several years, both at home and abroad, and had grown quite used to its life, quite a part of it at times, but somehow he had not expected to find it here in his old home town. Suddenly it seemed an impertinence here so near to the old home. It almost seemed as if he were seeing it with his mother's disapproving eyes.

He stood a little apart from the rest, holding a glass from which he had not tasted, which somehow he was strangely reluctant to taste. He watched his former schoolmates as they flocked in now, boisterously, each one with a noisy greeting. They were the same people. He could recognize them, in spite of their disguises of modern garments. Yet they seemed to have changed indefinably, to have coarsened and cheapened themselves, to have grown brazen and hard. It wasn't just that they were older—the make-up of the girls had hidden age to a certain extent—it was that they seemed to have lost illusions, to be without that eager look of youth with its natural hopefulness. They were not old enough to have lost those things. It was almost as if they had lost joy or all hope of it. He had seen that look on men and women of the world, but these who had lived in the home town and grown up with him, these ought not to have it, not yet anyway—not so soon. Why, in some cases it almost seemed as if they were wildly unhappy and were trying to keep the world from finding it out, as if their very laughter were hollow with pain!

And yet, they were Anne Casper's kind! He could not deny that! And Anne Casper was very lovely. Was it possible that under her beautiful veneer Anne Casper was hard like this and disappointed and selfish, and he had not seen it?

That little girl on the grandstand that afternoon had not had that look! How was it?

Yet all these would laugh at her, despise her perhaps. Certainly Evelyn had.

The evening was hilarious and Keith Morrell was weary. This was just the thing he had run away from in New York. At least, he had run away from the thought of Anne Casper, slim and willowy with her sleek black hair, long curly lashes, and her great dark eyes that could intrigue at one time and be so hard at another. Anne Casper who had laughingly but utterly refused to comply with his request; and who had, moreover, insisted that he ought to give up his lifework, which had been planned for him through the years by his father and mother and himself, and go into some gigantic financial speculation with her father, be rich and independent, and be free most of the time to play around the earth with her and her friends and give himself up to amusing her. Those were the conditions she had made for continuing their friendship, an ultimatum, in fact, though she hadn't exactly put it in so many words. He had been very angry when he went away, but he had not let her see how angry he was. He had only been stern and white, and had rejected her suggestions gravely, quietly, and gone.

He had thought when he left her that his heart was probably broken. That he would never believe in women again. For he hadn't been able to think, until she made a point of it, that she was really as money-minded as this. He could not believe it even yet when he recalled her loveliness. Surely in a day or two she would recall him. Of course, he had not yet actually asked her in so many words to marry him, but it had been well understood between them that such was his intention, his desire. Her beauty and her grace, her professions of interest in himself, all that marvelous startling experience of meeting her and being drawn into her friendship in spite of the environment which surrounded her, an environment which was not natural to himself, it could not be that that had not been real! All the way down on the train he had reasoned thus, had stared unseeing out of the window and told himself that if she did not retract what she had said life was done for him, happiness was no more!

But now as he sat at the long-drawn-out dinner that reminded him of many he had attended with Anne Casper, he suddenly realized that notwithstanding his supposed unhappiness he had not thought of her once all the afternoon. He stared at the thought with startled interest while he listened to Evelyn's empty drawl of old times, and really heard very little of what she said.

The thought puzzled him. He did not like to think of himself as vacillating, as easily throwing off and forgetting a love of which he had fully persuaded himself. No, he wasn't like that. If there was ever one thing his mother had drilled into him, it was to be serious about falling in love, not to be impetuous but deliberate, to be entirely sure he had chosen the right one and then to abide by it, be loyal to it, come what might.

But his mother would never have approved a woman who would test his love by a demand that he should go into a questionable business and throw aside all his preparations for life. And when he came to face it honestly, had he ever been quite sure that Anne Casper was the true mate of his heart? Hadn't he just been deliberately trying to make himself believe that her beauty was real and not merely of the flesh?

He had got so far in his thoughts when the general hilarity interrupted them. Some silly tale one of the men was addressing to him noisily. Keith had only toyed with his wine glass but the others had drunk freely, and gaiety was the keynote of the hour.

Suddenly, as he saw what the outcome of the story was to be, its utter silliness and sordidness palled upon him. Was this the thing he was letting himself in for by accepting Evelyn's invitation? Just a return to the atmosphere he had so wearied of in New York? And not even Anne Casper to relieve the situation! It was not his native element. It was hers, and he had stood for it that he might have her, telling himself that when she was his he would wean her away from it. But could he do that? Wasn't it too much a part of her, and without it for a background would she have the glamour?

Somehow at this distance, he wasn't so sure of Anne Casper. And perhaps he wasn't so heartbroken as he had thought! What was it that had got him? The coming back here to his old home, where he could remember his sweet simple life with his father and mother, his absorbing school and play, his ambitions for the future?

And suddenly he knew what it was, the picture of

himself kneeling by his mother's knee, with the firelight flickering over his mother's face! It was the girl, Daphne Deane, and her story of how she had watched as a play his own life, that had got him. Foolish, of course, child's play, not a thing that should influence a man grown. But somehow a great disgust for the thing he was doing now filled his soul. He wanted to get away from this lighted room, and these silly painted half-drunken former comrades of his, out into the coolness and darkness of the night.

"He's frightfully solemn, isn't he?" whispered Nell Harbison to Evelyn across her partner, with lifted eyes toward Keith. His head was turned toward the lady on his right who was rallying him that he was not drinking, and he did not hear.

"Yes," assented the hostess. "It's his mother's fault. She made him that way. I always said she would, keeping him so much to himself, and making him grind at his studies. But Nell, he's horribly good looking, you know."

"Yes, darling. He always was! But what a waste under a scholarly expression like that!"

When the company drifted out of the dining room at last Keith Morrell paused at the open door and gazed out into the night. The soft plash of a fountain, the sweet tang of honeysuckle from an arbor, drew him. He longed inexpressibly to get away. How could he manage it? It was only a step out there into the soft darkness where he could get his balance, get away from this eager pursuit of happiness. He could easily go and no one know where he was gone. But that wasn't exactly the courteous thing to do.

Evelyn came hastening toward him smiling. The orchestra was playing and already two couples were dancing. He didn't want to dance with Evelyn and he could see that was what she was intending should happen. Quickly he glanced down at his watch, and then as she reached him he looked up smiling:

"I wonder if I could make a phone call here in the

village?" he said pleasantly.

"Oh, surely," she said, leading the way to the instrument, and showing signs of intending to linger and wait for him.

"This is something I should have attended to earlier in the afternoon," he explained as he took up the telephone book and slipped into the little booth under the stairs. "I probably shall not be long. I'll find you in the other room when I am done. Don't let me keep you."

Reluctantly she drifted away.

There had been only one person in the town whom he could think of to call up in his need of an excuse, and that was an elderly woman, a friend of his mother's, a lifelong invalid, yet a shining saint. He hadn't thought of her in years, and he had no real obligation toward her. She was just a vague part of the dim background of his childhood, but it certainly would please her if he called up to ask after her health, though he wasn't even sure she was alive now.

But there was her name, Miss Emily Lynd. Why shouldn't he go and call for a moment? It would give him an excuse to get away, and really was the kind thing for him to do. She had been so fond of his mother, and of course had heard nothing except the bare fact of her death. It was one of the things his mother would have liked him to be thoughtful enough to do. Well, at least he would see if she was able to see him. She had been bedridden when they went away. Perhaps she still was. Perhaps it was too late to call up an invalid, almost ten o'clock! Well, he would venture it anyway.

So he called, and almost immediately the answer came, the same sweet fresh young voice he remembered of old. How had she managed to keep her voice young through all the years of pain she had had to endure?

"Yes? This is Miss Lynd."

"This is Keith Morrell, Aunt Emily." (Everybody called her Aunt who knew Emily Lynd at all.) "Did I call you too late? Had you retired?"

There came a flute note of laughter.

"Retired? Dear lad! How should I retire more than I am continually? Don't you know that I've been nothing else but retired for the last five years? But, have I turned my light out yet? No, I hadn't, and if I had I would turn it on again to hear you talk. It's great to hear your voice after this long silence. Where are you? Can't you come and see me?"

"I'm in the village, Aunt Emily. Yes, I'll come for a few minutes, if I'm not too late."

He hung up the instrument with a guilty sense that it would have been just too bad if he hadn't done this, and he probably wouldn't have thought of it if he hadn't been so bored with this dinner party.

He sought Evelyn Avery and made his excuses, pleading an urgent errand, and drew a free breath as he strode away from the house.

As he found his way down the fragrant moonlit streets he wondered what Daphne Deane had been doing all the evening? Surely now that she was grown she had to attend affairs such as he had just left. Didn't she have a social world that did the same thing? He wondered where she had been tonight. Now if she had been there, he would have enjoyed taking her off into a corner somewhere and talking with her, finding out what was behind that young look in her sweet wise eyes. Still, likely, if she had been there she would have been all dolled up with a hideous red mouth and smears under her eyes. Everybody did. If you went to such places you did as the rest did. Though it did seem rather incongruous to think of Daphne Deane smoking a cigarette or drinking champagne. He found the idea distasteful.

Well, best put it all out of his mind. He would take the midnight train back to New York. If there was an earlier one he could catch, so much the better. He would make this brief call on Aunt Emily Lynd, and then he would go back to New York and telegraph the agent in the morning to go ahead and sell the estate. What was the use in being sentimental? And as for Daphne Deane he probably would never see her again anyway. Why consider her? She probably wasn't real either.

Then he arrived at the little white cottage of antique build whose lovely old lines always filled Keith's beauty-loving eyes with satisfaction. Now in the moonlight its quaint loveliness thrilled him anew, and he resolved that some day he would come here and make a drawing of it to use in some of his future work.

But he found a welcome that was even more beautiful in the house itself. The moment he stepped inside the door he felt himself back in his boyhood. Soft perfume of rose geranium, sweet briar, suggestions of wild things like white violets—or was it wild grape blossoms?—and then as he went down the hall and entered the sanctum of the dear invalid, came the clean tang from a bowl of glowing nasturtiums, poignant with crisp homely sweetness.

How often he had come here with a basket of flowers from their own garden, flowers picked by his mother and sent to the beloved invalid, and those same pungent odors had clung to every breath he drew. Those old familiar odors assailed him now and gripped his spirit with something tender like unexpected welcoming arms.

And no less so the sweet face smiling from the pillows, framed in its lovely aureole of white beautiful hair.

Quick tears stung into his eyes, surprising him as he stooped to touch his lips to the frail hand she held out to him. It seemed as if other days had suddenly returned.

"How dear of you to take the trouble to come and see me!" said the sweet old voice that yet had that vibrant quality of youth in its fringes.

Keith's conscience gave a sharp twinge. She wouldn't be so gracious if she knew that he had only come as a refuge from something that bored him. And yet, wouldn't she? He remembered her as always having an understanding mind, and she would be grateful even for the little second thought that had sent him here. But why hadn't he thought of her before? Why hadn't he come here first of his own accord? He suddenly knew that this was something he might have missed that was greatly worth having and perhaps he would never have realized that he had missed it, not even after it was too late.

"It is good to be here!" He breathed the words with a veiled amazement, knew in his heart that they were true, and that he was glad he was here. It was like getting home after a long lonely journey. And then he wondered why he had not come before.

"It is wonderful here," he said with a tinge of wonder in his voice as he looked around. "It looks just the same as when I was a kid. You have not changed and your home is just the same cheery cosy place it always was. Sunshine flaunting cheer in the face of pain and suffering! It used to fill me with comfort to see you and hear you talk. I always came away with the feeling that there was no pain nor trouble, nor even death that need be feared."

"Why, how lovely to have been permitted to make you feel that way," she said, her fine sweet eyes kindling with a lovely light. "Now, I shall feel that it has been worth while to have lived, even such a useless life as mine, just to have that said to me. I feel like pausing right here to look up and say 'Thank you, Father!'"

"Well, it's true!" he said fervently. "And it's so good to see it all just as it was. Why, even the smell is the same! Perfume on the air. Flowers everywhere."

"Ah! Yes! Aren't my flowers lovely! I have to thank my friends for those. One especially. I wonder if you knew her. Daphne Deane? She keeps me supplied almost from day to day with some new bit of loveliness. Your mother used to do that for me from your garden, you know, and when she left us little Daphne took it up. I always thought her sweet quiet mother had something to do with it at first, when she was a mere slip of a girl, but since, we have become very close friends. Did you know her?"

A sudden light came to Keith's eyes.

"We were classmates for awhile in high school, you know," he said. "I met her this afternoon for a few minutes and walked along with her. I didn't know her so well in the old days, but I can see that she is all you say she is."

"You must know her," said the sweet old invalid thoughtfully. "She's rare!"

"I'd like to," he said with interest. "She impressed me that way, too. In fact I think I remember feeling she was out of the ordinary when she was in school. She was a bright scholar!"

"Brilliant!" said Emily Lynd. "Her father is a professor in the university, you know, and she has had an unusual upbringing. But there has been some adversity, and serious illness, and her life has not been easy, nor carefree. Yes, you must know her. Are you staying with us long? Or are you perhaps coming home to remain?"

"I'm going back to New York on the midnight train," he said wistfully, a sudden homesick pang striking him.

"Oh, I'm sorry! But you'll come again? You'll perhaps come often. New York is not far away."

"Not far," he said, "but I expect to be busy. I'm in an architect's office and must make good, you know."

"Of course. But—I'd hoped—perhaps I ought not to say that, but your mother and I used to talk about it. She was anxious to have you located around here."

"I know," he said sorrowfully, "but Mother is not here, and I had this fine opportunity. It seemed the only thing to do."

"I suppose so!" Emily Lynd's face had that faraway look as if in spite of facts she saw a vision. "Still," she added brightly, "the way might open for you to come back, you can't tell, and this is a good place in which to make good your early promise." She smiled at him. "New York is big and there is much competition."

"Yes," he said thoughtfully with a sudden wish that her suggestion might come true. Then it came to him to wonder what Anne Casper would say to that, and instantly he knew she would not like it. Not at all. Anne Casper would never fit into the old life here, either. Had he come too far astray for the dreams he and his mother used to dream?

When he left his old friend an hour later, making his way slowly down the pleasant, moonlit street, the thoughts of home and his boyhood life were pulling at his heartstrings, and though he put them aside as impractical, they gave him a queer startled feeling like having his face and hands washed clean, and his eyes suddenly opened to things that he seemed to have forgotten for a long time.

His way to the station led him past the back of his old home, and at first he hesitated and thought of taking a longer way about to avoid it, for somehow he shrank from passing the still empty dwelling in its quiet grouping of shrubbery, and seeing it so lonely and unused. There was something about moonlight that got you sometimes. Then he realized that he had stayed with Miss Lynd longer than he had planned, and it was getting near train time. He must not miss this train. He ought to be back in New York early in the morning.

So he resolutely held on his way. In a moment he would be passing the house where Daphne Deane lived. Across the street was the spot where he had stood that afternoon.

And now as he came opposite the gate he saw that two people were standing there, Daphne, unmistakably, and a young man. Also, as nearly as one could tell by moonlight from across the dim shadowed street, he seemed to be a well set up young man.

Well, of course that was to be expected. As pretty a girl as that! There would be a young man of course. But suddenly the idea annoyed him. Somehow he didn't want this interesting girl from his past to be tabulated and disposed of so quickly. Yet how ridiculous! Why should he care?

Then he heard a little trill of laughter, and the memory of her tone and the way she had looked up frankly at him that afternoon made him wish he might linger and perhaps step over and join in the conversation. He couldn't intrude, of course, even if he had time, but his footsteps lagged. As he passed by on the other side in the shadow of the trees, he heard the young man say:

"How about tomorrow night? Wouldn't it be possible then?"

"No, I'm sorry," she said clearly. "I have two lessons to give. Perhaps toward the end of the week—"

The young man spoke again in a low cultured voice, but he couldn't hear the words, and his feet by now had carried him well past them. As Morrell turned the corner into the street that led to the station he heard Daphne's voice calling a good night cheerily, and a queer fancy came to him that it was a good night for him, too. At least he would take it that way anyway, and he said in a low murmur under his breath: "Good night!"

Then came the distant whistle of his train and he had to sprint to catch it, and all else was, for the time being, forgotten.

4

KEITH Morrell arrived at the station half a minute ahead of the train, but as he came within sight of it he heard loud hilarious voices, and suddenly became aware that some of them were familiar ones that he had been hearing not so long ago. And loudest of them all was Evelyn Avery's, shouting at the top of her lungs. He sensed that the voices of all were much the worse for wear since he had left them. The whole crowd were silly drunk.

"Well, if he doesn't get here within the next second he'll miss it," shouted his recent hostess, and then he knew that they had come down to the train to see him off.

With a glance at the approaching train he made a dash in the darkness behind the station, vaulted the low fence, and reached the far end of the platform in line with the rear cars. As the train came to a halt he swung himself onto the last car. He had no taste for such a send off, and he wished heartily that he had not gone with Evelyn to dinner. How far she and her crowd seemed to be from the wholesome tender thoughts that had been in his mind during the last two hours. Why hadn't he pleaded necessity and gone to Miss Lynd's at once?

But when he was seated on the opposite side of the car, and the train was moving on its way past the noisy party on the platform, there came to him a sudden regret that he was leaving the place where he had spent so many happy years of his life. He was going back into his new modern world with alien associates, and strange ways, that were not according to the standards of his youth. Going back to his problems—and Anne Casper!

The more he thought about it the more he shrank from leaving Rosedale. It seemed to him that the work he had come to do was wholly unfinished, and there was an uneasiness in his mind about selling that home property without considering the matter further, without at least going through the house and looking things over. Just to let his mother's things go to strangers to sort out and throw away or resell was not the way to do. He ought to conquer his foolish sentimentality, go bravely into the house and look things over like a man.

As the train took him farther and farther away from the old home he became more and more loath to go on. The words of his mother's friend came to him, little hints about the loveliness of the garden, the dear old house among the tall elms, how much she enjoyed looking at it from her window, and how she could sometimes fancy she saw his mother walking on the terrace or picking flowers in the garden. It seemed a desecration to have it made into an apartment house. To fling it all away without a thought—a look at least. He could not go on through life shielding himself from memories of the past. He had to be a man.

As he looked back on the afternoon he began to see that the words of the young girl, Daphne, had rather expected that of him, implied it, though she hadn't of course mentioned such a thing.

He grew almost angry at himself, and told himself he had a case of nerves. Soon he would be on the New York express, flying back to his new world, his new life, and its perplexities. It was better not to go into the past again. He could not bring it back, and it could only open old wounds.

But still the heaviness about selling the old home hung over him. He tried to convince himself that it would be wrong to refuse such an advantageous offer. He needed the money. If he had that money at once, free from hampering investments, he could buy himself a partnership in some good firm, and be able to tell Anne Casper he had a future before him that promised well. In the not-far-distant future he could easily support her in fair luxury without giving up his chosen profession nor going into a money racket with some of her rich and questionable relatives.

Yet in spite of all these things the picture of the dear old house persisted, and when he closed his eyes and tried to forget, his mother's eyes seemed to be looking into his own and pleading.

What was the matter with him anyway, that the thing was getting him this way?

He picked up an evening paper that a man had left on the seat across the aisle, but he could not focus his mind on what was printed in it. Suddenly his eye caught a headline: "OLD HOME LEFT TO ONLY SON." He flung the paper from him back to the opposite seat, and turned his stare out the window into the darkness.

All at once the lights of the city began to gleam in the distance and then flash by rapidly and he suddenly knew that he was not going back to New York tonight. He could not go and leave this matter of the house unsettled. Somehow he must face the thing and decide it. He would go to a hotel, get a good night's sleep, and then he would go out to Rosedale in the morning and go through that house. Surely some conviction of what he ought to do would come to him as he went through it.

So he finally took a taxi to a hotel and went to bed, but not to sleep. His active mind went over and over the matter, recalling all he had seen and heard of the old home life, recalling the gentle smile of Miss Emily, the warm touch of her frail little hand, like a flower, her tone as she spoke of Daphne. And Daphne's face seemed to cross his vision, as he had first seen her on the grandstand, her look as she glanced up with recognition in her eyes changing to withdrawal as she realized that he really did not know her. The mischief in her voice and smile later as she told him that he had never taken her personality into his consciousness enough to recognize her after the interval. Somehow her look had stung him then, and his face burned in the darkness at the memory. She thought him a cad, and somehow it seemed to matter a good deal what she thought of him. Just why, he did not know, but it did. She had shown him the lovely side of herself afterward, and he did not want a girl like that to think ill of him. Especially a girl to whom he had been a child-hero! He wanted very much, he found, to live up to her first ideal of him, the ideal that her mother had given her. Of course she was only a stranger. Of course she would likely never touch his life again, any more than she had in the past, but he certainly would like to set himself right in her eyes before he passed out of her ken forever. He recalled the question he had asked of her which Evelyn Avery officiously answered for her, and his last word to her that he was coming back again to hear what she had to say. It hadn't meant much when he said it, but now suddenly he wanted very much to know what she would have replied. "Should you care?" he had asked with reference to his selling the old house, and that quick catch of her breath, the fleeting dismay in her face, came back now to his mind. Was her look perhaps what had made him feel vaguely that she thought him disloyal to all that the old home had meant? And all at once he wanted very much to get her answer.

Would she possibly be willing to go with him over to the house and see it for herself? Perhaps her presence with him would dispel the uncertainty, exorcise the demon of dismay that came to him whenever he tried to decide what he would do with the property.

At last he slept, soothed by the possibility that he might not have to go through the ordeal alone.

Back in Rosedale, Daphne had not recognized him as he went by in the darkness on the other side of the street. The shadows were deep and the moon had snatched a cloud and pulled it over her face just then. Besides Daphne was engaged in a slight argument with the new minister, and wasn't noticing chance passers across the street. Certainly she would not have expected Keith Morrell to be there, for she thought of him as submerged in the questionable gaiety of Evelyn Avery's party, and deep in her heart was disappointed in him accordingly. The Keith Morrell of her idealization would not have enjoyed a company of that sort.

The new minister, Rev. Drew Addison, was young and attractive. He had fine eyes and was more than interested in Daphne Deane. He was trying her out, feeling his way with her, trying to impress her with the fact that he was most wise and careful, and could choose a middle ground in the disputes of the church and the world, and yet be entirely loyal to the faith of his fathers. He argued that there was no sin in compromise, that the Bible said one must be wise as a serpent and harmless as a dove.

Daphne Deane closed her lips in a firm little line and gave a troubled gaze off into the shadows of the orchard in the dim moonlight. Was this minister going to be a disappointment when they had so hoped he was the right one? He had seemed to have so much about him that was attractive to the young people, so much enthusiasm, so much—well, was it really spirituality, or only a holy way of saying things that made them seem spiritual? She didn't want to think this. She put the idea away, and earnestly tried to feel that what he was saying was all right, that he just had an unfortunate way of expressing himself.

But when he asked her to go into the city to a symphony concert on the night of a notable Bible conference where a young earnest conference leader was to be the feature of the evening, and to which he knew she had promised to take a large group of young people from their church, her eyes grew troubled again.

"That's very kind of you to think of me," she said. "Of course, I'd love the music, but you've forgotten that I'm taking the group to the conference that night. Aren't you going yourself? I'm sure they expect you to be there."

"Well, I did think of it. I had a curiosity to see just what it is in this young adventurer that has made him the idol of the hour, but I hadn't really expected to go, at least not for more than a few minutes, just to look in on it. There is so much claptrap about such gatherings that it gets on my nerves. When one has been doing really serious work in the realm of theology it is a little hard to bear the rantings of a radio-crooner, you know. And, of course, that was before I got the tickets for the concert, too. I wouldn't miss this concert for anything. I'm a great admirer of the orchestra."

Daphne stood silent, making no reply.

"But you needn't feel tied down by any obligation about the young people, Miss Deane," he went on, "I'll gladly absolve you from your duties in that direction. There are plenty of people who would be glad to take your place as a chaperon and leave you free. I will ask old Mr. Simmons. I'm sure he would be greatly pleased to look after them, and you know I got these tickets with you especially in mind. You have a true musician's soul, and I have greatly anticipated hearing this special symphony in your company."

Daphne spoke quickly and crisply, lifting her chin a little.

"I'm sorry," she said, "but I wouldn't miss this conference for anything. I've been praying all the week for it, and have been hoping great things for the young people who are going."

"Really?" he said with a trace of amusement in his voice. "I sincerely hope you won't be disappointed. I shouldn't myself expect much good to come from anything as sensational as I hear these meetings are. I don't quite see how you can stand the strain."

"I don't know what you mean," said Daphne. "I've never felt that the meetings were sensational."

"You have heard this young preacher, then?"

"Many times!" she answered gravely, "and I know him well. He is one of the most utterly consecrated children of God I know, and his preaching is reaching thousands everywhere, and leading souls to Christ."

"Ah! Indeed? I *wonder!* In the ultimate reckoning those may not turn out to be real conversions after all. But—you wouldn't exactly call his ravings *'sermons'*, would you?"

He studied her face quizzically, amusedly, as if she were a mere child and must not be judged harshly.

Daphne felt herself getting angry, and she paused and drew a deep breath. Anger would never win a battle for right.

"Well," she said smiling, "having never heard him, what would you call them?"

He smiled broadly now, a bit condescendingly.

"I think that the utmost that could be said would be to call them evangelistic *efforts*. Even that would be stretching a point in my estimation—that is, from the standpoint of a scholar, you know."

"Well," smiled Daphne calmly, "it is sometimes a comfort to remember that the Bible says that God has hid some things from the wise and prudent and revealed them unto babes. 'Where is the wisdom of this world? Where are the wise?' Though in this case it happens that the young man in question is a graduate of a rather well-known university, and also of a theological seminary, and has several scholarly degrees to his credit. However, this isn't a very profitable conversation, is it? I am wondering if it is going to rain tomorrow? Do you notice it is clouding over since we came home from prayer meeting? I hope it will be pleasant for another day. I'm planning on washing curtains tomorrow, and I do want a sunny day to dry them quickly."

"You are rather quick on the trigger, aren't you?" said the minister, still amusedly. "Are you really as unsophisticated as you try to make out?"

"Perhaps I'd better leave you to find that out, if you think it's worth while," she laughed, bells in her voice again, and little crinkles of amusement about her eyes and nose. "I really must run in and see if my mother needs anything. She hasn't been well today, and I've been a little worried about her. There comes the moon again. Perhaps we're going to have a nice day tomorrow after all. Good night!" and Daphne turned and disappeared into the shadows of the lilac bushes that arched the walk to the door, never knowing that her good night had reached to other ears and was echoing in the heart of the young man running for his train.

5

BUT Daphne did not wash curtains the next morning, though the sun was shining brightly and she had made her brother bring the curtain stretchers down from the attic and set them in position for her. She had put on a little blue print dress, one of her plainest morning dresses, and was all ready to go to work, but instead she went to answer a knock at the front door and found Keith Morrell standing humbly on the porch, an eager look in his eyes.

"Good morning!" he said. "Are you very busy? Would I be a terrible nuisance if I asked a favor of you?"

"Why, no! Of course not!" said Daphne smiling, and feeling a sudden unexplained lifting of her spirit. "Come in, won't you? That is, if you don't mind the disorder. I was just taking down the curtains to wash them."

"Perhaps you'll let me help?" he offered eagerly.

"Oh, that wouldn't be necessary," she smiled. "They come down with a touch."

"But I'd love to," he said earnestly, "and I'll feel all the more comfortable afterward to make my request, if you'll let me help. I always used to do it for mother."

It was one of Daphne's lovely qualities that she never

made a fuss about things. So now when she saw that he really meant it, she went easily forward and let him help, till all the curtains were lying in a crumpled heap on the floor.

"Thank you so much!" she said breezily. "And now, won't you sit down and tell me how I can help you?"

"Yes, just as soon as we get these out of the way," he said, gathering up the heap of soiled muslin. "Where do they go? You have to put them asoak, don't you?"

"Why, how did you know?" laughed Daphne.

"Oh, mother always did," he said, drawing a quick little breath of a sigh. "Where do I take them? Is there a laundry?"

"Yes," said Daphne, matter-of-factly, "right out this way," and she led him through the dining room and kitchen to a small laundry where the tubs stood already filled with water.

He dumped the curtains in and seemed to enjoy poking them down, and making sure every corner was under water.

"Shouldn't we wash these right away?" he asked interestedly. "I'm not in a hurry."

"Oh no, they have to soak awhile first," said Daphne. "Let's go on the side porch and talk. It's pleasant and shady there."

So she led him to a vine-clad porch where easy willow chairs and tables, a few books, and a bit of sewing made it seem almost like an open-air living room.

"How cosy this is!" he said as he settled down in a big willow armchair and put his head back against a convenient cushion.

"We like it," said the girl with a quick glance around to see if the little sister who was supposed to put this room in order the first thing in the morning had done her work.

"It's a beautiful home!" said the young man wistfully. "I can't help looking back and wishing I had known it intimately when I was growing up."

"That's nice of you," said Daphne, giving him a swift glance to make sure he meant it. "I wish you had. It would have been nice for us."

Their eyes met and a warm glance passed between them.

"I've missed a lot," he said thoughtfully as he studied her more closely. Then with another bit of a sigh he smiled:

"Well, now I'd better get to my errand. I have to go over to my old home and look around to see just how things are, and I was wondering if you would consider it an imposition for me to ask you to go with me? I haven't been back since mother left me, and I thought it would be pleasant to have somebody with me."

There was a look of a hungry little boy in his eyes, that appealed at once to Daphne.

"Why, of course!" she said, springing up with a light in her eyes. "It will be wonderful! Just wait a minute till I can make myself a little more respectable for going out."

"Please don't go and doll up," he pleaded, rising and taking a step toward her. "It's just a dusty old house, you know, and I think you look wonderful just as you are."

His voice was very genuine and it brought the bright color to her cheeks.

"Thank you!" she said lightly. "I appreciate the compliment. But I'll just put on a clean collar, if you don't mind. We have a neighbor who would sound it abroad if I went out, even across the street, looking like this. I'll be with you in just a minute."

She was back in almost the allotted minute with a fresh crisp wisp of organdy rolling back from the neck of her blue frock, and her hair satin-smooth.

"Now," she said, her eyes starry, "I feel as if I were about to step into real fairyland!"

"I'm afraid you will be disappointed," he said, looking down at her admiringly. "The house has stood uncared for a long time and everything must be frightfully dusty, although I think mother did have covers put over the furniture before she went away. It seems to me I remember talk about it."

"It won't make any difference to me," said the girl eagerly. "I shall be seeing it with eyes of younger days, and it will be all glorified."

Keith Morrell's eyes expressed his admiration, though he made no immediate reply.

They went out the back way together, through a little gate that dated back to gardener days in the Morrell family. The young man helped the girl over the garden wall, to the great edification of Mrs. Gassner who never missed any unusual happening on their quiet street.

Daphne stopped for a moment at the top of the three steps that led down to the garden and looked across the tangle of color that had grown up according to its own sweet will, blue phlox and cowslips, candytuft and columbine pink and white and blue, coral bells and violets, growing together in an arrangement all their own, peering out brightly through masses of clambering honeysuckle vines and old-fashioned yellow roses.

"I came so far once to get Ted's ball when he was a little fellow," she said. "Mother wouldn't allow him to come in after it himself, lest he might harm something. It was breathlessly beautiful I remember. And over there there was a pansy bed, all purple and gold, and velvety brown and orange. And there was a fountain just beyond."

"That's right!" said the young man, leading her down an overgrown path, "it's right over here. Seems dreadful, doesn't it, having the garden all messed up like this? I didn't realize. You see there's never been a caretaker since Tim Maxon died. It didn't seem important to me then to have one. Mother was very sick, and I knew she wouldn't be with me long. And afterward—well it just didn't occur to me again. I'm sorry."

It was almost as if he were apologizing to her.

"But it's all here! See, there's a yellow pansy, and a purple one peeking out from this cover of shrubs. Poor thing! You want some air and sunshine, don't you?" She stopped and pulled the branches back, scratching the dead leaves away, pulling out a weed or two, and lo, a brave little pansy plant stood forth.

Morrell knelt beside her and helped, putting back a briar out of her way, and pulling up some strong weeds that had taken possession.

"It wouldn't be hard to bring it back to order again," said the girl. "It would be fun! I'd like to do it!"

"So would I," said Morrell. "I wish I had time to stay. I must certainly get someone to look out for it—that is—if I keep it!"

"Oh!" said the girl drawing in her breath as if his words had hurt her.

His hand lingered beside hers, just touched it among the warm earth and leaves, and something like a flame seemed to pass between them. All at once, he deliberately laid his hand over hers, gently.

"Would you care?" he asked softly. "Would it mean anything to you if I sold it?"

She lifted questioning eyes, suddenly clouded.

"Oh, yes, I couldn't help but care," she said honestly, looking into his eyes. "But of course—I've no right—" She dropped her gaze to the pansy bed again.

"I'm not so sure!" he said meditatively, clasping her hand more strongly and suddenly rising and bringing her up with him. "Last night Miss Lynd was telling me how she loved the old house and garden, loved looking at it, and remembering; and it came to me that perhaps the old house owed something to its friends and neighbors, something intangible, just by being there—"

He looked down at her with that question in his eyes. He was still holding her hand warmly with the soft bits of earth clinging between their clasp, and his eyes searched hers as if he would read his answer in them. Daphne, who did not make a practise of letting young men hold her hand, never thought about this. It seemed a kind of holy clasp, a culmination of the beautiful relation that had always been in fancy between the old house and her little life and interests.

"Why—that is a beautiful thought," said Daphne slowly, and then her keen mind seeing clearly through she added: "But of course there's no obligation like that!"

"Isn't there?" he said it with a troubled smile, suddenly dropping his clasp of her hand, and taking her arm quietly, to lead her on. "I'm not sure. I'll have to think it through."

She walked quietly by his side, his hand holding her arm, and Mrs. Gassner from the vantage point of a second story back window, watched them carefully, and murmured "I wonder—!"

There were little flowers peeking out from old borders, nodding for recognition as they passed, but the two walked on silently, strange new thoughts going through their minds, and Daphne wondered at herself to be walking thus familiarly with the son of this old house, the young man who had always stood to her as some great personage whom she would never know but in fancy.

They came at last to stand on the wide veranda that ran across the front of the house and gave onto the terrace below. The tall white pillars rose nobly to support the roof far above, and they both instinctively looked up.

"It needs painting," said the young owner, looking troubled again. "Father would never have let it get to looking this way, I am sure." It was as if he were thinking aloud.

He fitted the key into the lock and threw the door wide open. The sunlight flung a path of brightness over the hall floor and part way up the wide old staircase.

"Oh, it is wonderful!" said Daphne, one hand up at her throat in her excitement. "It is just as I dreamed it would be!"

She lifted her face and followed the winding of the lovely old staircase, with its sweeping curve of mahogany rail and fine white spindles. She looked at the staircase and the young man looked at her, seeing her beauty as he had not yet seen it, his heart warming to her appreciation of his old home.

They presently went on into the house.

The rugs were rolled up and wrapped in brown paper, lying along the walls, the furniture was shrouded in cotton coverings, the pictures veiled in white.

It looks like the ghost of my past," said Keith Morrell in a sad tone. "I was afraid it would be like this."

He went to the front windows, snapped up the shades, unlocked the sash and flung them up. Then he unfastened the blinds, throwing them open, and the sunlight rushed in.

"There! That is better!" he said with a sigh, and impatiently reached out and pulled off the coverings from a couple of chairs.

"Sit down," he invited grimly. "It's not a very pleasant habitation."

"Oh, but the spaciousness! The vistas!" exclaimed Daphne, her eyes sparkling with pleasure. "I love it! Such beautiful rooms! How wonderful to have lived in a place like this!"

"I wish you could have seen it as it was!" said the boy sorrowfully. "My mother always had everything beautiful about her."

"I'm sure!" said the girl, reaching out her hand and touching delicately the upholstery of beautiful old tapestry. "I know there must be things here one could study and enjoy for many a day."

"I suppose so," sighed the son of the house. "I really never thought much about them. There are some fine paintings, I know."

He flung aside one of the veils, and then another, and revealed rich coloring, handsome setting of gold frames. A ship at sea. A street in the orient with towers and mosques and wealth of native coloring. A great cathedral.

"Oh," said Daphne. "Things I have read about and always wanted to see!"

"I always liked that Rheims cathedral," he said, watching the glow on her face. "I'm not sure but it gave me my taste for architecture."

They went about from picture to picture, his eyes watching hers, as she drank in their beauty.

"But you ought not to uncover all these things for me," she said. "They'll all have to be covered up again."

"I like to," he said. "It is good to see them again."

He strode over to the south window.

"This was Mother's desk," he said, flinging aside the cover. "Here she used to sit and write letters. But when I would come home from school she would always stop to greet me and hear my news, no matter how busy she was—"

His face was tender now with memories, and Daphne's heart swelled with sympathy for him.

"Your smile reminds me of hers," he said slowly, more as if he was just thinking aloud.

"Oh!" she said, "I'm glad! That's dear, to think I could remind you of her."

He turned quickly away to hide some emotion, and went over to uncover the piano.

"That was her piano," he said, his voice husky with feeling. "How I loved her touch. She was a real musician. Do you play? I thought I saw a piano over at your house. Sit down and try it. It's probably all out of tune."

He drew the piano stool out and placed it for her and she sat down, her fingers running softly over the keys. He saw that she played well.

"It's not bad at all," she said, "after all these years of standing idle in an unused house! It's wonderful!"

Her fingers rippled into a Chopin Nocturne, and he

dropped into a chair and watched, his heart filled with inexpressible longings.

"You are a musician, too," he said, when she finally swung around to him and smiled.

"I love it!" she evaded, "and that is a fine piano! But I am taking far too much of your time, and we ought to get to work and cover up these things again. We cannot leave them this way."

"Not yet," he pleaded. "Play me just one more."

So she played a few minutes longer. He sat back and closed his eyes and listened, old memories sweeping over him and doing things to his soul, searching it of strange ways he had been going of late, pointing out changes in himself that he had not noticed before.

When she rose at last, decisively, he took her over the rest of the house, till they came at last to the nursery.

"Here," he said huskily, "was where you must have seen me kneel to say my prayers. Mother always sat in that low chair before the fireplace. And over there in that cupboard are all my toys, the electric train and the stone blocks and picture puzzles." He turned quickly away and she saw him brush his hand across his eyes.

At last she turned away from the window that faced toward her own home, and her own voice was full of feeling.

"Thank you for giving me this real glimpse of the thing I had dreamed about for so many years," she said gently. "It is even more satisfying than I had pictured it."

He came and stood beside her, looking down and speaking with deep earnestness.

"And I thank you for bringing back to me things that I thought were over forever. But now I see they were meant to be eternal things, a part of me which could never end. My mother and my home—yes—and my God! You see I had forgotten how I used to say my prayers."

Then suddenly he caught her hand and spoke brightly:

"Come! We must go over to your house and finish washing those curtains! Do you put them on stretchers? I know how to do that!"

"Oh, but you don't have to wash the curtains," she laughingly protested, as he pulled her down the stairs.

"I know I don't have to, but I want to," he declared, as he hurried around closing windows, while Daphne tucked the covers over the furniture and closed the piano tenderly.

"It's perfectly scandalous," said Mrs. Gassner a few minutes later, to her sister-in-law whom she had bidden up to her watch tower at the second story back window. "There come those two back across the garden now! Holding hands! Will you believe it? I wouldn't have thought it of that smug-faced Daphne Deane—and her as good as engaged to the new minister, if you can believe hearsay! And they've been over in that empty house alone for over three hours! I timed them when they went in and I haven't stirred from this window since, watching for them to come back. Times certainly are changed. I heard the piano going, too. Isn't that a crime? The first time he's entered his mother's house in five years, and allowing the piano to be played! That's heartless, I say! An only son, too! But children have no feelings these days!"

Mrs. Deane met them smiling as they entered the house.

"I'm glad you've come, dear," she said. "I was just going to send Beverly over to tell you lunch is ready."

"Mother!" exclaimed Daphne. "You don't mean it is lunch time! Why, I didn't dream we'd been gone an hour."

"Yes, but aren't you going to introduce me to your guest?"

"Oh, of course. But mother, don't you know him? It's our neighbor, Keith Morrell, and he's been showing me through the wonderful house."

"Oh, yes, I know him, but I didn't think he would know me," said Mrs. Deane, smiling and holding out her hand to the young man.

"I certainly am glad to know you now," said Morrell, earnestly. "You make me think of my mother. I feel I've missed a lot in not knowing you all before."

"You had a wonderful mother, and we're glad to have you here now, anyway," answered Daphne's mother. "Suppose we sit right down while everything is nice and hot."

"Oh, Mrs. Deane, I mustn't bother you for lunch. I didn't realize it was so late. I only came over to help wash those curtains after I had monopolized your daughter so long. I'm ashamed. I apologize."

"Please don't. We're glad to have you. It seems as if we had known you all your life, you have lived so near. I admired your mother very much, and I'm just glad to have an opportunity of meeting her son."

"Then it will be a pleasure to me to stay. Isn't this great! I'm having a real holiday!"

"Where's Ranse, Mother? I can't find him anywhere," said Beverly appearing on the scene out of breath.

"Why, I told him he might play ball till lunch time," said his mother.

"He isn't out at the diamond. I looked for him everywhere," said the little girl.

"This is my little sister Beverly, Mr. Morrell," said Daphne.

"I'm glad to know you, Beverly. But since you have all known me so long, couldn't I rate being called 'Keith' instead of Mister?" he said smiling at Daphne, as he took Beverly's shy hand and greeted her.

"Well, if you'll call me Daphne," said the older sister.

"Sure I will," said Morrell. "Weren't we schoolmates? Didn't you beat me in math once? I couldn't help it, could I, that you knew me better than I knew you? You took the advantage of me and kept rather in hiding, you know."

Laughing they sat down at the table. There was an instant's pause as the mother glanced at the guest:

"Will you ask the blessing?" she said quietly.

Keith Morrell gave a swift startled glance around the table, then bowed his head and after an instant's pause said:

"Lord, we thank Thee for this food, and for the pleasant companionship, Amen."

"That's the first time I've been called upon to do that since my mother died," he said with heightened color. "I—haven't been living—in that kind of a world." His eyes were studying the opposite wall thoughtfully, reading a lovely motto hanging there.

"Christ is the Head of this house," it read, "the unseen Host at every meal, the silent Listener to every conversation."

He read it through and Mrs. Deane watching him said quietly:

"Then we're glad you have got back to your own environment. Will you have cream in your coffee?"

"I think I must have needed to come," he said gravely. "Yes, thank you, cream please. My, how good this coffee smells! Like home!"

They were almost through the meal when they heard loud footsteps stamping up the front walk and storming in the door.

"There comes Ranse," said Beverly.

The boy came on to the dining room door, puffing and panting and utterly oblivious of the presence of a guest.

"Why, Ransom, my son, where have you been? What *have* you been doing?" said his mother rising in dismay and looking at her child.

He was covered with mud and blood from his heels to his head, his nose was swelled to twice its normal size, and one eye was closed and quite black. There was something resembling tears running down his face and mingling with the blood, but he did not seem to be aware of it. His one good eye was flashing fire of what he plainly felt to be righteous wrath.

"I been having an awful fight, that's what!" panted the boy.

"A fight? But Ransom, you promised me—!"

"Yes, I know, Mother, I promised you I wouldn't fight, not unless it was strictly necessary! But this was! Wait till I tell ya. That new kid, that Ted Gowney, that's just come ta our school, said his father had bought the Morrell place and was gonta make a race course out of it, an' a gambling joint of the house, an' sell liquor, and have a road house, an' a lotta things worse, an' I tole him he was a liar! I tole him that we knew the man that owned it an' he wouldn't *ever* sell his place for a thing like that! And so he laughed at me, an' said his dad had already bought it, or as good as bought it, an' there wasn't any man too good ta sell his place for *any*thing if he got enough money out of it. And then I—I—I just licked the tar out of him!"

Keith Morrell was on his feet, his eyes shining, his hand reached out to grasp the grubby fist that had been so valiant.

"Good work, young feller! I'm proud of you! I'm glad I have such a brave defender. I'm the owner of that place, and you can just tell that young boaster that money wouldn't buy that place of mine now, not even if the buyer had perfectly good moral purposes in view. Because, you see, I'm not selling that place to anybody, at present anyway. I'm keeping it for myself! And after you've mopped up a bit and had your lunch, we'll go out and hunt up that scum of the earth and make it very plain to him."

Then the boy's one good eye shone joyously in the midst of his ruined young face, and he shouted: "Oh, *Boy!* I knew you were the stuff! I knew I could bank on you! I knew you'd never sell that grand place to anybody! Not to a fella like that mutt's dad, anyhow!"

And then Beverly joined her scornful young voice:

"Of course not! He wouldn't do a thing like that! I

wouldn't a bothered to tell the poor fish. I'd just a laughed at him and let him wait ta find out how wrong he was!"

But Keith Morrell was watching Daphne's face. She was preparing a sumptuous plate for her young hero brother, but her eyes were shining like two stars, and Keith suddenly knew that Daphne really cared a lot whether he sold that house or not.

6

ANNE Casper lit a cigarette and dropped down on the chaise lounge in her own room.

She was attired in white satin pajamas embroidered with peacocks. She always wore some shade of peacock when she was angry, preferably peacocks with their tails spread. The vain birds seemed to have something in common with herself.

For the past twenty-four hours she had been very angry, and so she wore peacocks.

The room was a very lovely one, cool and delightful, as all of Anne's surroundings were likely to be. Two windows looked out to sea, and a sea breeze was blowing the filmy curtains now, billowing them in lovely dreamy folds.

The curtains were pearl color, almost ethereal in their texture. The walls were white with a tinting of rose in the ceiling that well set off the furniture upholstered in imported white linen tapestry, with great sprays of pink roses flung here and there like painted things. There were white rugs and other white appointments. It made a lovely background for Anne Casper's dark beauty and she knew it.

But she was not thinking about her appearance just now. She sat staring at a large photograph of Keith Morrell framed in silver that stood on a little white table formed of a slab of white onyx curiously supported upon the backs of two modernistic animals, dogs perhaps, or something wilder. Beside the picture stood a small jeweled clock, and occasionally her eyes watched the hour, and she frowned petulantly.

Then above the beating of the sea waves she heard a distant whistle, her brow relaxed and she gave an impatient sigh. The train was coming at last. Perhaps Keith would be on it. Anyway, her father would be coming and that would be a help. He had promised to come on that train.

All the afternoon Anne had been engaged in the much discussed fashion show at the beach, modeling the abbreviated bathing suits that Keith so much disliked. He had asked her for his sake to give up doing it, and she had lifted her stubborn young chin and flatly said, "I won't!" And then he had put that hard steely look in his angry eyes and gone away. She had laughed as he went, and told herself he would come back soon enough. She had fully expected that he would be present at the fashion show. All day she had watched for him, searched the cheery throngs of onlookers, but had not been able to find his fine aristocratic face anywhere among them. And when it was all over and one of the handsomest prizes hers, and she had come to the house to rest, she had flung the expensive bauble on her dressing table more vexed than she cared to own even to herself, arrayed herself in embroidered peacocks and sat down to sulk.

But still, he might come even yet. Now that it was all over he probably would come quietly. It was his way, that was somehow intriguing and different from the ways of other young men. Then things would go on as they had, and she would have won her point. At least she would have won half of it. The whole of her victory would have been won if he had come to see her in the much discussed attire. That would have been a real triumph, to have made him see and enjoy the exhibition, and make him own afterward that she had been so lovely in the costume that he forgot all about his objections. But at least it would be something if he came back as soon as the show was over.

So she sat and waited, angrily, impatiently, yet more eagerly than it was her wont to await the approach of any young man. There were usually too many at her feet for her to miss a mere delinquent. Perhaps his very refusal to give in to her every whim intrigued her all the more to conquer him.

At last she heard the car drive up, and her father's voice below, speaking to the chauffeur. She sprang up and went to look through the window. No, there was no one with him! Her face took on its vexed look again. Still, Keith had only met her father once, just for a moment. He might not have made himself known at the station. It would be like his pride to take a cab, or perhaps walk, or—he might even be waiting till after dinner and calling more formally. But of course that would show that he was still holding some of his anger.

She turned and went back to her place by the table where she could study again the face of the young man, her latest victim, who was by way of rapidly becoming more to her than she had ever really intended.

Sometime later there came a tap at her door and her father entered.

Almost at once after he was seated his eyes wandered about the room and rested upon the picture.

"Your young man didn't come to the office today. I thought you were going to send him."

"I was, but you see I didn't get that far with him, Dad. He's horribly stubborn! I'm very angry at him!"

She drew her beautiful brows into an angry scowl.

A shade of something like amused satisfaction crossed her father's face as he watched her.

"So!" he said grimly, "you've found somebody you can't bend at a word, have you? He must be a pretty good man if he can stand out against you."

"Now, Dad!" reproached the daughter with a furious glance at her amused parent, "I thought you said you were a hundred percent for *me!*"

"Oh, so I am! You're all right. Chip off the old block and all that. Only I can't help admiring when I see a better man than I am."

"What do you mean, a better man than *you* are? I didn't say anything like that."

"No, I know you didn't, but I know it must be so. Any man who can stand out against you and do something you don't want done is a winner."

Anne lifted her proud head nonchalantly.

"He's not a winner with me unless I choose to let him be!" she stated, with much more assurance than she felt. "I'm not sure I want to take the trouble to bother with him. I'm frightfully angry at him."

"What's the cause?"

"Oh, he undertook to tell me what to wear at the fashion show! Or rather what *not* to wear!"

"He did? Well he has more courage than I'd have. What is he, anyway? A man-dressmaker? Or one of these long-haired artists that want to combine mud and garbage and call them artistic."

"Oh, no, nothing like that!" said the girl. "He's just old-fashioned. Didn't want me to go out in public in a stylish bathing suit. He'd be perfectly satisfied, I suppose, if I'd staged a long-sleeved high-necked black dress with a skirt and stockings for swimming."

Her father looked at her quizzically.

"Ummm! I'm not so sure he isn't right after all. It makes me hot under the collar sometimes to see you cutting around with nothing on but a scrap like a skimpy pocket handkerchief. It wasn't the way your mother would have dressed you!"

"Oh, Dad! You're hopeless! My mother would of course have dressed me as other girls are dressed."

"I'm not so sure!" sighed the unscrupulous man of the world. "Your mother was an unusual woman."

"Well, I wouldn't have stood for it if she had tried to put me into anything queer."

"I've a notion you would, Babe! I think you would have come up with a few different ideas, if she had lived. And I guess I'd have been different, too! I guess I've been a mighty poor hand to train a girl-child! All I knew was to make money and hire other people to do the training."

"Heavens, Dad! Don't call me Babe! And why the sob stuff? You don't feel sick or anything, do you? I thought you came up here to help me in my difficulties, but instead you seem to have taken the other side."

"Oh no!" said the man with a sigh and a settling of his heavy frame deeper into the big chair, "I was just talking. But go on with your tale. What's the story? Why didn't the young man turn up at the office today as you promised me last night he would do?"

"I *told* you. We had a battle. He got angry and I couldn't get anywhere with anything else after that."

"You mean you didn't tell him?"

"Oh, I told him, all right! But I might as well have told it to a stone wall for all the impression it made."

"You mean he didn't answer you at all?"

"Oh, he answered me. He answered me plenty!"

"What did he say. Wasn't he grateful that I was willing to let him in on some deep stuff and put him on Easy Street?"

"I should say not! Anything but! He as much as told me that such get-rich-quick schemes weren't honest!"

"*What?*"

"Well, not in so many words. But he gave the effect all right, and then he said he was an architect. I gathered that he considered himself foreordained from all eternity to be an architect, and that he would be committing sacrilege to be anything else."

The father's face was a study. He was divided between indignation and a kind of admiration for the young man who had the audacity to take such a stand.

"Well, how did he think an architect was going to support you in the manner to which you are accustomed?"

"I put that idea across to him," said Anne meditatively, "and he held his proud head high and went off!"

"Perhaps he intended to allow me to continue to have that privilege." The father gave a brief derisive grin. "Like several others of your brilliant followers."

"Oh, no!" said Anne sharply. "Nothing of that sort. In fact, he made it very plain to me that anybody who married him would live on what he could make, or not live at all!"

"I see!" said the father, "one of those proud-but-poor and intends-to-stay-so! Well, and so you didn't actually tell him at all that I was willing to meet him this morning, that it was in the nature of an appointment?"

"No!" said Anne scornfully. "He was too mad! He was simply furious about that bathing suit! And when he gets furious he freezes up like an icicle. I didn't want to waste my ammunition on a coat of mail."

"I see!" said the father thoughtfully. "Perhaps he's one who needs to be taken by guile. Invite him here to dinner and make a careless approach, startle him by a few facts, and a real proposition in actual figures. He is likely only ignorant. I think I could probably explain away his fears about dishonesty. He needs to understand modern methods of finance. If that will help you any I'll be glad to do what I can. He seems to be an interesting chap even if he is stubborn. He must have some backbone. Anyhow, I'd like to make a study of him since you're wasting so much time on him. I don't want you to get stuck with some dummy!"

"He's no dummy, Dad. He's got entirely too much

backbone to suit me! I haven't the slightest intention of getting myself a keeper. And I intend to order my own costumes always whether they happen to suit anyone else or not."

"Of course you would," said the father grimly, "but all the same it wouldn't hurt you to have a keeper. However, whatever you want to do I'll try to co-operate. I can arrange to be down here in time for dinner tomorrow night, I think, if you care to plan something then."

"Thanks awfully, Dad! You're sweet! I'll think it over. At present I'm rather furious at him. Besides, I don't know how to get in touch with him. I telephoned three times today and left word for him to call me, but I haven't heard a thing. He may have jumped off the Woolworth building by this time, though I suppose we'd have heard of it before now."

"Don't worry," said the father dryly. "Young men with backbone aren't jumping off the Woolworth building every day. You'll probably see him again when he gets his mad worked off, and a little absence will perhaps make him more tractable. He isn't by any means out of a job, is he? That might be helpful."

"No, he's got himself a place in an architect's office, and thinks he has a prospect of buying himself a partnership."

"Not a bad idea, but what with?" asked Mr. Casper.

"I don't know. He doesn't talk much about himself. I think he has a little money. I don't know how much."

"Family?"

"I don't really know. Family is the smallest part of my worries. If I didn't like his family, I could freeze them out."

"Maybe! It's not always so easy. But I think I'd better begin to look into things. What firm is he with?"

"I think the name is Sawyer."

"Not Sawyer, Poole, and Jewett?"

"That's it."

"Well, I might be able to work something with them. I

hold a good many operations in my power, and if I promised to throw certain contracts in their way, I'm sure they would find it convenient to let even a promising young man know that they had no further need for his services."

Anne Casper frowned.

"Wait a little, Dad, before you go so far. He's pretty headstrong."

"All right, just as you say. But I think I could work it. It wouldn't need to be known who was the power behind the action, you know. And sometimes a little starvation is a good thing to bring down a proud spirit. If he had no job at all and no prospect of one, he might not hold up his head so high, especially when a good proposition and hard cash was offered him. I know plenty of young men who would jump at such a chance as I'm ready to give him if you say the word."

"So do I," sneered Anne Casper, curling her too-red lips in disdain. "I'll think about it, Dad, and let you know developments. Meantime, keep tomorrow night open for dinner and be here early if you can."

A servant entered just then with a tray of tinkling glasses, and the matter was discussed no more. But while Anne Casper sipped her pleasant drink, she was planning a campaign.

Meantime the young man in question was a hundred miles away helping to wash curtains, and not once thinking of her the whole afternoon.

And over across the lawn from a second-story side window, Mrs. Gassner watched greedily as the young man and the girl, with the help later of a little sister and a young brother, and then still later an older brother, worked gaily, stretching curtains out in the shady side yard.

7

THE expedition after Ransom's adversary did not prove successful. It was reported that he had gone to visit his aunt in the city, and there seemed to be nobody around belonging to him, nobody who knew anything more about him, so Keith Morrell returned with his young defender just in time to see the curtains coming out of the washer.

With enthusiasm he plunged into the work of putting them on the stretchers, despite Daphne's protests that she could easily do them alone.

"But I want to do it," he insisted firmly. "And look how I wasted your time this morning."

"It wasn't wasted," she declared, "it was a real holiday for me, and to have actually seen the inside of the dear old house is something I shall treasure, because now I shall have a real picture of it as it is, and not just a conjured vision from my imagination."

"And you have given back to me something I thought I had lost forever," he said earnestly. "Now, give me that curtain! Is this the hem that goes to the bottom? This isn't going to take long. We'll have them on the frames in a jiffy, and then while they are drying can't you and I go over to my garden and find some flowers for your mother?"

"Why, how lovely!" said Daphne, her eyes sparkling. "Mother will love it."

"Fine!" said Keith with a boyish smile. "And then— you'll let me stay long enough to put up the curtains again at the windows, won't you? I'd feel happier if I might."

"That would be grand," said Daphne, "but we've already taken a lot of your time."

"I'm not going back to New York till evening," he said with sudden decision, "so why mightn't I call it a holiday, too?"

She gave him a swift searching glance.

"You call this a holiday? All right, you may help, if you'll stay to dinner afterward," she said gaily.

"I'd like nothing better, but wouldn't that be an imposition?"

"We'll love to have you, and I know Don will be disconsolate if he gets back and finds he didn't get in on your visit."

"I'll stay!" said Keith happily. "I liked him."

"You won't have such a grand meal as you had last night at Evelyn Avery's," warned Daphne gravely.

"I'll bet it will be *better*," said the guest. "I'm fed up on these formal dinners. They all taste alike. I enjoyed my lunch here a lot, and I certainly didn't want to go last night, but I couldn't seem to get out of it very well. I got away as soon as I could and went to call on Emily Lynd."

"Isn't she a dear!" said Daphne.

"She certainly is! My mother loved her. And she thinks a lot of you. She told me how you bring her flowers, and she couldn't say enough in praise of you."

"I love her," said Daphne simply, "and I do enjoy seeing her eyes light up when I bring her flowers."

"I wish our garden were as nice as it used to be. I'd like to think you would take her some of mother's flowers, too."

"Oh, may I? I'd love to."

"You sure may! I'll have to see to getting someone to clean up the beds a bit, and perhaps the plants would bloom better."

"Oh, don't bother to get anybody. Why not let Ranse and Beverly go over there and weed the beds occasionally? They would count it the privilege of a lifetime."

"Would they? Then I give them carte blanche to do whatever you say, and tell them to keep an expense account for tools and so on and I'll come down some day and settle with them."

"They certainly will be delighted!" said Daphne, a light of pleasure in her eyes.

"But say," said the young man as he carefully slipped the last inch of curtain into line on the frame, "don't we have to wash the windows while these things are drying? It seems to me that was a part of the ceremony of washing curtains."

"Oh, mother had Maggie, the cleaning woman, do that this morning. They're all ready for the curtains," said Daphne, laughing. "But it's nice that you know about little homely things like that; it sort of rounds out your character as our hero of nursery days."

"Say," said Keith, grinning boyishly, "if I stick around here much longer you certainly will succeed in making me think I'm something great!"

Mrs. Deane up at her window heard the gay laughter, and looked out indulgently, perhaps a trifle anxiously. What a good time those two were having together out there stretching curtains! How nice it would be if her girl had a friend like that! And yet she hoped Daphne wouldn't get any foolish ideas. For even though she had made a story out of the big house and its family, she had always taken great care to have no sentimental nonsense about it. And now of course these children were grown up. Oh, it mustn't be that what had been a seemingly harmless game of watching the neighbors, should turn out to hurt her girl, her dear wonderful girl! For this young man, no matter how well he had been brought up, was rich and had traveled and had advantages that they had never been able to afford for their children. He would have but a passing thought for a quiet little girl in his home town. And alas, she herself had set the stage with romance for her girl. It had been very wrong. She wished now that Daphne had not invited the young man to lunch. But he would soon be gone back to New York of course, and they probably would never see him again. One day couldn't possibly do any harm!

And then, of course, there was the new minister. Not that she liked *him* so much, herself, though he was good looking, and had the good taste to like Daphne. Daphne herself seemed to be very noncommittal about him so far. But at least it wasn't as if Daphne had nothing to take her thoughts away from this pleasant interval.

She sighed as she thought of the minister. What was the matter with that minister, anyway? Or was it just that she was a silly old romanticist herself, and couldn't see glamour in a modern, matter-of-fact egotist? Well, the Lord would guard her child! And she lifted up her heart in a brief prayer, and turned from the window with a smile. It was nice to hear the pleasant voices down on the lawn.

And over in the next house, Mrs. Gassner had transferred her point of observation to the sewing room window which was on the side of the house overlooking Deanes' lawn, and she missed nothing, not even when Keith called Daphne to help him with a troublesome corner that had stretched itself out too long for the frame.

"H'mmmm! I wonder what the minister would say to *that!*" she murmured to herself.

Presently the two young people took a basket and went off across the back fence again to the Morrell garden, and Mrs. Gassner hurried back to the second-story back bedroom.

"Well, of all things!" she said as she presently saw the two lifting branches that had overgrown their bounds and searching out blossoms from the borders of the paths. "What on earth can they be doing now? Probably they lost something this morning, a wrist watch or a ring or something. I do wish I had my spy glass that I loaned to Mrs. Brower the last time she went to the shore. I wonder why she doesn't bring it back. I'll send Elvira over after it the first thing when she gets home from the city tonight. I'm missing a lot!"

It took a long time to find the right flowers. Keith kept remembering some pet plant of his mother's and searching to see if it had died out. But they finally came back to the house with a well-laden basket, and spent another half hour arranging them.

And then the curtains were dry and they took them off the frames and hung them at the windows in crisp folds.

"They look great, don't they?" said Keith standing back when it was all done. "Say, this has been more fun than I've had since I left home to go to college. It seems as if there hadn't been any real home anywhere since that. Of course, I enjoyed college, and the travel, and all that, but it wasn't like home!"

Daphne watched his face and felt a thrill of joy that he was measuring up to her ideal of him, hour by hour through this delightful day.

Keith drew a sigh of pleasure, and grinned at her.

"Well," he said happily, "I'll put this stepladder away and get those frames taken apart and then we'll call it a day."

It was while he was taking the curtain stretchers apart that Donald arrived, swinging stalwartly over the back fence and coming across the lawn.

"Hello, there!" said Keith, "I'm here yet, you see! Hung around to tell you how good you are at baseball."

"Oh, say, is that you again?" said Donald delighted at the

unexpected guest. "Say, this is great! You haven't come back to your house to live after all, have you?"

"No such luck!" said Keith, his smile sobering. "I work, brother. I have a job in New York. I'm due at the office in the morning at nine o'clock. I ought to have been there today, but business detained me and I had to send a telegram instead. But I've had a grand time today. Wish you'd been here. I'd like to try my hand at catching a few of your whizzers. Though I don't suppose I'd be much at it now. I haven't had a chance to play a game for almost three years."

Don grinned.

"Pitch ya a few after supper," he said, with a delighted grin. "I gotta go and get washed up now. Been driving a bus all day and I feel crusty!"

When Keith came back in the house he found Daphne setting the table.

"Please let me help," he petitioned, giving a swift survey of the table and then reaching into the sideboard drawer for more forks, anticipating Daphne's next move. "You know it's great to feel I belong somewhere, even if it's only for a single day."

She lifted laughing eyes.

"We certainly can't be said to have made you feel like an outsider today!" she said.

"No," he said thoughtfully as he laid the spoons carefully at the right. "No, you haven't. You've been wonderful to me. But that wasn't the way you began yesterday. You know you rather resented my speaking to you." He gave her a mischievous glance.

The color flushed her cheeks, and then she lifted her steady glance.

"You know that you hadn't the slightest idea who I was when you spoke to me," she said quietly. "You didn't even *think* you'd ever seen me before. And I didn't like to think you were like that. I—was disappointed—in you, if you must know the truth.

And now it was Morrell's turn to flush.

"Please!" he said earnestly, "I'm *not* like that! I don't go around picking up strange girls. I really don't. I can see how it must have looked to you, but—well—when I first saw you there on the grandstand you looked up as if you were going to speak to me, which was perfectly natural, of course, since we were old schoolmates. But I had been watching you·for some time, trying to think who it was you reminded me of, going over the list of all my former associates, and I had just about decided that it was my mother of whom you made me think, when you turned around and almost spoke, and then froze up and turned away."

"Well, you see," said Daphne, quite rosy now, with downcast eyes, a bit embarrassed, "when I turned around to look for father who had said he might come to the game if he got through in time, I saw you watching me, and for just a little instant I thought you recognized me. And then I knew at once you didn't—and of course I knew you wouldn't be likely to anyway—so I just turned away. And then when you spoke I couldn't bear to think you were just flirting—"

"Oh, I say now, *please!* I don't want you to think that of me! I don't know why I spoke to you the way I did. I hadn't the slightest intention of it. But I did want to find out who you were. Your face haunted me with a resemblance, so I slipped around back of the grandstand, intending just to watch and find out if you were somebody I ought to know, and then before I realized how it would appear to you, I spoke. I do hope you won't hold that against me!"

Daphne laughed merrily.

"Oh, no, I don't! We've had a good time today and I've forgotten all about it. We're just old schoolmates."

"But—I don't want you to be disappointed in what you grew up thinking I was."

"I'm not." Daphne's eyes sobered. "I guess I was too prim or something. After all, we did know each other well enough to have spoken, even if you had forgotten. I guess it was just my pride. Let's forget it."

She smiled at him and just then the professor-father came in and was introduced.

"Well, I'm glad to meet you, Mr. Morrell," said Mr. Deane. "You've changed a bit since the days when we used to see you over in your garden. But I remember your father well. I thought he was one of the finest men I ever knew. He was my first acquaintance in Rosedale, and he certainly was a friend to me in those first days when we came here and needed friends. I felt it keenly when he was taken away. He was a true Christian gentleman!"

"He was a wonderful father!" said Keith, his face kindling tenderly.

Daphne gave a quick glance at the two and slipped out into the kitchen to help her mother get the meal on the table, while they settled down on the wide couch in the dining room and talked. Daphne could hear them as she went back and forth putting things on the table. Something swelled pleasantly in her heart. She told herself that she was glad that the hero of the years was running true to form, and that the fairy story she had learned as a child had not been rudely proved to be a fake.

Donald came down and stood listening, putting in a word now and then, asking a question. Keith was speaking of the relative advantages of education at home and abroad. The mother glanced through the door and smiled. It was a pleasant atmosphere of home and friendliness. How well this guest fitted into the family life. Would he stand the test of intimacy, she wondered vaguely? Oh well, it was just for a day, but pleasant to remember.

Then they all sat down at the table and Keith thought again how nice it was to be here, how much more congenial than the Avery crowd!

Donald and Keith went out for a few minutes of ball play before the dark came down, and when they came in again the dishes were finished and Daphne had slipped upstairs and changed her dress. She was wearing a little pink cotton frock, filmy and crisp, that gave her the look of being very young and sweet. Keith looked at her and was reminded of high school days and the girl who had dropped into his classes in the middle of a semester and outstripped them all. What a fool he had been not to have cultivated her acquaintance then. But as she had explained, she had been scarcely ever available except for classes.

And now he suddenly realized that his day was almost over and he was loath to leave.

Daphne sat down at the piano and touched the keys lightly, wandering into an old melody that reminded him of his mother. They all sat down and a sort of holy hush came over them, as if it were a special time, a ceremony which they expected. And now Keith noticed the Bible Mr. Deane was opening. Family worship, of course, but it had been so long since he had even heard of the custom that he had forgotten. Dimly in his early childhood he could remember his father, too, with an open Bible, and his mother's arm about him while they knelt in prayer. His heart was deeply stirred. He felt as if he were in a dream of other days, and he began to dread the awakening. Tomorrow there would be New York, and—what? Anne Casper? His two worlds did not belong together. But this one was something he had lost long ago. In a few days it would be but a memory again.

After the prayer they sang a song or two, old hymns that he was surprised to find he knew. Then suddenly the living room clock struck the half hour and Don jumped up.

"I've got to beat it!" he declared with a wistful note in his voice. "I'm driving Mrs. Houghton into town tonight to the symphony concert, and it's time we were on our way."

"That means you'll be late coming home again," said his mother anxiously. "You need your sleep."

"Not necessarily," said Don with a wry face. "She may not stay long. She only wants to be seen in her private box awhile and then she may come home. She does that sometimes. I gather she doesn't give a whoop about the music itself. She may not know a symphony from a permanent wave, with a majority in favor of the wave. And that daughter of hers is a pain in the neck if there ever was one!"

"Donald, you shouldn't criticize your employers."

"I know, mother, but it's true. Good night, Mr. Morrell. Hope you come again. I'll vote for you to join our sunset team if you will."

"Thanks awfully, Don," said Morrell, "I appreciate that and if I ever get the chance I'll remind you of it. But say, haven't we known each other long enough for you to call me Keith? I'd like that."

"Sure, if you don't mind," grinned Donald, "but I'm a lot younger than you are, you know."

"Now, don't remind me of my age!" laughed Keith. "I can't help it, you know."

Merrily they separated, and then Keith suddenly remembered that he had heard Daphne tell the minister last night that she had two music lessons to give that evening. There used to be an eight o'clock train to the city and of course he should take it.

With a blank feeling of disappointment in his heart as if the light of a nice pleasant day had suddenly been put out, he said good night and hurried away. It was almost time for that train, and of course he ought to take it. Why did he feel so reluctant? By this time they must think him a great nuisance, though they had all eagerly invited him to return whenever he would.

Mr. and Mrs. Gassner were sitting on their vine-clad porch in the soft darkness as he passed their house and Mr.

Gassner was very hard of hearing. His wife was giving him an account of the day, while she kept an eye out toward the Deane home.

"Well, for goodness sake, if there he doesn't come now!" she was saying as Keith Morrell came within hearing. "*At last!* Do you know he's been there this whole blesssed day, hobnobbing with Daphne Deane! I thought she had better principles than that, and her as good as engaged to the new minister—if all they say is true, and I guess it is!"

Then the train sounded afar and Keith Morrell had to run, but he carried that sentence with him, and wondered as he swung himself on the last car why he should care even if she was engaged. She was just an old schoolmate. He had had a pleasant day, yes, but tomorrow night—or was it the next night?—Daphne Deane was going out with that prig of a minister he had seen at her gate last night, and he was going back to New York.

And Anne Casper?

8

THE train was well on its way to the city, when Bill Gowney arrived at the house of the real estate agent, William Knox, and rang the bell.

The agent was just on the point of going out to escape him. He hadn't expected him quite so early. Gowney's other visits had been made about nine o'clock. Knox wasn't anxious to meet Bill Gowney until he had that promised telephone call from New York. It was going to be embarrassing to explain the owner's reluctance to come to a settlement, and Knox felt that he must handle this matter cautiously. He couldn't afford to miss the fat commission on a sale like this. It must go through!

He came into his small parlor reluctantly, at the call of his angular wife, who resisted his mild effort to get out the back door unseen, and personally shepherded him down the narrow hall to the parlor.

"Oh, hello, Gowney! That you already?"

"Yeah. I thought I'd come in and sign them papers. You said you'd have 'em ready by last night, ya know, but I couldn't make it then. Had a little business up the state. But I had my son telephone. You got the message, didn't ya? Got the papers here?"

"Well, no, not to say *here,* Gowney. You see there's been a little hitch in the matter. It may hold ya up a day or two, but it'll come out all right in the end."

"Hitch? Whaddya mean?" Gowney got up and stalked over to the desk where the agent sat and scowled down at him.

"Well, you see the owner was here himself yestiday. I found he wasn't just ready to fall in with our plans, not to say *ready,* not as ready as I had been led to expect by his letters."

"You mean he wasn't willin' ta take the offer? You mean he wanted more money?"

"Well, I 'spose that's about what it amounted to," said the agent cautiously. "He didn't exactly say so in so many words, but he wasn't impressed with the figures offered. Not as impressed as I expected him to be. You see he's been away in New York and Europe and other places, and I suppose he's got pretty big ideas."

"Well, why didn't ya offer him more?"

"Well, I did suggest that you might be willing to raise the figure a little, but I didn't get anywhere. You see you have to have a definite offer to get anywhere with a young man like that."

Gowney strode to the window and stared out into the dark a minute and then he whirled around.

"Well, offer him another ten thousand," he said, biting his words off shortly. "Things have gone too fur for me to go back, an' I gotta get this settled right away. Time's a big object with me. When's he gonta let ya know?"

"Well, he didn't exactly say."

"Know his telephone number?"

"I have his New York address," said Knox. "I could get him on the phone, I 'spose. But there ain't any hurry like that, is there? Long distance phone calls mounts up quick, ya know."

"Get him on the phone, I tell ya. I gotta get this settled right away. Several things has come up an' I wantta be able to tell somebuddy I'm taking possession tonight."

The agent looked startled at the haste.

"I cud get him in a letter by airmail," he suggested.

"I gotta know *right away,* I tell ya. Call up right now! Whadd' I give ya that retainer for ef I ain't got no rights? Get busy there an' call 'im!"

The buyer was ominously still while the call was put in, and while they were waiting Knox tried to be affable.

"Nice day it's been," he remarked dropping into a chair by the telephone.

But the caller only grunted, and then after a second he whirled around with stormy eyes and asked:

"You think ten thousand more'll satisfy him?"

"Well, I should think it would," said the agent blandly, seeing his commission rise. "Of course I wouldn't want to guarantee it would. But I can't see why he wouldn't be satisfied with that. It's really more than I would expect ta get myself if the property was mine, but young folks have ideas, ya know."

The caller sat down stiffly in a straight chair and stared at the agent.

But presently the ring came, with the message that Mr. Morrell was out of town and was not expected back till late that night, or even tomorrow morning.

Gowney made some strong remarks, then, and the agent looked anxiously toward the hall door hoping Martha hadn't heard them. Martha had a way of appearing and speaking her mind at times, and this was too momentous a matter to run any risks. What if it should be all off and he should lose that commission? He would have missed the chance of his lifetime.

"Tell you what," he said mildly. "I don't see any harm in your tellin' your friends you've taken possession taday. Of course, it is a little irregular, but ef you saw fit ta pay a small down-payment, ya know, I should think it would work out all right. I should think he might feel a moral obligation ta let it go at that!"

Gowney's sharp little eyes twinkled as he studied the mild face of the agent.

"O.K. by me!" he said and flung down a roll of bills. "You'll stand by me if I take possession tanight, so ta speak?"

"Well, I'll do my best—," said Knox, with an uneasy memory of the young owner's face as he left him the night before. Perhaps he might be getting himself into a jam by making these tentative promises. But then, *surely*—all that money! No young man in his senses would hold out for more, and he had never heard that the Morrells were so awfully wealthy. No, of course it would be all right. But he sincerely hoped that Martha had not heard this last transaction. He stuffed the roll of bills hastily into his side pocket and tried to talk in a genially quiet tone.

"Well, I'm sure it will be all right. Of course, I'll—I'll return this—in case the deal—falls through!"

"Falls through?" shouted the bully. "It can't fall through now! I tell ya I've *got* ta have that property, an' you gave me your guarantee that it was as good as mine. I'll hold ya responsible! I'll knock anybody's block off that stops me now, an' I don't mean mebbe!"

Knox found he was trembling a little as he opened the door to usher his visitor away, but he drew a long breath and soothed him with a few smiling words of assurance. Then he turned with relief to come back into his bright little room and close the door behind him, and there was Martha standing in his way, her lips drawn in a thin line and her gray eyes full of apprehension.

"Now *William!*" she assailed him. "What's that man going to hold you responsible for? He looks to me like a jailbird!"

And while the temeritous Knox was taking a grilling from the capable Martha, Keith Morrell was leaning back in the train with his eyes closed, thinking with relief that he didn't have to sell his house. Of course he wouldn't sell the old home. He must have been crazy to even think of it. It had just been that dread of going through it alone and having his feelings harrowed. But now he was glad he had gone, glad that wonderful girl had been willing to go with him and give him a picture of his boyhood that somehow had been slipping, fading from his mind. He must not ever lose that. It was too precious a heritage.

Later that evening, after both her pupils were gone, Daphne went and stood in the window of her own room which looked out across the back yard and into the Morrell garden. It was from this window that as a child she had learned to watch for the movements of the little boy in the great house, and to idealize his life.

The darkness was soft and sweet as it was wafted into the open window. Breath of honeysuckle and lilies from the dewy garden, old-fashioned pinks and mignonette. Daphne drew a deep breath of it, and it seemed like the essence of the day, a beautiful happy day with no shadows and doubts in it. It seemed like something perfect that she could put away with her treasures of memory and keep, a jewel that had no flaw in it.

Likely he would not come again. It was not to be expected. Though he had asked if he might. But that of course was just his courtesy, his pleasant appreciation of the day. He was in business and that would hold him. And he likely had a lot of worldly friends and interests. Oh, he wouldn't come again, of course, but it was nice to feel that he had been all right, not spoiled in any way, from the boy he had promised to be when she had known him in school. It was like closing the covers of a delightful book that one had enjoyed. Looking over the story and finding it good to hold in memory as a part of the beauty of life. She would think of it many times, perhaps, with pleasure, but the reading of it was definitely over of course.

Well, it was more than she had ever expected out of the childish visions, that they should come to a finish so gaily.

She drew a little wistful sigh as she looked out at the familiar lines of the dear old house across the garden, a lovely dark etching under its tall old elms, against the night sky, and there came a warm feeling at her heart that now she knew it both inside and out. She could vision the desk where the mother had sat, and the eager boy coming home from school to his welcome. She could see the fireplace before which the little boy had knelt to pray at his mother's knee, and the room as it must have looked with the toys scattered over the floor. She had a background now for all the stories her own mother had told when she was a child.

It was characteristic of Daphne that she was thinking more now of the boy she had not known intimately than of his real self with whom she had spent the long bright day. The little boy had belonged to her, but the young man was someone who lived afar and whom she would not likely see again, at least not often.

But suddenly as she stood watching the dim old house in the sweet darkness, a speck of light winked through the shrubbery. She watched it with alert eyes. A firefly? Only *one?* If it were a firefly, there would be more than one surely, and she searched the darkness intently for others. Perhaps this was only the advance guard.

It winked about in a circle, hovered over the same location, danced about a bit, disappeared, then steadily glowed in one spot for a moment, and was gone! A curious way for a firefly to act. There! There it was again! It was almost like the beam of a tiny pocket flashlight. Could it be that Keith had gone back to the house after all and was out there hunting for something that he had dropped in the darkness?

But no. The train had gone, and he had been insistent

that he must get back to New York. Besides, he hadn't any flashlight with him. She remembered his wishing for one when they went into the house, and he had been searching for the fastening of the shutter in the dark parlor, for, of course, the electricity was not on in the house.

There! There it was again! Just a wink. Oh, of course it was only an erratic little firefly, and she was a silly. She must go to bed.

But she did not turn on her light. Instead she undressed in the dark, breathing in the garden scents and keeping watch toward the old house. Once she thought she heard a grating sound like the pushing open of a door that stuck, and once she saw a wider flare of light. But when she went closer to the window all was dark, and of course it must be only her imagination working, the way it often did if she let it go.

After she lay down in her bed she thought she heard that creaking sound again, or was it more like the slam of a door? But when she went quickly to the window there was only still darkness, no more fireflies. She went back and lay down.

She was going over the day bit by bit now, examining everything that had been done and said, and enjoying it, as one would pick up a book of poems and glance at a sentence here, a phrase there, and sense the loveliness of each.

Usually she fell asleep at once when she lay down, but somehow tonight she couldn't. She told herself she was too excited. And why should she be excited over the mere dropping in of an old schoolmate whom she didn't know very well? Well, that perhaps was just the effect of her upbringing, her quiet life, filled with home duties and studies and little errands of kindliness. It was late when she did at last doze off, very late she knew, because Emily Lynd's light which always burned long after midnight, and which usually she could barely see from her pillow if she lay over to the extreme edge, was gone out. She was just slipping over the border into dreamland—or had she been over and come back?—when she was roused by some unusual sound.

It brought her broad awake and blinking toward the window again. Perhaps it was only some sliver of a dream mingling with her waking thoughts before she fell asleep.

What was that? A car? Surely yes, a motor running! Perhaps a truck. Perhaps the milkman. But no, the darkness of the sky showed it was not near enough to morning for him, and even as she reasoned the little clock on her mantel chimed three silvery strokes. Still that motor throbbed in low subdued tones. It was almost a stealthy sound, as if the motor had become human and was trying to whisper, and hold its breath. Now that was queer. Why should that be?

She stole from her bed again and tried to pierce the darkness, but though she could now distinctly locate the sound, she could see nothing but dense darkness. It had hidden itself in the blackest depth of shrubbery, and as nearly as she could tell it seemed to be standing just behind the big house. But there wasn't a light on it, there wasn't a sign of anything human, beside that furtive throbbing.

Stay! Wasn't there a movement, stealthy, but unmistakable? A footstep! The low murmur of a voice? Or was it?

She was growing weary as she knelt beside the window, and chilly with excitement, when at last there came a sound like a key turning in a rusty lock, a stealthy movement. Then a dark shape moved slowly across the night. The chugging of the motor was plainer now, and less furtive. Whatever it was had been parked behind the Morrell house, just opposite the low door to the cellar, she knew the exact spot, and now it was backing out of the drive! It had reached the road, and suddenly the sound of the engine went soft. It was coasting down the gentle slope that went past Emily Lynd's house to the highway! And it grew bolder as it went. But strain her eyes as she would she could see no light on it. They were traveling without a light.

Then suddenly a light shot out from Emily Lynd's window. Ah! Emily had heard that stealthy traveler too! She was not dreaming. Tomorrow she would take some flowers from the garden and go and call on Emily Lynd, and they would perhaps talk it over.

There was no sound of the soft throbbing of that motor any more. It had coasted smoothly down the grade and was thundering away into the night. And at last Daphne crept shivering back to her bed. Perhaps it was only some tired truck driver on a long trek from Washington to New York or somewhere, and he had just driven into the unused driveway to snatch a nap, lest he should fall asleep at his wheel.

She turned over comfortably and went to sleep.

9

BY the time Keith reached the city he had succeeded in dispelling to a certain extent the dismay that had seized him when he found himself really going away from Rosedale. He hadn't been able to explain that dismay to himself. He told himself that it was homesickness, and the memory of his mother, but he congratulated himself that he had come awake to his own feelings in time to save the house. He realized that it would have been in the nature of a disaster to have waked up some day and discovered its loss after it was too late to get it back again.

Funny little kid, that Ranse, to go fighting for an idea that had been given to him in his babyhood! Because that empty house couldn't really have meant anything to a child like that. But he was grateful to him for fighting against the thought, and for wanting to save a place that had been idealized for him.

He must keep in touch with that family. They were rare. The father was a most unusual man, not at all a modern man of the world. He must be famous in his line or a modern university would not keep him nowadays. A man who had family worship in his home, and spoke of

God as if He really existed! He must look him up and see just what his line was. A scholar he was surely. And the children all showed that they were bright. He let his mind run back and remember Daphne's quickness in the classes, the way she so easily outstripped most of her mates—and the way they were jealous of her and held aloof from her, just because she was different. They called her a grind, and pitied her. And now he saw that she was as far above them all as a star. Well, he wished his mother had known her well. It was curious why she hadn't. But he could see that the retiring nature of both Mr. and Mrs. Deane, and their desire to bring their children up in their own way and not just exactly after the pattern of all others, might have been a barrier not easily overcome. He remembered that his own mother had been of a retiring nature also.

When Keith Morrell got out of the train in the city station to take the New York express he almost ran into an elderly man who was walking in the other direction. He righted himself and apologized and suddenly recognized one of his father's closest friends.

"Oh, Mr. Dinsmore, I'm sorry!" he apologized. "But I'm so glad to have met you. It's good to see one of father's friends."

"Why, it's Keith Morrell, isn't it?" said the older man, grasping Keith's hand warmly. "Well, I declare! You're grown up! And aren't you the very image of your dear father as he was when I first knew him! I've been wondering where you were. You know I used to tell your father that I had my eye on you to come into our firm when you got ready. You always said you were going to be an architect, you know. Have you got over that?"

"No, I'm doing my best to be one," Keith smiled. "I wish I'd known there was a chance for me with you."

"But why didn't you come back and ask?"

"Well, I guess I shrank from coming back where there

were so many memories. And then I got a chance to go into an office in New York—but I wish—"

"Well, perhaps it isn't too late yet, boy! New York, eh? Who are you with?"

"Sawyer, Poole, and Jewett."

"Not half bad to have landed with them. Partnership, is it?"

"Well, not yet," grinned Morrell.

"Well, things turn over in this world, and maybe you'll want to make a change sometime. If you ever do, look me up. I don't want to influence you against your will, but I've always had a liking for you."

"Thanks awfully!" said Keith. "I'll keep that in mind. I'm not so sure but there might come an upheaval of things somewhere soon, and I might take you at your word."

"Good! Glad to hear it!" said the older man fervently. "I've always looked on you as a sort of half-son of mine anyway, and I'd like nothing better than to have you around all the time. By the way, are you selling the old home? I met that agent out in Rosedale the other day and he said he was selling it for you."

"No," said Keith firmly. "I'm not selling. He wrote he had a customer, and I came down to look things over, but I've decided to keep it. Maybe I'm foolish, but I can't quite make up my mind to part with it."

"Good boy! I'm glad of that. I'd hate to see it pass out of the family. I know your father cared a lot for it, and sacrificed to get it back. You know he was born there, and it had belonged for a couple of generations back to the Morrells. Your father was proud of its history. It was his dream to leave it to you."

"Yes," said Keith with compunction in his voice. How could he have forgotten all that, and let himself think for a moment that he could sell the dear old home?

"Well, I'd like to see you married to some nice girl and living there," said Mr. Dinsmore wistfully. "Like to see you coming in town every day to our office. Taking over after I'm gone, perhaps. I think we could work together, boy! Think it over! I'm getting old, you know, and I'd like to see somebody around that sort of belonged."

"You're very kind," said Keith, feeling suddenly as if he were a little boy again and this old friend was offering to take him to the zoo.

"I'm taking the train for Chicago tonight, and I'll have to be moving. It's almost starting time. But think it over, boy, think it over. And run down sometime and see me, anyway."

Then he passed on through the gate to the Chicago train, and Keith Morrell stood staring after him, finding something like tears in his own eyes.

Suddenly it came over him that he was glad he had come down, glad he had stayed over another day and started home just at this time. If he hadn't, he never would have met this kindly friend, never have known the friendship that was still his, and somehow it touched him greatly. He wouldn't have missed that warm grip of the hand, that kindly tone as he said, "Think it over, boy" for anything in the world.

Thoughtfully he boarded his own train for New York. He had bought an evening paper but he did not look at it when he sat down. Instead he pulled his hat down over his eyes, put his head back, closed his eyes, and just thought, feeling himself in the grip of an emotion that was sweet and yet rather overwhelming.

It was strange how those few words recalling his father, and the home he had sacrificed to buy and save for him, had changed his attitude toward the old house. He wanted now to keep it for its own sake. Not just for mere sentimental reasons, but because it represented the abiding place of three generations of his family. It stood for fine noble things, for sweet homely old-fashioned God-fearing standards, and for clean living, right thinking. He had a sudden desire to live there some day himself and continue the traditions that had made the place respected.

It was likely that the tale young Ransom Deane had brought home from his bloody fight had been very much overdrawn. It was unthinkable that any man would dare to come into that staid old quiet suburb and attempt to make a road house and gambling den or worse of a respected old house, but it would be bad enough just to have a place that had been a landmark for a century or two, turned into a noisy apartment house.

But anyway, no matter what the intention, he was definitely not going to sell it. That was settled. He had given his word. And the minute he set foot in the Pennsylvania Station in New York he would send a telegram to that persistent agent in unmistakable language, once and for all. Some day—*some* day, he would go back there and live. He smiled ruefully as he remembered Dinsmore's picture of his wife living with him there. His wife! Well, if Anne Casper was to be his wife, which of course was by no means certain now, he was quite sure she would never live there. He could see her lip curl and her nose tilt at the thought of quiet little Rosedale, and even if she came there she would feel that the old Morrell place was on the wrong side of town and would want to build on Winding Way or Latches Lane as Evelyn Avery had suggested.

Oh, Anne Casper! Why couldn't she be different? Why couldn't she be sweet and serviceable like the girl he had been with all day? He'd half closed his eyes and watched the darkness whirl by, interspersed with flashes of lights in small towns, and remembered Daphne's face as she had looked around upon the rooms in his old home and loved it. How she had caressed every old bit of polished furniture with her glance, and her tone had fairly lilted with pleasure in each room. How she had helped the old days to return, and memories to troop around and people the rooms again. How she had brought back even the sweet little drama of his own evening prayers and revisioned it for him as he stood there beside her. She, a little neighbor girl, who had made pleasant playtime pictures of his home and rejoiced in them!

Why couldn't Anne Casper be like that? Why couldn't her eyes grow misty over the tale of his childhood? But they wouldn't. He knew they wouldn't. It wasn't in her to be anything but bored by such a recital. He couldn't fancy himself telling her these things, these sacred things. Or if he did he couldn't fancy her doing anything but laugh at them, laugh them to scorn. She would call him a sentimentalist. He could hear the tones of her voice, and he winced over the thought. Why had he ever got tangled up with Anne Casper, anyway? She wasn't his kind and he wasn't hers. She wasn't a girl his mother would have loved. And she would never have honored his mother and her standards the way a girl he loved should honor them.

And yet—she was very beautiful! And sometimes she seemed to care for him a great deal!

Well, he was probably done with Anne. She had given her ultimatum, and he had turned it down. If she gave in and called him back to her—but she wouldn't, not Anne, with that stubborn pretty little chin. But if she did, it would prove that she really cared for him, wouldn't it? Or would it? When he tried to judge Anne he was perplexed. She seemed to be an unknown quantity. Perhaps that was one reason why she intrigued him so much.

And what would life be, lived beside a woman like that? Tempestuous? He wouldn't like to live in the midst of tempest and uncertainty. He wanted a calm peaceful home, filled with love and sunshine. Was it conceivable that Anne could fit into such a background? Could help to create such an atmosphere?

He found himself thinking of the home where he had been all day. The sunny atmosphere, the free harmonious life of the whole family, all working together, all interested in the same things.

But *work!* Anne didn't work. She had probably never done anything harder in her life than to play a set of tennis, or sail a boat, or win a swimming match. She wouldn't want to work. She might even feel degraded if she had to work. He couldn't think of her taking down curtains and washing them and putting them on stretchers. He had never seen her tried, of course, and he might possibly be misjudging her, but his feeling about it was that she would scorn such employment, consider it menial.

And yet what a good time he and that other girl had had today working side by side. How utterly unspoiled she was, how sane and wise she seemed! Now that was the kind of girl his mother would have approved as a friend for him.

But Daphne Deane was "as good as engaged to the new minister." The words still echoed unpleasantly in his mind from the vine-clad porch of the Gassner house, and reached him over the miles that were rapidly multiplying between himself and the delightful day he had spent. Involuntarily he sighed. Whatever the new minister was, he hoped he was good enough for Daphne. And of course a minister would be very well suited— No, he would put it the other way, Daphne Deane would be an ideal minister's wife. He could see that in a flash. But he grudged her that life unless the minister were also an ideal minister. Well, perhaps he was. Why should he care anyway? But he did. Probably just because it was all a part of the old life that she had given him back again, and he hated to think of anything imperfect connected with it. Anyway, he must stop thinking about it. The thought of that minister whom he had visioned but dimly in the moonlight was somehow spoiling the brightness of the day he had just spent, and he didn't want it spoiled. It was something unsullied and lovely to keep in memory. And besides, he had Anne Casper to think of.

Or did he? Well, at least he would write a letter to Daphne, thanking her for the day. That would be expected of him. And he had promised dear old Emily Lynd to go down sometime soon and call on her. He could run in on the Deanes for a few minutes' call, and then—well, probably he wouldn't see them any more, but it was nice to have them on his list of friends. And he must never forget that Daphne had given him back the most precious things of his youth, the things he might otherwise have forgotten utterly till it was too late to regain them.

As he sat thinking he began to enumerate in his mind things that he ought to change in his habit of living. Prayer. That was among the most important. He must get back to some sort of prayer. He wasn't just sure how much he still believed of the old religion his mother had taught him, but he had a feeling that prayer, at least, was an essential, that it would somehow clarify the atmosphere of his life, and help him to see things more clearly in their relative values.

He tried to think back and remember when he had stopped praying, and decided that it was somewhere along in the second year of his college life. He had a roommate who never prayed, who jeered at the idea in a pleasant gentlemanly way, and who was a swell fellow in other ways if there ever was one. Had he let that influence him? The swell fellow had had a brief and brilliant career, married a famous beauty, a youthful divorcee, before his graduation and three weeks after his marriage had plunged from an airplane and ended his bright career. It all came back to Keith now, that first night that he had knelt to pray with his friend Estabrook in the room. The caustic sarcasm, the mild amusement in his handsome eyes. He had prayed hurriedly, secretly, after that, anxious to please his mother and keep his promises to her, and yet not get caught again on his knees. Fool that he had been. *Young* fool! Extremely young! Not afraid of his friend, of course, yet unwilling to seem a sissy!

Of course, he couldn't have had any very deep conviction himself about prayer or he wouldn't have been a coward before a fellow-student. But yet he could remember back even when he was a boy in high school, what utter faith he had had in prayer. How he had resorted to it on all occasions when he felt a need of any kind of help, how often he had thought he received distinct answers to prayer, and felt a throb of thankfulness. How implicit had been his faith when he was quite young! And where had it gone? Had it really gone, or just been mislaid? Covered up by the rubbish with which he had chosen to clutter his life? When had it disappeared? He couldn't quite remember. There hadn't been any distinct time when he abandoned it. He just forgot all about it, in the cares and interests and sorrows that the years had brought.

But now that he recognized its absence he had a definite idea that he ought to do something about it. The son of his father and mother had no business going around like an atheist. He knew better. He recognized that that interesting college chum of his must have been a sort of atheist or he never would have lived his life as he had, died as he had. He remembered sharp-flung words that voiced his unbelief. They hadn't bothered him at the time, but he saw now they should have done so. If he had not allowed his Christian faith to become dim, a lot of things might have been different in his own life. Perhaps even this perplexity of Anne Casper would never have been there to vex him! And dimly it came to him that his own life might have counted for more in its contact with the lives of others. Perhaps something had been expected of him when in the course of human destinies his life had been sorted out in a pair with Harold Estabrook for two long years. Estabrook was gone beyond his power to reach now, and his own life was at least two years back in its moral tone from what it had been then. He could not go back and undo any of it! That was an appalling thought!

He went on with his list. Prayer. He must begin to pray again. That is, if it was possible to get back to praying terms with a God whom he had forgotten so long.

His Bible? Well, of course that too had been packed away in a trunk that same year with his discarded prayers, and eventually been given away to the Salvation Army, hadn't it? No, perhaps he had kept it after all. He seemed to remember that at the last minute he had found an inscription written by his mother on the fly-leaf, a precious personal word, and for that he had kept it. It must be packed away somewhere in the old house. Sometime he would go down again to Rosedale and hunt it up, just for the sake of reading his mother's tender words.

Then there was church service. He hadn't attended a church service in a long time. Of course there had been chapel in college, but it was always more or less of a form and quite elective. Even when he went he had usually used the time to glance over the headings of some theme that he must be ready to discuss in a following class. But gradually he had ceased even the occasional form of attendance at chapel.

Of course when they were in Europe he sometimes went to a church with his mother, but more to admire the architecture of the building in which they were supposed to be worshiping, than with any idea of worship.

He resolved that he would start going to church again. Not that he was especially interested in doing so, but merely that he might cultivate a Christian character such as his father's son might be supposed to have. He felt that all these things would be in the nature of anchors to keep his life from drifting against dangerous rocks, and into unknown harbors. It was not that in any sense he felt that he was a sinner, and needed a Saviour. He was merely bringing his life to conform once more to the path in which his parents, who had been successful and respected citizens, had set his young feet. He felt that they were pretty safe guides to follow.

By the time that the train reached the Pennsylvania Station in New York Keith Morrell felt with self-respecting relief that he was well on his way to becoming everything that his mother could possibly expect of him.

He went at once to the telegraph desk and sent his message to Knox couched in no uncertain terms.

> Have decided not to sell my property in Rosedale. Please take it off your list. Do not even care to rent at present. Send bill for any expense you may have incurred in the matter.
>
> Signed,
> Keith Morrell

Having paid for his message he turned away satisfied that he was well on his way back to his mother's teaching and his mother's God. If he felt anything more about it at all, it was that God would be well pleased to see him coming back. He had perhaps been rather impolite to God for a time, but he was going to make it all up now, and refusing to sell the old home was the first step in setting his spiritual house in order.

He slept well that night, though he dreamed toward morning that Anne Casper sent word that she was coming to his office to see him, but when he went out to greet her it was Daphne who was there, rising to meet him, putting her warm hand in his, the way it had touched his in the sunny garden among the loam, and it thrilled him with a strange happiness. But she only looked up at him with those wonderful beautiful brown eyes of hers, and smiled at him, a strange wistful smile, and then suddenly she was gone, and it was Anne Casper standing there frowning and flashing her eyes at him. And he might not let his eyes search for Daphne in the shadows of the room, for Anne Casper was demanding his attention!

But all day long, at intervals, he remembered Daphne's look, and try as he would, he could not shake off that thrill of pleasure he had felt in her presence.

10

WHEN that telegram reached William Knox he was sound asleep in his bed, snoring the snore of the just, his over-fat pocketbook safely hidden in a little steel-lined compartment in an innocent-looking box, with his important papers. No one, not even Martha, had access to it, because he was the only one who knew the combination of the lock.

He had been snoring for approximately two hours when the telephone rang, and Martha, whose mind had not been at ease since the visit of Bill Gowney, was the first to hear it. In fact, William Knox seldom heard that telephone bell when he was in bed. He always left it to Martha to answer and to call him if it was necessary. But sometimes, especially in cold weather, she shook him awake and compelled him to go and answer it himself.

Tonight, however, having lain awake conjuring up all the possibilities of trouble that might come through that veiled threat of Bill Gowney's, she was alert and curious. It was not like any of William's clients to telephone at this hour of the night, unless it was that dark-browed man who had been so angry earlier in the evening. Of course, there was always the possibility that Harvey Knox, her stepson, might be in some sort of trouble. Maybe he was trying to get a surreptitious message across to his father when he thought she was asleep. Perhaps he was wanting to come home with his good-for-nothing wife, and live with them. And William Knox was just soft enough to say yes before she found it out. But somehow tonight that possibility did not loom quite so large as it often had. She was more afraid of that ugly-jowled man who had threatened William, and said something would be his responsibility. Perhaps this would be he again, and she could find out something more about it.

So she stole from her bed into the hall, shutting the door carefully behind her, and went to the telephone, answering "Yes?" in a tone that would have intimidated almost any mere telephone operator.

She caught the word "Western Union," and pricked up her ears.

"Yes," she said under her breath. "Yes, this is his home. I'll take the message."

She made them repeat it until she had written down every word and then she studied it under the hall light a full minute until she had memorized it, and figured out just about what it might mean to William Knox in the light of that threat in the early evening. Then she marched into the bedroom, thrust up the light like a banner, and stood over the snoring William, a gaunt figure in a high-necked nightgown and crimping pins, the severe lines of her face unsoftened by even her plain daytime garb.

"William!" she said, shaking him firmly with one hand while she held the paper containing her notes in the other. "Here's a telegram! *Telegram!* Do you hear?" she shouted in his good ear. And William turned over and said:

"Eh? What? A telegram?"

"Yes, I said a telegram! And now what do you think? You certainly have got yourself in one nice mess if ever!

What was it that Gowney man said to you about responsibility? Well, you've got it now, all right, and I expect this is going to ruin us at last. I've always told you you would do it, with your everlasting softness, always trying to accommodate everybody, even though you knew it couldn't be done. And now you've got your comeuppance!"

"Now, now Martha!" deprecated William Knox, "suppose you stop getting excited and just let me understand what you're talking about. Where is this telegram you're speaking about? Who brought it?"

"Brought it? Brought it!" sniffed Martha. "As if a telegram had to be brought in these days! We've got a telephone, haven't we? I took it, of course."

"But why didn't you call me, Martha? The wire was for me, wasn't it? You should have called me. Business calls should always be given to me."

"Yes? Well, do you want me to try to wake you up in time to take a message when it might have been somebody had died or something, and you snoring like the seven sleepers?"

"Well, then, Martha, where is this telegram? Who is it from? Are you going to tell me, or shall I call up Western Union and get them to give it over again?"

William Knox arose with all the dignity he could muster in his plaid pajamas.

"Well, it's from that Morrell man. He says he doesn't *want* to sell his house, and I heard you tell that Gowney bum that he might take possession tonight! *Now,* if you haven't got yourself in a jam, then my name's not Martha Knox."

William came over to his irate wife, took the paper she was holding and walked downstairs to his desk in the living room to study it. Martha followed him with questions, getting little satisfaction from him, whereupon she took to giving advice.

"If you ask *me,*" she volunteered, sitting half way up the stairs with her nightgown wrapped around her feet, "I'd say you better get that young sprig on the telephone at once and tell him it's too late. You found you had already sold the house before he got here, or something like that. Or else I'd get my clothes on and go out and rout up that bum of a Gowney and tell him he *can't have* the house! You better take along whatever it was he gave you, and tell him you've been thinking it over and you can't feel to accept it. If it's money, I'd better go along. It isn't safe for you to go out so late with money alone, and I don't trust that Gowney anyway. If you'd asked *me—*"

"Well, but I *didn't* ask you, Martha! This is *my* affair. Will you let me handle it?"

"No, William," firmly, "I know my duty. You've got yourself in a jam and much as I disapprove I'll stand by you. I'm going with you if you are going out."

"Martha Knox, will you go back to your bed and try to get some sleep? This is my jam, isn't it? And I'll get out of it somehow. Now, *go!*"

Eventually, after she had said her say, Martha went because she knew she had faithfully said all there was to say. But William sat up till almost dawn trying to figure his way out of the affair. Then, when he found his head going around in circles he succumbed to sleep on the living room couch, and was snoring away serenely when Martha came down to get breakfast in the morning.

But over in the cellar of the old Morrell house, with cellar windows well draped in burlap to keep the light from sifting through, strange things were going on.

"William!" said Martha Knox, standing over him severely. "Did you call up that young Morrell on the telephone last night?"

"Well, no, Martha. I didn't want to upset him last night after a long journey."

"Well, what are you going to do about it?"

"You just leave that to me, Martha," said William. "I've got the matter all thought out. You leave it to me."

"Yes, leave it to you and who'll you leave it to?" said Martha angrily as she slammed out to the kitchen. *"Such works!* A man with no backbone and no common sense! Always getting into a jam!"

She waited until William had eaten a hearty breakfast before she mentioned it again.

"Well, aren't you going to call New York now? It would have been a lot cheaper to have called him in the night, but I suppose you figure since he's paying the expenses it doesn't matter. I don't call that being exactly honest, but at least you ought to call him now."

William cast a withering glance at the clock.

"I didn't want to call him at his apartment. It's better to do business at his office."

"Well, it's after nine o'clock, isn't it? He's surely there by this time. I do wish you'd get busy. You make me nervous as a cat."

"Well, you see, Martha, I'm a business man and I know business ways. It's never well to disturb a man the first thing when he gets to the office. There's the morning mail that has to be attended to and he can't be interrupted."

"Fiddlesticks!" said Martha. "What mail will that young sprig have to attend to, except letters from girls and invitations? Have a little sense, William, and go to that telephone at once!"

But William stuck it out until ten o'clock before he gave in to the haggling, the truth being that he couldn't quite decide just how to handle this important matter so that he would not lose his own share in the transaction. At last, unready though he was for the important conversation, he was driven to it.

But by this time Keith Morrell was off to Boston.

It hadn't been in his scheme of things at all to take

another journey, especially to Boston. But when he arrived at the office he found, instead of his regular routine work of drawing plans and making front elevations, that he had to pack a grip hurriedly and take the train in half an hour. The member of the firm who would naturally have gone on such an assignment had been taken suddenly ill.

"You'll have to go, Morrell," said Sawyer. "It needs somebody who thoroughly understands the plans. All instructions are in this envelope. I had them written out last night after you telephoned you would be in the office this morning. These people don't understand about the extra expense involved in making those changes they wanted. I think you can make it plain to them. I would have sent Hendrickson only he has not had anything to do with this contract, and I was afraid he wouldn't understand."

So Keith had been hurried away and surprisingly found himself removed for the time being from any necessity of meeting Anne.

Now Anne had written him a note inviting him to the shore for the week-end and promising him a good time in her most caressing manner, not even mentioning their differences of opinion. She had sent the letter to the office, that it might reach him sooner and it had arrived while he was in Rosedale. But in the hurry of getting him off, the office clerk had forgotten to give him his mail, so he did not have that on his mind either. As the office had provided him with plenty to do in the way of preparing for the coming interview in Boston, perhaps it was just as well.

So he sat in his Pullman chair with a table before him and papers spread over it, figuring away, drawing an outline now and again, making notes of the different points he must present. He realized that this was an important commission he had been given and he wanted to make good. It might help him to rise more quickly than he had hoped.

There is nothing like a lot of good hard work to make a young man forget girls, even sweet serviceable girls who know how to work and can bring to mind long forgotten prayers. Perhaps Keith had a realization of this as he put aside all other thoughts and worked away mile after mile. He was having his chance now, a small chance at least, and he was going to make the most of it and do this thing well.

His work in Boston was interesting, going over matters step by step with the firm who were giving the contract, figuring and redrawing and figuring again, telegraphing back and forth for instructions, and returning at last feeling that he had succeeded in what he had been sent out to do. It was somebody's fault of course that he didn't get Anne's letter at once, even the morning he reached New York again. It didn't get to his attention until late in the afternoon, after a day of good hard work that had given him a sense of satisfaction, and an added self-respect. He frowned as he read the letter, studied the date, and realized that it was this very evening for which she had invited him, hoping that the week-end could begin Friday night instead of Saturday. The last train for the shore would leave in just three-quarters of an hour.

He was in no mood to be thus easily placated. He had been working too hard and doing too well for the last few days to have an inferiority complex. He didn't care to let Anne patch things up lightly without any apology for her disagreeable imperiousness. She needn't think she could recall him as easily as that, with just a smile and the snap of her pretty little fingers. She wasn't to play fast and loose with him any longer.

Besides, there was a full morning's work waiting for his attention tomorrow, maybe longer than a morning's work, even if it was Saturday. He didn't intend to suggest to the office that he take a half-day off at this important stage of the game. Rather he would stay all the afternoon and work Saturday every hour and minute it contained than give the impression that he was an idler who was only hanging around for a holiday.

He shut his lips firmly, gave a perplexed minute or two to thought, and then almost haughtily betook himself to the telephone booth.

He told himself that he didn't care whether he got Anne or not. Just as well if she wasn't there. He would leave a message for her if he couldn't get her, and let things come out as they would. She would probably be furious at him for not replying sooner, but she might as well understand now as later that he was a working man and couldn't sit around and await her pleasure, nor dance to her piping all day long.

But Anne was there. She had not gone far from the telephone these last few days. She had almost been afraid that this new man-fancy of hers had more character than she supposed, and perhaps was really angry now. She answered at once, breathlessly, with that little pleased rising inflection she knew so well how to assume at times.

Still a bit haughty he explained that he had been in Boston on business and had not received her note until a few minutes ago, and that he was sorry but it would be utterly impossible for him to run down to the shore this evening. He was having to work hard all day Saturday.

"Oh, Keith—!" there was disappointment and a caress in her tone that soothed his ego. She had known they would. Yet his voice was still curt as he explained that he was a working man.

She did not dispute that as he had expected she would; instead she put on her sweetest voice and coaxed, insinuating that her heart was breaking for a glimpse of him, although she didn't say so in so many words, and that he had been away a very long time.

At last he relented so far as to promise to run down Saturday evening. Yes, he would come in time for dinner *if he could*. But he wasn't at all sure he could remain more than the evening.

She had to be satisfied with that.

He hung up feeling that he had at last scored a point with her. She had not once been imperious nor resentful. Perhaps it had been a good thing that he went away as finally as he had gone. Perhaps it had made her realize that he was a man with a will and character of his own, and not a piece of putty that she could mold to her will. And perhaps when she came to realize that it might bring her to a sweeter more reasonable attitude, to the kind of attitude a right-minded girl should have toward her lover's life-plans. He told himself that he had always hoped that perhaps she would one day put aside her spoiled selfish ways and prove to have a soul beneath the surface as lovely as her face, and that if he had not had that hope he would never have allowed himself to become as intimate with her as he had. It had been only in the solemn night-watches when they were not on good terms that he had owned to himself that she was selfish and spoiled and probably never would change.

But now, as he hung up the receiver, he set his lips firmly. He wasn't going to let her pull the wool over his eyes any longer. Either she would give in and be reasonable and look at things as he did, or else he was done, and he meant that she should understand that from now on. He would go down to dinner tomorrow night, this once, and see how things were, and he would be very careful not to let her compelling mood melt his resolve. He would take precautions with himself, put on a sort of life preserver of moral fiber. Perhaps—he paused in startled wonder at the thought as he opened the door of the telephone booth—perhaps he might even pray about it before he went! Would that do any good? Could he expect a neglected God to take any interest in a thing like that? Of course, though, prayer might at least have a reflex influence upon himself, even if God were not listening. He had heard a wise and learned speaker say once that the only good in prayer was its reflex influence on the person who prayed.

Well, if even that were all, at least he might try it. But he had a strong feeling that there was really more to it than that, and that if he was going back to prayer as his mother had taught him he must at least have some faith in it.

"God!" he said with a swift uplift of his heart. "God, do you care?" Then he went back to his work feeling that he had made the first move toward getting back to prayer.

All the next day as he went about his work his mind was occupied with so many matters that he had no time to worry about the coming interview with Anne. What would be the use of thinking, anyway, he argued, when once it occurred to him that he wasn't getting ready any line of action; Anne always set the stage for her own scene, and it was next to impossible to anticipate her movements. He would just have to trust to his wits to know what to do when the time came. His wits—and prayer! And he had a curious reverent wonder in his mind as he added that. For twice now he had attempted to pray. Last night before he retired, and this morning before he left his room to come down to the office. But he hadn't got on so well. It had been more like a reverent pause, than anything else. He couldn't of course repeat any of the prayers he had used as a child. "God Bless mother and father and make me a good boy today, Amen!" His eyes grew misty as the old familiar words came to his mind. There was no father and mother to be blessed any more, though wistfully he would have liked to add the last phrase. A good boy he would like to be, but he was no longer a boy, he was a man, and a man ought to be good himself, oughtn't he? He oughtn't to expect a God to make him so, ought he? He felt a bit vague about that. His early teaching hadn't been clear along those lines, and it had stopped when he was about seventeen and went away from home to college. But at heart he felt still a wistful little boy who wished that vital things could be made plainer, and he could somehow be helped to order his life aright.

In the final outcome of matters at the office, Keith offered to stay all the afternoon and get some drawings done that had been promised by early Monday morning. He could see that his offer made somewhat of a hit with the elder, worried partner who was greatly relieved that it was going to be possible to fulfill the promises made about a difficult contract.

So he worked away happily, whistling softly to himself fragments of melodies his mother used to play, some of which Daphne had played when they were together for that little while in the old house.

He was just looking at his completed drawings, making sure that every measurement was according to specifications, when the janitor of the building looked in.

"Well, say, you are staying late," he remarked. "Didn't you know this was Sat'day? You're missin' out on yer half-holiday aren't ya? D'ya know what time it is?"

Keith looked at his watch in dismay. There was barely time for him to rush to his apartment and change and catch the last train for the shore, and he had promised Anne he would try to get the earlier one so they might have a little time on the beach before dinner. Now, Anne would be furious again, and he sighed wearily at thought of battling with her. Somehow it had been restful to get away from everything and just work, at clean wholesome work. That was probably the best thing in the world. Everything else was hectic. That was probably what kept Daphne Deane so sweet and wholesome, she wasn't afraid of work, and absorbed herself in it, and didn't have time to think about herself and become morbid. He wondered if the minister would be keen enough to appreciate how fine she was.

These thoughts went rampaging through his mind while he was rushing frantically through the motions of getting dressed and hurrying to the station.

Then on the train he leaned his head back and closed his

eyes and tried to get some kind of poise for the evening that was before him. There was just one resolve firmly fixed in his mind, and that was that he wouldn't be placated. He wouldn't be persuaded to do what she wanted him to do. It was a dishonorable way to earn one's living according to his standards anyway, and while he didn't want to say in so many words what he thought of her father's methods, he could never approve them, and he must maintain his own right to independence of thought or there could be no hope of future happiness. Also he clearly saw that if he gave in to Anne's blandishments and allowed himself to be deceived by her present yielding attitude, he would find himself involved before he knew it.

How was it that he was suddenly beginning to see and acknowledge these things to himself now, when he had always put such thoughts away from him before? Was it that getting back to the old home and simpler surroundings had cleared his vision?

Did he really love Anne enough to marry her? Or was it that he loved her, but did not trust her? Perhaps that was it. He had felt since he first knew her that if he could once get her away from her surroundings she would be very different. But would that be possible? Were not her surroundings a part of her very self? He wasn't sure. But this much was certain. He must not marry her until he was sure. And perhaps this evening would be the testing time. Perhaps his absence had brought her to see how wrong her attitude was.

The train slid into the station, and among the expensively attired throng suddenly he saw Anne Casper. She was wearing something white and softly transparent, that drifted about her in the breeze and gave her the look of a Greek goddess! Keith stared at her startled! He had never seen her look like that. It was amazing! Usually the clothes she affected were smart, excessively so, but she wore them with an arrogant air as if to compel respect for them in spite of their disregard of all the laws of real beauty. But this lovely garment she was wearing now was all gracious flowing lines that softened her whole appearance. Even the brief trifling jacket of the same cloudlike texture had simple sleeves that fell away from her rounded arms with exquisite charm. The regal little head that usually was so sleek, like shining black satin plastered in severe lines about the face, had somehow changed its character to long loose waves that seemed the perfection of only nature itself, with little soft curls framing the face, soft loose black curls that gave her a pensive sweetness he had never seen there before, a sweetness that not even the daring brilliancy of her small red lips could deny. And there were shadows delicately circling her great dark eyes and enhancing the mystery that always seemed hidden there. It never occurred to him to wonder how much of her various moods was makeup. He would have been indignant had anyone suggested such a thought. Though if he had been observant he might have wondered how she so quickly attained that lovely pallor with only a hint of rose when sometimes she seemed to glory in the deep tan she had acquired.

But however that was, she stood there awaiting him, one lovely arm lifted to wave a greeting, all in white, with a single gorgeous jewel hanging on a thread of platinum about her neck, and her soft dark hair beaten by the wind into a frame for her lovely face. She was a new Anne Casper. No, not new, she had never shown him this side of her nature before, that was all. Suddenly his heart leaped up with a strange thrill. Was this then the real Anne Casper, this peerless girl? And was this true love that was shining from her dark eyes till they looked like twin dusky jewels above the diamond at her throat?

She was standing in front of a beautiful shining car that was blue with chromium finishings, and a chauffeur in livery to match was in attendance. She was a notable figure even in that sophisticated crowd at that exclusive shore station, and he went forward to meet the greeting in her eyes with wonder and a question in his own. Was this the real Anne Casper, and had their brief separation brought her to understand true values at last? Was she trying now to show him that she was repentant? Almost he seemed to see that in her eyes.

When he reached her side, coming through the cheerful crowd, some of whom were acquaintances, it almost seemed that Anne lifted her face as if she expected him to kiss her. Of course she didn't, of course that was only an illusion of his excited brain. Anne Casper was not sentimental. She was keen and quick and clever. But this new Anne he did not know, so sweet and gentle and winning, perhaps she was purposely trying to show him a new side, one meant for him alone.

He got into the limousine beside her, and they rode away into the soft pink light of dusk. Winding down the white pebbled drive among the flowerbeds maintained by the railroad company, bowing to this one and that as other cars passed them, gay laughter, bright costumes, to Keith it was suddenly like another world. Electric lights were beginning to spring up on the station platform, garish in the twilight. Lights were shooting out from the drug store, on the corner of the beach drive, lights from the tea room where late comers were idly drinking tea, and quiet pink lights subduing the gold and pink and turquoise of the evening sea, whose waves seemed barely to be whispering as they slid up the far stretch of sand. And then a pale glow of light sifted from the frail ghost of a moon that was rising steadily higher and higher out of a silver sea.

As Keith took in the beauty of the scene and then looked down at the beautiful girl beside him, he felt that he had somehow stepped into a dream. He couldn't realize that it was actual. Where were all the tumult of vexation and unhappiness through which he had passed, all the anger and bitterness that she had roused in him at their last meeting, the hours of brooding, and his own perplexities? Here she was by his side looking up at him with liquid lovely eyes, and no sign of the fury with which she had sent him away. The scorn of her eyes was changed to gentleness, and there was about her that lure that he had felt when first he met her, that slow sweet lifting of those long lashes, the deep meaningful glance in her eyes as if he were the final answer to all her dreams. What did it mean?

He did not entirely forget his high resolves not to yield too easily to her charms. He was not trusting all this at once. There was grave perplexity and question in his glance as he regarded her, the look and question of a man who has been getting back to first principles and trying to feel firm ground beneath his feet.

He was not returning as the eager lover who had been summoned back to be forgiven, and handed another chance. He was meeting her gentleness with grave and distant conversation, about the beauty of the sea, the last regatta, the swimming meet, and—"You're looking well, Anne."

As the car swept into the wide gateway between the tall hedges, and up to the palatial summer mansion he saw her father standing at the top of the marble steps on the wide veranda to welcome them, and he gave a startled look at him and then a quick glance at the girl. She had implied in her letter that her father was away in Boston for the weekend and she was alone with an ancient aunt. It had been one of the reasons why he was willing to come down, because he might have some chance of seeing her alone and clearing up their differences, if such a thing could be done. But now with her father here the occasion would necessarily be more formal.

He gave her that one quick searching glance and her lashes fell and then rose again with a lovely sweep and a smile on her lips.

"Dad came back this afternoon unexpectedly," she explained quickly, as if in answer to that searching glance. And then there was no time for more for Mr. Casper came down the steps to meet them, and Keith Morrell, on guard at once when he looked into the face of the man of the world, answered the greeting with a quiet noncommittal aloofness.

Just what was going to be the outcome of this meeting? Had this all been planned? Was the father here to look him over?

Almost a sternness came into Keith Morrell's eyes and about the set of his lips. The stage was set in this stately mansion by the sea, with the rhythm of the waves for accompaniment, and the rising moon for lighting. Anne Casper in white robes and a great diamond, dressed for her part. But where and how did he come in?

WILLIAM Knox had been enduring agonies during the last few days. He had not been able to attend to any other business excepting the matter of the Morrell estate. His wife had seen to it that he did not. She nagged him until he scoured the town to get in touch with Bill Gowney and failed utterly. It began to seem strange even to mild-minded William Knox that people who were supposed to know more or less about Bill and his family, simply shut up like clams when they were asked where he was, and with furtive glances at one another faded out of the picture as quietly and unobtrusively as possible.

After he had searched every possible place where Gowney might be found he came home in a panic lest Gowney would call upon him and ask if he had made the ten thousand raise offer to the owner. He tried again to get Keith Morrell on the telephone. Failing to reach him he sat down and wrote a letter to him under the strict supervision of Martha, stating that the house was already sold, and the matter had gone too far to stop it. The buyer had already taken possession. For

Martha had been considering what it would be to have that fat commission, and knew exactly how she wanted William to spend it.

But William was so excited over the whole matter, and so annoyed at Martha for her interference, that he made a mistake in the address and wrote it Rosedale instead of New York, so it was returned to him the next day by the canny Rosedale postmaster. Unfortunately it was brought to the notice of Martha, which made matters still worse, and William began to look worn to a thread.

Matters were at this stage when Daphne went over to call on Emily Lynd one morning with a fresh supply of flowers, some of them out of the old Morrell garden.

She found her old friend had not been very well for the last few days.

"I haven't been sleeping as well as usual," she said. "A queer thing happened. I got an idea I saw a light in the old Morrell house one night. You know I can look out of my window from the bed here, and see it, and I always used to get such comfort out of watching the lights in that house. When Mrs. Morrell was living I used to watch for her light in her bedroom window every night, and when it went out I knew she had gone to bed and it was time for me to put my book away and go to sleep. It came to be a sort of habit with me, to look across out of the window toward that house every night. I've missed it a great deal since they went away."

"Yes," laughed Daphne, "so has Mother, and in fact all of us children. You know mother made a sort of a fairy tale for us when we were little, out of the old house and its people, and it really was a shock to our young minds to have it all closed up and ended."

"I know just how you felt," said Emily Lynd smiling. "And you can imagine how startled I was a few nights ago, I think it was Tuesday night, to glance across the meadow and see a small bright light staring at me like an eye."

"Why, how strange!" said Daphne, thinking of her own experience.

"Yes, wasn't it?" went on the old lady. "I couldn't believe my senses at first. But it shone on, quite steadily for a long time, till I finally got out my field glasses and looked at it. And there it was, a little speck of a bright light beaming away, and I couldn't understand it. For it wasn't upstairs in Mrs. Morrell's window, you know. It wasn't even in the first story, it was away down quite near to the ground, as if it might have been in one of the cellar windows. I decided it must be that someone had been in the house and left the light turned on in the cellar, and I wondered if I ought not to send word to the agent and have it looked after. But the next night I looked and it wasn't there, so I didn't know what to think."

"It couldn't be the electric light," said Daphne, puzzled, "because the current is turned off. I know because Mr. Morrell was at our house Tuesday and asked me to go over with him and look around. I had never been in the house, you know."

"Oh," said Miss Lynd, "I'm glad you saw it. It is such a lovely old house. I used to go over so often in the days when I could still get around a little. I'm glad you know Keith. He's such a dear fellow."

"I only know him a little," said Daphne. "We were in high school together, you know."

"Yes, he told me. I hadn't remembered that. Well, perhaps he left a candle down in the cellar and it burned out. That might explain it, except that last night I saw the light again! You see I had kind of got in the habit of watching for it."

"You *did?*" said Daphne, her eyes wide. "How very strange! I wonder if it has anything to do with what I heard!" and Daphne told of her experience.

"And last night I heard the same noises again, although I didn't see any light," she went on. "Do you suppose that it is just some truck driver from a distance who drives in there to rest a little while? And mightn't he have gone around to the front terrace to smoke a cigarette? Could it have been the bright end of a cigarette you saw?"

"Oh no, it was bigger than that. Brighter than that!" said the old lady decidedly. "I just couldn't make out at all what it could be. I suppose there is some explanation but I couldn't understand it at all. And of course, I, like a silly fool, had to lie awake and try to think it out."

"Well, I've been in the same fix," said Daphne, "only I haven't seen any more fireflies. I guess we'll have to ask Mrs. Gassner what it is. I'm sure she'd have some solution of the mystery. She always seems to know everything that's going on in the neighborhood. She came over to borrow some salt yesterday just to try and find out if we knew why Mr. Morrell came home last week. She said she heard he was going to turn his old home into a summer hotel and start taking boarders and she wanted to know whether he had asked mother to take charge of it. She said if he hadn't she might like to apply for the position herself. She said she thought she could run it and still keep her own home going, it was so handy, but she didn't want to snatch the job from mother if she planned on taking it. Mother told her she didn't think Mr. Morrell had any idea of using his ancestral home for a hotel, that he didn't speak as if he had any such intention. She must have been misinformed. But isn't she the limit?"

"Yes," said Miss Lynd almost gravely, "she is. I'm afraid she makes a lot of trouble for people. I understand she's spreading a terrible story about that poor motherless little Cassie Winters, just because she sees her walking the street arm in arm with Archie Reamer. The poor child hasn't any other place to meet her friends since her home was broken up! She was in here the other day on an errand for Mrs. Mathison, the woman she works for over on the south side, and she was crying as if her heart would break to think that people would say such mean things about her. I declare I was indignant! Mrs. Gassner ought to have been a fiction writer, the way she invents stories about people. And she has only to say 'I shouldn't wonder if—' and in half a day it is all over Rosedale as a fact. Sometimes I think I'll send word·for her to come over here and just reason with her about it. Then I think maybe it would be better just to pray about it and let the Lord work. He never makes blunders the way I do. And while we're praying I wish you'll remember Cassie Winters and Archie, Daphne. He's a steady sort of lad, but he's out of a job. He wants to marry her and have a little home of their own, but that good-for-nothing brother-in-law of his got angry with him and dismissed him from the lumber yard and Archie can't seem to find another job. I think they're both Christians of a sort but they've never learned to trust the Lord, and it goes hard with them. And then, Daphne, there's Keith Morrell. I'm sure he needs the Lord. I've known him since he was a baby, you know, and I love him as if he belonged to me. He's in the world a good deal. He told me a few things when he called on me last week and I can read between the lines. We'll pray for him, too. You lead off, dear."

So Daphne knelt beside the bed with her hand in the soft warm hand of the invalid, as she had often knelt before, and they two brought their petitions to the throne. They had these little times of prayer together now and then, and Daphne, though shy about it at first had grown to love the fellowship greatly.

And when the prayer was ended Miss Lynd pressed the young hand tenderly, looking into the bright lovely face of the girl.

"Now, tell me, dear, all about the old house. I haven't been there in so many years. I'd like your impression of it. I'd like to see it again through your eyes."

So Daphne told it all, how wide and high the rooms had seemed, how the light swept down the lovely old staircase from the great arched window on the landing above, what joy it had been to look at the fine old paintings, and recognize the characteristics of some of the old masters. How she had loved playing on the sweet-toned piano, and getting a glimpse of the beautiful furniture. How interesting it had been to see the playroom with its fireplace where she had often visioned toys on the floor, and a child playing, when she was small. But she didn't mention the little boy kneeling at his mother's knee. That seemed something she had no right to mention even to so dear a friend of the Morrells as Miss Lynd.

Then she told about the garden and how the vines and plants had made a lovely entanglement everywhere, but how the children were starting to weed and trim, and it would soon be in order. Then she pointed out the bright blossoms that she had picked there this morning among those she had brought.

When at last Daphne had to go, the invalid lay thinking about her. A sweet child she was, so unspoiled, so fine of mind and spirit. Oh, why couldn't Keith have fancied her? Why hadn't he been intimate with Daphne in school instead of that Evelyn Avery where he had gone to dinner the night he called upon her? Why hadn't his mother fostered a friendship between him and Daphne?

But then she remembered the days when Daphne's mother was so ill, and she had been much at home. Of course it was all explainable. Only she felt so sure that Keith's mother would love this girl, if she were here today. And yet, what of Keith? How had he developed? Was he worthy to be the friend of this wonderful girl? Well, it wasn't for her to try to plan for God in such matters. She loved them both, but she mustn't meddle with romances even in thought. That was dangerous business. God had his plans for both of them. She might only pray that they be guided aright to do His will in the days of earthly life that were before them.

And then she turned back to that question about the light in the old house. If it came again she must surely call the police and put it in their hands. She couldn't lie awake every night and get sick over it. It was not her responsibility anyway, except to report and let the police investigate.

Then she picked up her field glasses and studied the view from her window carefully, trying to locate the exact spot where that light had shone. It seemed to her that it had come from behind where the coal trucks stopped to deliver coal. Would it be possible that there was a window on the other side of the cellar opposite the coal chute where the light from the back street could shine through?

But no, for then it would shine every night, and she would have noticed it before. Also, this light was not visible till late at night. Well, it was very queer, that was all.

Meantime, rumor was hard at work spreading more tales.

"Yes," explained Evelyn Avery eagerly to an enquiring friend, "it's true. I happen to know. Keith Morrell is selling the old house. He told me so himself. He was here to dinner the other night. I happened to come on him just as he landed in town to sign the papers or something for the sale and he told me about it. We had a grand time talking over old times."

"Well, I suppose he won't ever come back, then," said the friend disappointedly. "I always liked Keith Morrell. Of course, he was rather studious and all that, but I imagine he's over that by this time, as much as he's been abroad. Did he say anything about coming back to live? But of course he wouldn't if he is selling that lovely old house."

"I'm not so sure," said Evelyn lightly, "he might. He feels, you know, that a house on that side of the town is quite impossible in these days. Everybody worthwhile has moved over to the hill. He might build. He spoke of Winding Way or Latches Lane. It's so exclusive up there, you know, and he naturally would want to be with the best people, and near the Country Club, after his years abroad. It seems to me I remember he was a great golfer even when he was young."

"Oh, you don't mean it! Latches Lane! Wouldn't that be wonderful! I suppose of course he inherited all his parents' estate. And weren't they fabulously wealthy? I always supposed so, leaving a nice home like that and living in Europe so long."

"Oh, of course!" said Evelyn, who didn't really know a thing about it. "But wouldn't it be wonderful if he should come back to live?"

"Is he engaged? He'd be quite a catch!"

"Well, some say he is, and some say he isn't," said Evelyn quickly with downcast eyes. "I wouldn't want to say what I know. He might not want it talked about. But being engaged isn't being married, you know," and she giggled significantly.

"Well, I'm sure I hope he doesn't bring any impossible foreign bride here for us to have to swallow. I think he ought to be loyal to his native town and come back and take one of his old girls."

"*One* of his old girls!" said Evelyn with asperity, "and who were they, I ask you? His mother never gave him a chance to have any girls. She was terribly snooty. A girl had to walk a chalk line or she wasn't worthy of her precious son."

"Well, she's out of the way, anyway, thank goodness, and I imagine he's changed all that by this time. I always thought he was terribly good looking, didn't you?"

And presently the girl went out to spread forth the news of the coming new Morrell estate on Latches Lane, with a possible bride-to-be in the offing. So the story spread until one day it reached Mrs. Gassner, who shook her head ruefully and exclaimed: "Well, *I* think somebody ought to warn that bride before it's too late, him running around holding hands in gardens with that sly little Daphne Deane who pretends to be so religious. Why, you know they say she doesn't even go to the movies, and yet what did I see with my own eyes, right out my second story back window!"

12

KEITH Morrell seated at the elegantly appointed table across from Anne Casper could not understand the changed atmosphere, the unwonted cordiality on the part of Anne's father, the genial friendly attitude. What did it mean?

And what was the matter with himself? Why, if this had happened two weeks before when he had gone away from this girl for what he thought was the last time, prepared to eat his heart out for love of her, to consider his life ruined, his rosy future a blank, how happy he would have been if he could have known that in a short time he would be back in her good graces, dining with her and her father as if nothing had ever come between their friendship! And now he didn't seem to feel so happy. Somehow his heart was anxious, uneasy. Did he really love this girl after all?

Oh, she was lovely, there was no doubt about that, brilliant, gifted, desirable, and yet somehow he couldn't thrill at sight of her as he used to do before they had their difference. Yet she was more lovely in her present garb than ever he had seen her before, and there seemed to be a gentleness upon her that he had never associated with her before, of which he had never thought her capable.

What had happened to him during the interval? What power had awakened him to look beneath the surface, to doubt her, to wonder if after all, even though she gave in to his convictions and went his way, she was desirable—for him? He hated himself for these thoughts. It did not seem loyal, stable, honorable, to accept them in his heart. He didn't like to think of himself as changeable.

He was looking across at Anne as she talked, her eyes wide and beautiful, the diamond in the hollow of her throat catching the light and flinging it over to him in a dazzling point, bringing out the beauty of the girl who wore it. Yet it all seemed unreal. It was a picture that was being held out to him, and he was waiting there to see what it all meant.

He would have been surprised if he could have known that Anne herself had much the same feeling, as if she were seeing him actually for the first time. There was a gravity about him, a dignity that he had never shown to her before. He had been a charming courteous gentleman, a little bit too fastidiously formal, perhaps, in his manners, but now he seemed to have taken on an awesome maturity in these few days since they had been separated. He seemed like a man upon whom responsibility sat, and to whom life meant more than just a continuous round of amusement. She wasn't sure whether she liked it or not. It frightened her just a little. That set of his jaw, that firmness about his lips, that look of a man whose mind could no more be made up for him. She gave a swift furtive glance toward her father, wondering how he would cope with this. Would he be able to move a man who stood on his own and was not cringing to success as represented by her father's large income? Or would he lose his temper, which was so uncertain toward any who did not fall in with his plans at once? Would he fling down an ultimatum as she had done, and expect to conquer that way, and get—*nowhere* with Keith Morrell?

But—did she like Keith all the more for this quality? Perhaps—if she could conquer in the end. If he was to be hers she would like him to be unconquerable except by herself.

But see how she had got nowhere by her own independence! For she could read in his manner that he had not given in one inch. He had taken things up just where she had laid them down two weeks ago, and was not counting on any truce, even though she herself had ignored everything and was ready to forget and begin all over again. To her surprise this quality in him seemed only to intrigue her the more. Perhaps she was one of those women who could only love a man who could conquer her!

The talk at the table was pleasant, interesting. Keith found himself relaxing a little and actually enjoying his dinner. They spoke of his travels and theirs, places they had both visited, people they had met abroad, told incidents of the way, finding mutual experiences and acquaintances. Keith began to forget that there was a situation here which he would inevitably have to face before the evening was over. He talked well. Mr. Casper, watching him closely, noted that his manner was easy, his smile engaging. And of course since this was what his daughter seemed to fancy for the moment he was out to get it for her. He always got anything for her she wanted. Money would get it. Money would get anything if you bid high enough. This young man would be no exception. He might simply need a little careful handling because he was high-spirited. That was not a bad thing in business. It might even prove a great asset. One needed to carry things with a high hand and be ready to take risks. He judged that young Morrell had taken risks for his own opinion, setting his will up against Anne's. A man who did that was usually a winner if he was handled right.

So Anne Casper's father set out to "handle" Keith Morrell.

Adroitly he questioned him concerning his early life, his parents, his fortune, his hopes, and listened respectfully, if somewhat amusedly, when Keith told of his interest in his chosen profession.

"Yes. Well, architecture is a good line of course, if you're willing to plod along and waste a lot of years in good hard labor—"

"I am," said Keith quietly.

"Now, look here, young man, that's all very well, and I admire your spirit, of course, but why waste the years? Why not take an easier way and let your money work for you? Then you could dabble in architecture on the side, do what you want to do instead of being forever at the beck and call of others, carrying out their whims that do not coincide with your ideas of beauty and utility. For instance, you say you have some property of your own, even if it is only a small amount to start with. I could let you in on a proposition that I have on hand now that would net you—almost at once—" and he named what seemed to Keith Morrell a fabulous percentage to come from a small start.

Mr. Casper smiled benevolently.

"You see," he said, "it's this way," and he went on to give a few astonishing facts—at least he said they were facts—and to draw conclusions, and lay bare clever methods that seemed to Keith nothing short of rank dishonesty. Keith sat there with stern eyes watching the other man, not showing by the flicker of an eyelash his rising wrath.

"Then," said the rich man leaning back and tapping the arm of his chair with his eyeglasses, "with a capital of that amount you would be in a position to build your first house and build it the way you want it, build it for yourself to live in! And meantime you could be perfecting the plans and having them all ready for the time when you would begin to build. Of course you could amuse yourself later designing other buildings, too, and keep your hand in for the really bigger things you would do.

Why, man!" he said waxing eloquent, "think of the hospital buildings and churches and orphanages you could be designing with all the latest ideas, and building them to *donate* to some worthy organization. There are so many needy causes in the world," he beamed philanthropically. "Wouldn't that be better than worrying along for years before you had an adequate income to live in the style suited to a man of your talents? Well, what do you say, Morrell, shall I enter you in the lists and put you in on the ground floor? You would not need to start with much if your funds were not immediately available. In fact, I could lend you enough to start with. What do you say?"

Keith's voice was almost brusque as he answered:

"Thank you for your interest, Mr. Casper, but I should not care to get my money in that way."

There was a hardening in the elder man's face and a quick glitter of anger in his eyes.

"Are you presuming to criticize my methods of business, young man?" There was coldness in the voice and an utter withdrawal of cordiality.

"No," said Keith bravely. "It is not for me to criticize you. I only know that this would not be according to my standards."

"Why not?" The question was like a sharp knife with an icy edge.

Keith's eyes were down, but they came up in a moment and met his antagonist steadily.

"It would not seem honest to me," he said quietly. "I couldn't get my money from bleeding others. I want to work for it."

"And so you are presuming to call me dishonest!" rasped the older man, rage gathering in his eyes and voice.

Keith was silent for an instant and then he spoke quietly.

"There was a verse in the Bible I learned long ago when I was a child. It seems to me a good answer. 'To his own

Master he standeth or falleth.' I guess that's the only answer. I've no business to call your actions and standards in question. I'm only responsible for my own."

Anne Casper sat staring in amazement at this astounding turn of affairs, wondering over the young man who suddenly seemed to have become a stranger. He had never been like this before. How did he dare to talk to her father this way, and what would her father say next? She could see he was very angry.

"And who, pray, may *your* master be?" he asked after a significant pause, his voice hard and cold and biting.

Keith was quiet for a moment, looking down thoughtfully, and then with a deep quick breath he looked up and there was almost a whimsical glance in his eyes.

"I guess that would be God!" he said, but there was awe in his own voice as he spoke the last word. Then, as if his words had taken even himself by surprise, he added:

"Perhaps that may surprise you. I don't suppose I've been paying much attention to Him lately, but when you come down to it I suppose I would own Him as my Master."

There was sudden humility in the young man's voice that astonished the girl. She sat petrified, till suddenly her father's voice broke furiously into the silence that followed Keith's most extraordinary statement:

"And I suppose, young man, you would say that the devil is my master, would you?"

There was scorn and fury in the words, but Keith lifted his eyes gravely, almost haughtily.

"That would not be for me to question," he said steadily.

There had been wine served at the table, and cocktails in the living room beforehand, but Keith had not drunk. Neither had Anne, though Keith knew that she usually did. He wondered about that. But her father had made up for them both, emptying his glass several times as the conversation grew more strenuous, and now he filled his glass to the brim and tossed it down.

"Well, young man," he said, his voice rising wrathfully, his face red with anger, "this conversation is not very profitable. I asked you here to offer you a favor, and help you on your way. I know many worthy young men who would give all they have to be able to get in where I was ready to put you. But you have not chosen to accept my favors. I've only one question to ask, and then I'm done. How in the world, with those fanatical ideas, would you ever expect to get on in the world and support a wife and family? How could you possibly expect to support a girl—say a girl brought up as my daughter has been brought up—on a mere architect's salary? Would you expect to live on her private fortune? Or would you expect her father to do the dirty work and support you while you played around drawing pictures?"

Keith Morrell's eyes grew dark with anger. This was insult. For an instant he longed to take the old vagabond by the throat and shake the breath out of him, but he managed to keep his lips closed until his senses came back to him, though his face was deadly white.

"Sir!" he said, standing up and lifting his chin haughtily, "that remark is beneath your dignity. I think you know that I would never marry a girl and live on her private fortune. In fact, private fortunes in connection with any girls I knew have never entered my mind. I know that there are girls, and always have been girls, who are willing to begin at the basement or cellar with a man they love and work shoulder to shoulder on up. I don't imagine life with any other kind of girl would be very tolerable."

Suddenly Anne Casper jumped up, her face almost frightened, as she gave an imploring look at her father!

"Now, Dad, you've said enough! You've been drinking too much and you don't realize what you've done. We're stopping right here and Keith and I are going out to walk on the beach!"

She slid her hand within Keith's arm and drew him toward the door; and hesitating, with a lingering look at his antagonist, Keith allowed himself to be led away.

They did not speak as they walked arm in arm down the marble steps and out to the silver beach where the light of the full moon was beating down and touching the sea with brilliant quivers across its wide wonderful expanse.

Down the beach they walked straight into the full light of the moon, close down by the water where little licking waves were lapping along the rim and almost kissing Anne Casper's silver shoes, and neither of them said a word. Anne had great faith that the moon could do things to people, and she was letting it work.

She was very lovely there in the moonlight, with her trailing robes of chiffon, and that one great glorious jewel reflecting its gleam in thousands of prisms. She had never been so lovely before, perhaps, with the soft cloud of hair about her face and her eyes starry and wistful. But Keith Morrell was not looking at her. He was hearing her father's sword-like voice cutting down upon his visions and telling out in unmistakable words truths that Keith had drifted along without perceiving before. He was seeing a lot of things now, as he had never thought of them before, knowing that one cannot make two wrongs a right by wishing them so. Knowing that he himself had been falling from his own standards or he would never have got so far as to be part of a scene like this.

They were almost to the lighthouse when he spoke:

"Your father is right," he said, more as if he were thinking aloud, "absolutely right. I had no right for a moment to think that I could ask you to marry me. I had no right to think that I, and the only life I could give you, would satisfy you, instead of the things to which you have been accustomed."

"But listen, dear," she said, and her voice was honey-sweet as he had never heard it before, "there is absolutely no need for you to take the matter in that heroic way. There is absolutely no need for you to be a martyr, poor but plodding. I told you that before. Father has been trying to make you see that tonight. He will put you in a year's time where we can be rich and independent, and live our lives as we please. He wants to do that for me. He is entirely willing to do it for you, because he sees that you are a bright young man and able to——"

But Keith stopped short on the sand and looked down at her.

"Don't!" he said, and his voice almost frightened her. "I told you before that I could *never* do what your father has suggested. I could *never* take money from poor, helpless, duped people no matter how legally it appeared to be done, nor how well I got away with it. I would not have come here tonight if I had known this was to be brought up again. I do not want a wife who has to be a martyr, nor one who thinks I am a fanatic. If married people do not think alike and work out their lives together there is nothing ahead of them but sorrow."

"Oh, there is always divorce," laughed Anne gaily with the idea of making light of the whole matter.

"Not for me!" said Keith quickly. "Never! I would not go into marriage with such a possibility ahead."

"But Keith!" she said, and suddenly threw all her young passion into her voice. "Do you love your profession better than you love me? Don't you love me? Don't you *want* me?" and she suddenly flung her soft arms about his neck reaching up to draw his proud head down to her, and lay her warm cheek against his breast, her body clinging close to his as she looked up into his face, yielding herself to his nearness as she had never done before.

Startled, he looked down at her, saw her beauty, but saw something more, her determination, the cunning way in which she was wielding her power as a woman to force a victory. Almost the flesh leaped up to meet her call, almost the temptation of her loveliness in his arms broke down his barriers, and she saw it, and pressed her advantage.

"Keith, I love you so!" she whispered. "You will do this for me, won't you? You *won't* be so proud and stubborn. You will yield and do as Father says, just for a little, *little* while, and then we'll be rich and happy and—"

She had lifted her face till her lips could reach his and she laid them warm and tender upon his mouth and kissed him, with such a kiss as all hell's most beautiful temptations could not rival. But suddenly he drew back, lifting his head away from that kiss, putting up his hands to take her arms from about his neck. It was as if some power outside himself were compelling him to this action.

"Do you mean you could not love me unless I was rich? You would not have love enough to work side by side with me, and wait for my success when it came?" His voice was stern, his eyes searched her face for the truth. He stood, holding her delicate wrists, looking down at her, the little pretty thing with her white trailing robes there in the moonlight, with her kisses spurned upon her lips, and an angry light flaming up from the deep mysteries of her dark eyes.

"Oh, Keith, don't be silly! Why should I when there's no sense nor reason in your folly? If you really loved me you would not be willing to let me go in poverty for long months or years, and you would *never* really get where you could have the things I want. You know you wouldn't. Keith, don't you love me better than all those silly ideas?" She tried to lift her arms again and put them about his neck. "Don't you love *me*, dearest?"

She breathed the words softly, with lure in their caressing notes, but Keith held her hands firmly down before him, and looking into her beautiful eyes could find nothing in them to trust.

"I'm not sure that I do!" he said slowly.

Anne Casper stood aghast staring in horror and growing disgust at him for an instant, and then she cried out in wrath:

"You unspeakable fool!" she said, and wrenching her hand from his grasp she lifted it and struck him sharply across his mouth. Then she turned and fled down the silver-sanded way in the moonlight, her white robes floating around her like a ghostly cloud, and twice she turned her head and shouted back, "I hate you! I *hate* you!"

He watched her go into the silvery distance, with the vast sea beating in soft rhythm at her side, and the great white marble mansion that was her summer home in the distance. Above that melody of the sea he heard her voice again, more faintly, echoing back: "I—hate—you!" as she mounted white and ghost-like the marble steps and disappeared into her father's house.

13

KEITH Morrell, as he stood for an instant where she had left him on the sand, and watched her vanish into the marble palace, had a feeling that he had just been standing on the brink of a deep abyss, into which he was about to be drawn to great depths of calamity, and that a Power behind him somewhere had suddenly reached out and drawn him back into safety.

He didn't understand it. He didn't try to reason it out. He was filled with a great awe and humiliation. Awe that he had been saved in a way he didn't understand, humiliation that he had ever got himself into such jeopardy.

Then he came to himself and began to walk. Straight on into the silver distance he kept his gaze, and took great strides across the hard sand. Past the marble mansion where he had just been dining, without looking back at it, with no thought for his hat and bag which he had left there. He did not look to the right nor the left. His only thought was to get away. If the girl who had but a few minutes before said in such dulcet tones, "I love you!" was watching him, at least she would have no satisfaction in his passing. Her words of hate were still ringing in his ears, and his face was still smarting where she had struck him. There was a long scratch where the jewels on her hand had gouged his flesh, but he was not aware of it. His spirit was too deeply shaken to notice mere physical stings.

Yet it was not merely what the girl had done to him that stirred him so deeply. It was that he felt it was all somehow his own fault and he was ashamed. He should never have gone after a girl like this in the first place. He had got away from his own natural standards that were his inheritance from both father and mother, or he never would have gone after such a girl. He had known from the start that she was not his kind, that the world and its interests were foremost in her thoughts, that she had no visions of home and little children and a loving relationship with the man she married. As he walked on through the bright night, mile after mile by the sea, he was seeing himself as he had come down through the months since he had first met her, to this night. How she had caught his fancy at the first, by that slow lifting of her lashes, the too-intimate way she had of looking into his eyes, giving him the feeling that her soul had leaped to his at first sight.

Fool that he had been! How he had conjured the hope that her eyes had meant what they said. That they spoke of a great and sudden passion for him that she had never felt before for any man, a passion that would carry her anywhere with no limit at all so she might please him! How she had made him sure that she was the answer to all his dreams!

As he looked back he could see that she had never given him much joy of companionship in all their brief acquaintance. Their intimacy had consisted only in that tantalizing lure that was ever leading him onward to hope for precious things ahead that never quite came in sight. He remembered how she had never let him kiss her when he asked, but only held him off as if when she finally gave her lips they would be so much more precious because of the waiting.

He shuddered as he walked along to think of those red lips upon his own just now, and how falsely they had been set there, only to lure him to go against his conscience. He didn't question whether there had really been love in her heart just now when she had kissed him so ravishingly. He didn't seem to care. She had suddenly turned to clay before his vision, mere clay, and all her passion unholy.

How was a man to live with himself after a revelation like that of what he himself had done, of how he had been deceived?

Yet he must not blame her. She had only been acting out her true self, and in a sense he had never been deceived in her, he had only conjured a vision of her which if he had listened to his own common sense he would have known long ago was not true. Perhaps he had known it all the time, only he didn't want to believe it.

As he walked on mile after mile, the breeze blowing in his face, gradually his mind was clearing, and he began to see himself as he had never seen himself before. He began to see everything with a clarified vision. His whole life passed in review before him, as if God had been trying to show him a part of the original specifications of himself in the mind of his Creator.

Not that he put this in so many words. Not that he at all understood that it was God doing this. It wasn't as definite as that. It was just like seeing a picture or reading a story, but through it all a truth dawned upon him that if there was a Creator, and he had never really taken on modern ways enough to doubt that basic truth, then He must have had some idea in creating souls; and if God had indeed created them as individuals, as he had been taught in his early youth, then He must have had some reason for it all, some plan in mind. What that reason was Keith had no conception, but dimly he could realize that because of the parents he had been given, and his early training, the plan must have been something entirely different from the one

Anne Casper had for him. If that was so, a man hadn't a right to break through God's plan and give his life an entirely different turning, had he? It would be like that man up in Boston who was so insistent on sticking an annex on the building they had planned for him, an annex that would have been utterly out of harmony with the original plan, already well under way.

He went on and on thinking these strange new thoughts, passing many beautiful seaside places of millionaires like Mr. Casper, taking no note of them save to realize that they were of the same alien world from which he was walking away. He did not stop to think where he was going, nor what he was going to do next. He just walked on, a tall personable young man in a dinner coat, bareheaded, with his hair blowing in the sea breeze, his face stern and white and set ahead.

The fine estates and wide private beaches were past now and a boardwalk appeared on the land side, but still he walked on upon the sand, keeping as close to the water as possible. People were still walking on the boardwalk, and long lines of electric lights still outlined the shore. Occasional bursts of dance music were wafted from colossal hotels and piers jutting out to the ocean. At last one of these more extensive than the rest stopped his progress and drove him from the sand. But still he walked on, striding rapidly as if he had been sent for, as if life and death depended upon his going.

He was passing through one resort after another now, and it was very late. He did not realize how far he must have come. The lights were out in most cottages though most of the hotels were in full swing. But there were fewer people abroad, and the general air of night shutting down at last was about him. He suddenly realized that he was very tired. He felt as if he had come halfway across the continent, and it came to him to wonder why he was going on at such a hectic pace, and what he was going to do next anyway? Why was he so upset? Did he care so much for that heartless girl who had breathed her love and her hate almost in the same breath?

Then it came to him that it was something deeper even than love or hate that had stirred him. It was his own awakening to the fact that he was a fool that hurt, and he was dazed, because he had regarded himself heretofore as a rather wise and cautious person with high standards and fine vision. And now he knew that he had not been any better than others who had not his standards and vision, and he was mortified at himself. He had got no farther than self, as yet, but the revelation had shaken him greatly.

Having owned this much to himself however, he felt exceedingly weary. He wanted to lie down and sleep before he thought any more about it or made any plans. But it was very late and he was in a strange district. Moreover he had no hat nor baggage. Would they take him in at a hotel that way? And if they wouldn't, how far must he walk before he found a train or trolley or bus available at that hour on Saturday night?

The realization of his predicament brought him to his senses and back to a practical world. He stepped into the next hotel he came to and asked a few questions. The sleepy night clerk shook his head. Not a room left, and he didn't know any nearby place either that had rooms left. It was a busy season and a popular resort. Yes, there was a bus line to New York from the next village, about a mile and a half farther up the coast. He called up for the schedule. The bus was supposed to stop there at three A.M. He glanced at the clock. He might make it if he hurried. No, there were no taxis around here, all gone for the night.

Keith hurried out and started his weary feet springing on to the next village, and just missed the three o'clock bus by a half minute. He saw it wending a hurried way down the highway as he came almost within hailing distance. But there was a night watchman crossing the street to climb into his car and he told him there would be another bus at five o'clock, so he settled himself on a hard bench by the sea and prepared to wait the two hours.

There was plenty of time now to consider his past, his present and future, but strangely a languor crept over him, and he didn't seem to be able to think of anything except how good it would feel to stretch out in bed and sleep. Presently the sea before him grew vague and several times he dozed off, coming to himself with a start and a memory of Daphne Deane's laughing face smiling at him as they gathered flowers together for the supper table in her home. A nice home! A rare family, where he might have found friendships. But somehow he felt shut out from everywhere now. What would Daphne Deane say if she knew what he had been living through, knew that it was all his fault that he had got into such a mess? Besides, Daphne Deane was interested in a minister, so why should he think of her? She was no more of his world than this other girl. Her world was a safe sane sweet home place where people lived honestly, happily, thought often of God, and remembered little boys praying by their mother's knee. He had somehow unhomed himself and didn't belong anywhere. In allowing himself to consider getting into the big selfish social world he had even lost his hold on the world that was his own. He was like a man without a country. He didn't belong anywhere.

The bus finally ambled up and he got on board and went to sleep again, a deep desolation in his heart.

It was still early morning in New York when he arrived at his apartment, disheveled and weary, thankful only that there was no one about and he might get into his bed at last.

Meantime, down at Rosedale, Daphne Deane had awakened early as she often did on Sunday morning to have a little quiet time to herself putting the final study on her Sunday School lesson for her class of girls. The morning was dewy and sweet, and as she looked out of her window toward the old Morrell house she could see the dew on the grass down by the garden paths and across the lawn, and she noticed with some surprise there were places where the dew had been brushed away as by a heavy foot, in regular footsteps coming from the back of the house and crossing the well-cut lawn on which Donald had spent a good part of his Saturday afternoon. She studied the footprints in perplexity, for they were distinctly marked as the dew glistened all around on the short turf. They went straight from the driveway by the back door, across the lawn in front of the garden, and over to the far fence that led to the other highway. Could they belong to Crowell's great Saint Bernard dog who sometimes roamed the neighborhood? No, they did not look like a dog's tracks, they were distinctly a man's footprints. But perhaps it was only a milkman taking some bottles across-lots to a house on the other road. She dismissed them from her mind, and took up her Bible.

But before she opened her Bible she knelt to pray, as she always did before her Bible study, and strangely the thought of Keith Morrell came to her mind, like a heavy burden pressed upon her. Probably it was looking at the old house that reminded her of him, or glancing across to Miss Lynd's cottage on the other side of the meadow that made her remember her promise to pray for him. And so first on her lips was a petition for the young man.

"Oh, Father, if he doesn't know Thee, or if he has just wandered away, take the veil away from his eyes and heart so that he may see Thee, and come to know a precious fellowship with Thee, his Lord and Saviour. And if he be in any perplexity, or doubt, or temptation, wilt Thou keep him, and free him from the power of Satan. Oh, Lord, I claim Thy victory on Calvary over Satan, in his behalf."

She lingered several minutes upon her knees praying, and when she rose there was a lovely peace on her brow and in her eyes. She went and stood a moment again at the window looking out and thinking of the young man, wondering why it was that she could not get him out of her mind. She noticed that the footprints were not so plain now as they had been a few minutes before. The sun was fast pulling up the dew and erasing them from the grass. Perhaps it had only been a dog after all. Then she turned away and sat down to her study. The quiet peace of the morning stole in at her window, free from the clatter and rumble of the waking world that would presently begin. There was only the high sweet note of a bird in a treetop nearby, the sound of an early church bell a mile away, and the breath of the honeysuckle under the window.

Now and again Daphne lifted her eyes dreamily to the window, her glance far away to a distant hill she could just glimpse, as some great truth from the Word broke upon her consciousness. And sometimes she thought about Keith Morrell, and wondered why God had sent him back to them for that one day. Was it possibly to round out the picture of the other house in which they had always been so interested? Then she would resolutely turn her thoughts away from him. She must not spoil her ideals by trying to get too close to them and bring them down to earth. Of course she would never be likely to see him again, and she did not want to spoil her memory of him by any personal thoughts.

When she heard the far faint bell ringing again she knew it was time for her to go down and help with breakfast, and with a lingering wistful look at the sweet morning distance she closed her Bible.

The dew was mostly gone from the sunny places now and she noted that the mysterious footprints were entirely obliterated. Perhaps they had all been in her imagination. She was getting too sensitive to that house and all things associated with it. She must snap out of it. She was no longer a child to subsist on fairy tales.

Then after another moment upon her knees, asking strength and guidance for the day, she went downstairs humming softly:

I have seen the face of Jesus,
Tell me not of aught beside.
I have heard the voice of Jesus
And my soul is satisfied.

14

TWO hours later the Reverend Drew Addison paused smiling beside Daphne Deane as she sat at the head of her Sunday School class of girls, and bending down said in a low tone:

"I want to see you for a minute after church service. Wait around, won't you, and perhaps I can walk down with you. I have a sick call to make out in your direction, and I want to ask you something."

Daphne nodded pleasantly and went on singing, and the minister walked up to the platform to offer the opening prayer.

Daphne as she bowed her head was wondering what he wanted of her now. She had been to the symphony concert on Friday evening and would have had a very enjoyable time listening to the music, except that her companion made incessant remarks and criticisms. He didn't like the guest-conductor, he criticized his interpretation of the music, he had a good deal to say about the first 'cellist, comparing his technique unpleasantly with other famous 'cellists he had heard, and he made himself so obnoxious to the people sitting near that Daphne could not but be aware of the cold glances that were turned in their direction. He might be a far better musician than she was, and have heard many more famous players, but he certainly was a most uncomfortable companion. So now she was troubled. Was he going to ask her to go to the concert next month, or did he want her to prepare a program for the Rally Day service? Either of these things was equally objectionable to her. She delighted in good music and would have liked nothing better than to hear a concert each month, but not in the minister's company, not only because of his habit of interrupting all the loveliest passages, but also because she did not wish to be singled out from the congregation for his exclusive attentions. The minister's brief whispered word made a decided ruffle in the peace of soul wherewith she had begun the day.

He preached an eloquent sermon on improving the talents and enjoying the gifts that God has given. He said that art and music and beauty had been given by God to widen and polish our souls, and that no man had a right to ignore these things. Every man, although he was a day laborer, should own at least one lovely picture, should go often to picture galleries, and to hear good music, or get it over the radio. He likened it to a soul-bath, and said God had put the arts into the world to make man more fit to live in heaven by and by, and the man who neglected these things was as bad as the man who broke the whole ten commandments. He used many original phrases and forceful words, and made up in well-rounded sentences for his lack of real spiritual truth. He took as his text: "Every good gift and every perfect gift is from above and cometh down from the Father of lights, with whom is no variableness neither shadow of turning."

Daphne grew more and more troubled as she listened, and finally closed her eyes sheltered by her hand and began to pray.

She was gravely serious on the way home, still troubled

about that sermon. But the minister did not seem to notice her silence. He was eager about the beauty of the day, impatient that his duties prevented his using it for an outing.

"Such days are rare, you know," he said enthusiastically. "They ought not to be wasted in every-day routine. There ought to be a law declaring holiday in especially lovely weather."

Daphne met his bright look with a troubled gaze.

"It's a lovely day to worship the Lord," she said with a warm smile.

"Yes, of course, there is that side, too. It does bring better audiences and that makes it more worth while to make an effort to get up better sermons. Brings better collections, too, and that counts for a good deal. But still, it always goes hard with me to have to get up and preach twice a day and go to Sunday School and all the extra meetings, when the day is so charming that your soul is just longing for the wider reaches of the great out-of-doors. Just to lie in a canoe and watch the clouds go by, listen to the bird songs, watch the hemlock boughs dipping into the lazy water. You have such a charming creek here! I'm going to enjoy it a lot. I've bought a canoe and I hope you'll enjoy it with me sometimes."

Daphne gave him a troubled smile.

"The creek is lovely, of course," she said. "We have a canoe ourselves and often go out when we have the time. But it's always such a delight to me to have a whole day to spend on things of the Lord, instead of things of this world. It seems to me a priceless privilege to tell others of His grace and glory. And don't you think the church services can be just as restful and refreshing for our spirits, as the creek is to our tired nerves?" she suggested. "I think that when a message makes me feel the presence of the Lord Jesus, and gives my eyes a chance to look beyond the things of this life into the far reaches of eternity, it irons out all the wrinkles of my soul, and gives me new hope and joy and comfort."

"Well," said the minister a bit amused at her earnestness, "that's a very pretty way to look at it, but I doubt if you would if you had to preach twice on Sunday with a lot of extra trifles thrown in. You see, though my profession necessitates keeping my head in the clouds to some extent, I still have my feet on the ground!"

"And *how!*" murmured Donald to himself, turning his gaze toward the mountains and scowling.

Daphne was silent. It seemed as if she was always having to disagree with this new minister. As if somehow she was continually putting herself in the position of mentor to him, and she could see that it only amused him.

Donald had dropped behind them now, and the minister lowered his voice and spoke more confidentially:

"By the way, what I wanted to speak to you about was this. Are you busy on Tuesday evening?"

"Well, not necessarily," said Daphne pleasantly. "I was planning something, but I could perhaps put it off for something important. Was there something you wanted me to do? You're not having that committee meeting then, are you?"

"Oh, no!" laughed the minister. "It's not work, it's something better than that. It's recreation. I wondered if you wouldn't like to run up to New York with me just for the evening? We could take the midnight train back to the city and get a taxi out to Rosedale. We could take the five o'clock train up and eat our dinner on the train, and then have the evening in New York. You see there's a very charming play that is being given there and I thought it would be pleasant for us to see it together. My brother wrote me about it and said I really ought to see it. It is exceptionally fine. It's on Warren Housing's new book *Soul Strivings*, and the author has handled his subject in a very daring manner. The psychological conclusions are quite enlightening and the actors are all stars. Of course, it will likely appear later in our own city, but that's the bore of being a clergyman. One has to be so careful not to offend a few prudish fanatics in the church, so I generally choose such outings away from home. Then I can relax and really enjoy them. Do you think you would like to go?"

"Thank you, no, Mr. Addison," said Daphne quickly. "I never attend the theater."

"Oh, well, of course I don't either, not here at home, not habitually, but when I'm away on vacation I think I have a right to a little wholesome amusement and I take it. Of course, I'm careful not to transgress anywhere near enough to home for word to get back to any straight-laced elders." He laughed whimsically. "But you don't consider it a sin to go to the theater, do you?" His eyes challenged hers with one of his cynical little smiles.

"A sin?" said Daphne, lifting her serious eyes to his glance without wavering. "It isn't a question of sin, is it?"

The Reverend Drew Addison lifted perplexed brows.

"What else, then?" he asked.

"All things are lawful, but all things are not expedient," quoted Daphne quietly. "We are here to witness for Christ, aren't we? 'If meat make my brother to offend I will eat no meat while the world standeth.'"

"But surely, Miss Deane, you wouldn't take that literally. You wouldn't think it was right to deprive yourself of all harmless amusement just for the sake of some weak sister who can't take the good things of this world in moderation, would you?" He was smiling down at her in superiority, as if he were trying to show a little child her mistake.

But Daphne looked up earnestly:

"Shall the weak brother perish for whom Christ died?"

"But my dear young lady, you are carrying things too far. Besides, I was proposing that we go to *New York* to enjoy this play. No one would know we had gone. There seems no possible way that knowledge of our action could come back to our parish."

"Perhaps not," said Daphne, "but I've just been trying to make my girls understand what it means to reckon themselves dead to the flesh that Christ may live in them. Do you think I could go on talking and praying with them along those lines if I were doing the very thing that I happen to know is pulling some of them into the world, making them forget God? And besides, Mr. Addison, there's something deeper than even that. It is my own personal relation to Christ. I'm satisfied that things that are openly acknowledged even by the world to belong to the world, are not helpful to a Christian. You see, I want to lay aside all weights that might hinder my running, or my fellowship with Christ."

"Oh, my dear girl!" said the young man in a vexed tone, "you are taking life much too seriously. I seem to recognize a lot of cant phrases that are being bandied about today by so-called evangelists and Bible teachers, and they do not sound well on your lips. You are too intelligent to say such things. Why, my dear friend, you are young. You are just starting out in life, and it is your right to have a grand good time and not go around with a continual long face. You should be happy and unhampered. You should enjoy all the good things that God has put upon this earth for your happiness. They are all broadening, educating arts, and they were meant for your use. If you had not been so narrow as to set your stakes down against the enjoyment of life, you would by this time have seen enough of the good things of life to know how silly you are to refuse them. You would understand by experience what richness and delight you are passing up in refusing so-called worldly amusements. A minister of course has to walk circumspectly on account of malicious gossips who do not understand the relative values of these things, and have a mistaken idea of true religion in the daily life. But a girl in your position should have no hindrances and no limitations to her enjoyment of life, within respectable reason, of course. You are making a very grave mistake my dear, and I feel it my duty to warn you against fanaticism and prudery. You will certainly hurt your influence among young people if you try to order your life along such lines, and you will miss the joy out of life."

Then Daphne lifted her face radiantly, in her eyes the shining of one who has caught a vision that others have not seen.

"Mr. Addison," she said, and her voice was clear so that Donald, standing just within the gateway, leisurely picking a flower from a shrub and fastening it into his buttonhole, heard every syllable. "'I have seen the face of Jesus. Tell me not of aught beside. I have heard the voice of Jesus, and my soul is satisfied.'"

The minister studied her face for a moment with that superior smile of his. Then he lifted his chin a bit haughtily and said with the tone of one who was far wiser and better informed than she was:

"Well, I certainly am disappointed in you. I had thought better things of you than this. I had thought there was at least one young woman in my church who had had a broad and artistic education, but it seems I am mistaken. And you won't be persuaded to come with me this once to New York and see for yourself what you are missing, and how harmless it is?"

"No," said Daphne firmly, the radiance still in her face, "I cannot. And—I do not *want* to go into the world. My soul is really satisfied with Him!"

Drew Addison studied her face for a moment more in a kind of wonder and speculation. Then he lifted his hat a trifle haughtily and turned away. Daphne with her cheeks glowing and her heart beating a little wildly, turned and found her brother walking beside her.

"Great work, Daffy," said Donald, suiting his step to hers. "Proud of my big sister. She stood out agin the preacher and *won out!* My hat! How did we ever happen to call that piece of cheese to our church? What's he think he's got ta preach about anyway? My eye! Where did he get his so-called education? He doesn't seem ta know the first principles of being a minister, and I don't believe he even knew you were quoting the Bible either. I was watching his face and he looked kind of startled as if he didn't know what you meant. My little sister standing out agin the minister! Ain't that grand!"

"Oh, but it makes me so ashamed, Donald," said Daphne almost ready to cry, and putting her cold hands on her hot cheeks.

"Ashamed? My word! What've you got ta be ashamed about, I should liketa know?"

"Why, me, daring to speak out against something that an ordained minister says!"

"Ordained minister my eye!" sneered Donald. "Who ordained him? Just men! And what did they ordain him for, I'd liketa know? A man that would talk the way he did! What would old Dr. Shaw say if he heard? Why, Daffy, d'you realize what he said? He actually said he thought better things of you than that you should be satisfied with the Lord! That's practically what he said. Yes, he did! I'll tell ya what I think, and I'll bet a hat I'm right. I don't think that man ever knew the Lord himself, or he couldn't talk such fool nonsense."

And the minister walking away by himself, somewhat baffled but not discouraged, was thinking to himself:

"That girl has a fine mind! A little careful instruction will make her into a fine woman. What eyes she has. She would be a beauty if she were fixed up a little. Not much. It isn't her type. Just a touch of rouge, a mere suggestion of lipstick, shadows under those eyes, and she would be magnificent! I must see what I can do for her. I must order my sermons so that they will unconsciously mold her thinking. It may even be that my message this morning stirred her to this antagonism by its very opposite viewpoint from what she has always held. But when she thinks it over she will see the truth of what I said. It won't be an easy task to change her but it will be an interesting one. She needs a certain pleasant sophistication, which I feel sure I can give her, and then what a success she would be as a minister's wife in some rich city church! It certainly is worthwhile trying."

So he went on to visit his sick parishioner, quite satisfied, and planning a series of educative sermons that should do the trick of turning Daphne Deane into a young woman of the world.

But Daphne went into the house greatly troubled. Was this the minister to whose coming they had looked forward with so much eagerness? They had felt that he would be such a wonderful influence on the young people in the community. He was said to be so full of life and so sympathetic with the young. She seemed to remember the exact phrases used by the elder who was chairman of the committee appointed to select a minister. Other phrases from his report concerning Mr. Addison kept coming to her mind as she went slowly upstairs to take off her hat and put on a house dress to help with the dinner. He had said that the young man was broad and progressive and had the name of gathering the young people around him and getting them into church work. But now that she thought it over there had not been a single word about his spirituality, his consecration, his wisdom in winning souls. They had just taken all that for granted and read them into the endorsement eagerly, so glad to have found a minister at last after almost a year of candidating.

But it was too late to go back over that now. He was here, called and installed, established in the church and community. There was nothing to be done about it but pray, and after all that was the greatest power a Christian had in any matter. God held even the hearts of kings in His hand, and He could make this all come out for the best.

Arguing and disagreeing couldn't do any good, but God
could change anything. With God all things were possible.

So before she went down to the kitchen Daphne knelt
beside her bed and prayed for the young minister who was
just then planning a series of educative sermons for her
benefit. Then with the burden laid down she arose and
went downstairs with a serene brow.

15

BY Sunday night William Knox was almost beside himself, for Martha was on her high horse riding him to death. She had got out of him exactly how much money the man Gowney had given him, just how he had worded the receipt he had given, and where William had put the money. Indeed, she had made him let her count it, and examine each ragged dirty bill critically, although Martha would not have known a counterfeit twenty-dollar bill if there had been one there. And then she had made him rummage through the old tool box in the woodshed till he found two chain bolts which she had him put on front and back doors. After which she had sent him forth again to find news of Gowney, since it was of no further use to try and get in touch with young Morrell until Monday, as they had only his office address.

While William was gone she sat with nervous alertness by the telephone, ready to call the police in case anybody seemed to be getting into the house to steal that money.

And while she waited she figured out just what they would do with that money in case the sale should go through after all, and whether they were in duty bound to tell young Morrell about what Gowney had given privately to William to let him take possession, or whether it was really all right for them just to keep it and shut up about it. Of course, a lot depended upon Morrell's attitude to the sale. And besides, she had always prided herself on being an honest woman. She wanted to do the right thing, but if the sale went through smoothly, what right had young Morrell to that extra money when he didn't know a thing about it? And of course he would be having *his* extra ten thousand anyway. That is *if* Gowney was not a crook, which she strongly feared he was.

But late in the afternoon William came back reporting that Gowney had gone out to Chicago to his grandmother's funeral, and might be gone several days yet. Martha sniffed unbelievingly and settled down to another night of anxious watching and waiting, while William, worn out by the unusual strain, ate a hearty supper surreptitiously from the pantry shelf, helping himself to a double portion of apple pie which Martha was saving for the morrow. Then he went to bed and to sleep. He hadn't had such a strenuous time since the gangsters kidnaped Bennie Stebbins and hid him in the old Forrest place on the edge of town, and he was held responsible because he had it for rent while the family were in Europe. He had been supposed to get a caretaker for it, but had been economizing by doing it himself, that is, he drove over that way once a fortnight and looked toward the place from a distance. That had been a really tight place when they tried to connect him with the kidnaping as an accessory, and Martha certainly had rubbed it into him then that she might have married any one of three better men than he had proved to be. He thought of it sadly as he eased his weary body into bed and sank down on the pillow gently. He wanted to make sure of being asleep before Martha discovered he had gone to bed, or he would certainly have a night of it. If he could be really asleep Martha would not try much.

She knew how hard he was to wake.

As he sank off to sleep he took comfort from the fact that he had finally got out of that kidnaping scrape, and probably some way would eventually be provided to get him out of this, but anyhow he was going to have one more night's rest.

But along toward midnight when he was blissfully in his soundest, Martha shook him until his teeth chattered, and shouted in his good ear:

"Wake up, William! Wake up! Something terrible must be happening over at the Morrell house, and likely you're in for another awful time. You'd better wake up and think what you're going to say when they come for you!"

But William, inert, gave a carefully calculated snore and turned over into his pillow. Long practice had made him perfect in this sort of thing.

What had happened was this. Martha, attired in an old bathrobe over her daytime clothes, her feet thrust into large fleece-lined slippers and her hair in curlers had established herself in the old Morris chair beside the telephone for the night. She had turned out the lights and put her flashlight on the table beside her. But in spite of her firm resolves she had fallen asleep in her chair.

Suddenly into the midst of her dreams the telephone sounded out piercingly, and she was awake and on the job at once.

"Is this William Knox's residence?" asked a sharp feminine voice, for which Martha Knox was wholly unprepared.

"It is!" she said stiffening visibly in the dark, and fumbling on the table for her flashlight which continually evaded her.

"Well, is he there?"

"He *is!*" said Martha severely, as if her husband had been insulted by the suggestion that he would not be in his bed at that hour of the night.

"Well, I'd like to speak to him at once."

"Who is this?" demanded Martha irately.

"Why, this is Harriet Gassner," was the answer. "Is this Martha Knox?"

"This is *Mrs*. Knox, yes," said Martha haughtily.

"Well, I thought so. I thought I knew your voice. Well, would you just call Mr. Knox, please? It's about the Morrell house. Doesn't William, I mean doesn't your husband, have charge of that?"

"Oh, no!" said Martha with sudden apprehension in her voice. "No, indeed! He doesn't have charge of it. He never takes charge of houses. He merely has it for sale or rent. He's the agent, you know. Did you want to buy it? Because, I'm afraid—" Her voice trailed off into uncertainty as she realized that she must not tell anything she knew.

"Oh, mercy no! Buy that house? At this time of night? Well, I should say not. I'm Mrs. Gassner, you know, back on Emerson Street. I merely wanted to say I saw a light there and I thought maybe I ought to report it."

"A light!" said Martha catching her breath. "Well, perhaps the young Morrell who owns it has come home."

"No," said Mrs. Gassner, "I don't think so. He was just home a few days ago, and went away. I happen to know for I saw him running for the train. And I went over to Mrs. Deane's where he was all that day and asked her was he coming back to live, and she said she didn't think so, that he had gone back to New York. So, I'm sure it can't be him. Besides, the light is in the oddest place, away down near the ground. I thought at first it was a cat's eyes reflecting the light from the street, but then I saw it was larger than any cat's eyes. There are two lights, you know, round and a little way apart, and they are steady. They don't move. You see, I've been watching them a long time and my husband thought I ought to do something about it. At least I was going to call the police, but he suggested your husband might be able to explain it."

Martha struggled with the frightened lump in her throat.

"Well, that's very queer, isn't it?" she said trying to sound affable. "But don't you worry. I'll tell my husband and he'll attend to it. Of course, since he has the house for rent I suppose he'll say it's all right for him to see what is going on. The cellar, you say? No, I wouldn't call the police if I was you, they're so nosey. I wonder if the plumber was down in the cellar fixing a leak or something and left the light on? Maybe my husband will know."

"Well, I hadn't thought of that," said Mrs. Gassner. "I was afraid it might be tramps got in."

"How did you happen to be watching the house this time of night?" asked Martha the keen ferret suddenly. "I shouldn't think you could see so far."

"Well, I don't sleep sa good, and I can see the house from my bed, and light travels a good piece, you know."

"Yes, I s'pose it does. Well, you better get back to bed. My husband will look after it if he thinks it's anything to worry about!" And so she had eased off the other woman, and hung up, shaking with cold and fright, and had hurried to waken William.

It was not until she had poured the whole story out incoherently several times that William decided it was time for him to appear to rouse and get the particulars.

It was perhaps an hour later, and a streak of dawn was beginning to appear in the sky when William Knox, attired in trousers over his pajamas, and carrying an old-fashioned lantern which Martha kept ready for emergencies, started out on his furtive pilgrimage. Martha wanted to go along until he persuaded her that she should stay at home and look after the valuables and be ready to send assistance in case he didn't return in a reasonable time. But he extinguished his lantern as soon as he was out of sight of the house, and he made a wide detour around the block in the dark, viewed the old Morrell house from a safe distance, and went home to reassure Martha.

"It's that Gassner woman. It's her imagination, Martha. You might have known that. There wasn't a sign of light anywhere!" and he crept comfortably into bed again and slept till Martha roused him in the morning to get ready for the new day which she feared was going to be full of trouble.

But Mrs. Gassner was not the only one who had seen the mysterious light on Sunday night. Emily Lynd had seen that low spot of brightness that could be just glimpsed afar over her window sill more than once since she had told Daphne about it. And in spite of the fact that they had both decided there must be some simple natural explanation to it, she could not get it off her mind. As she lay praying after her light had been turned out and her nurse was sound asleep in the next room, she could not help opening her eyes now and then toward that light that came and went so mysteriously.

It had not been there for two nights, but now this Sunday night it shone long and steadily, low down just above the terrace, always in that same place. If she were only well and able to be up she would be out the first thing tomorrow morning and she would walk straight to the place to satisfy herself what it could be. But she was bound here on this bed, and could only watch and wonder.

She could not get to sleep at all that night, so she spent the time praying for the son of her old friend Nellie Morrell. But when the morning came the matter of the light was still on her mind and she decided to write a little note to Keith. That would be better surely than giving the matter to the police. If Keith thought it was anything that ought to be looked into he would know what to do about it. So she wrote her note and had it posted early in the morning, sending it special delivery.

Keith Morrell got William Knox's letter Monday morning when he went to the office, and he answered it promptly by telegram:

Will not sell at any price. Cancel immediately and return retainer.

Then he went grimly about the day's work with set lips. He would have to write that man Knox a letter sometime during the day when he had time and tell him he did not need his services further. Even if he changed his mind sometime and decided to rent he would not bother with this agent.

But later in the morning came another telegram from Knox.

Buyer away for several days. Cannot cancel till he returns.

Keith felt vaguely uneasy about it all the morning. He didn't like the situation at all. A large sum had been paid down and he did not know what the law was in such cases. He might have trouble about it. And more and more he was determined not to sell the old home on any account. It had begun to seem nothing short of a catastrophe to lose the property, at any price. Of course the extra ten thousand offered would make it entirely possible for him to buy a partnership and really establish himself in his profession. But he wasn't so sure that he wanted that keenly any more. His whole attitude toward life and his work here in New York had changed.

As the day went on the senior partner in the firm spoke to him about the nice work he had done in Boston, but the commendation no longer had the power to fill him with the elation that it would have had a few weeks ago. He wondered what was the matter with him? He wasn't grieving over Anne Casper, surely! If he was it was entirely possible to go back to her. It was he who had walked away from her.

But he found he did not want to go back. All life as he

had been living it had grown flat and stale to him. Even his ambitions were on a different basis, a more wholesome foundation. Mr. Casper's talk about wealth and success, instead of urging him on, had filled him with a fine disgust for this sort of standard. He had a feeling that he would rather swing far to the other extreme and live where tension was not so high, and one had a human kindly outlook on life. He could never rise by using others as human stepping stones.

Emily Lynd's letter did not reach him until late in the afternoon. He looked at the delicate script in perplexity. He had never had a letter from her before and did not recognize her writing. It couldn't be Knox writing him again so soon! It wasn't his hand. He tore open the envelope hurriedly. He was just about to leave the office for the day.

Dear Keith:

I've been a little worried about something I've seen and thought I ought to tell you.

I've been seeing a light at night over by your house, or perhaps it is in the house, I'm not sure. It is a low light about the level of the cellar window, and I would have thought you or somebody had been in and forgotten to turn it out, only it isn't always there.

At first I thought I would let the police know, and then I thought perhaps that might make unnecessary publicity, for it may be just some silly little thing that is perfectly explainable if I only understood. If I had my two good feet I would go over there and try to investigate, but as I can't I thought I would let you know, and if there is anything I could possibly do for you in the matter I'll be glad to serve you as well as I can from my couch.

Of course, I'm an old bedridden woman, and it may be I'm just seeing visions at night, for the house seems to be standing there as natural as ever in the morning, quite intact. But as I heard that one or two other people have seen a light (though one of them was Mrs. Gassner!), and as Daphne Deane told me that twice she had heard a car with a muffled engine and no lights driving into the back driveway, I thought I had better tell you.

I look back to your brief call a few days ago with great pleasure. I hope you will be coming this way soon again, and will remember to give me a good visit with you next time. I'll have Rena bake you some of the cookies you used to love so when you were a little boy, if you will come.

Very lovingly,
Emily Lynd

Keith read this letter with increasing anxiety. What in the world was going on in Rosedale? Had Knox really given possession to somebody in spite of his commands?

His first thought was to telephone the police and put it all in their hands, and then it occurred to him that it would be better if he could go down himself and see what it was all about, though he didn't like to ask for absence again so soon. But while he was studying over the matter the senior Sawyer came out of his office, hat in hand, and crossed to the hall door.

"What's the matter, Morrell?" he asked teasingly. "You look as if the affairs of the nation rested on your shoulders."

Keith looked up, his stern young face relaxing into a smile.

"Just a little complication about my property in my home town. I suppose it will straighten itself out somehow, though I really ought to run down there tonight and see what's the matter."

"Why not?" said the older man kindly. "You've had

some strenuous days lately. Go ahead. We can get along all right for a few days without you, now the Boston work is all straightened out. Run along and take a holiday."

"Thanks," said Keith lifting troubled eyes thoughtfully. "Perhaps I will if you don't mind. I might be able to get back by late tomorrow morning if everything goes all right."

"Don't try," said his chief. "You deserve a few days' rest. I'm more than pleased with the way you handled that fellow Phelps up in Boston. He was all set to make us trouble, and we might have lost thousands of dollars. Go on. I'll answer for you with the office staff. Good night!"

And so it turned out that in a few minutes Keith was seated in a Pullman diner ordering his dinner, a warm feeling at his heart for the elder Sawyer's kindness, and a strange elation at the thought that he was going back home again so soon. He hadn't analyzed that elation yet. He suspected that it might have something to do with the possibility of seeing Daphne Deane again, who was "as good as engaged to the new minister," and of course that wasn't quite right, especially not so soon after the severance of his interest in Anne Casper.

But he wasn't going into motives just now. He had enough to do to plan the campaign ahead of him, and of course though he appreciated Mr. Sawyer's kindness, he did not intend to abuse it. He must rush this business through and get back as soon as possible.

16

KEITH Morrell had had just time to stop at his room, fling a few things into a traveling bag, and catch his train. He was glad he had thought to bring his flashlight. He would go at once to the house and look carefully around to see if there was any possible explanation of the light which Emily Lynd had seen. It was likely explainable but still he was taking no chances. It might be that tramps had dared to encroach upon the premises. He ought long ago to have put someone in charge, had them sleep in the old stable loft, and let it be known that the house was guarded. With all those valuable pictures and rugs and that wonderful old furniture he ought to have protected it. Of course, it was insured, but even so some of those things could never be replaced. He began to realize that everything connected with the old days was infinitely dear to him. Why hadn't he realized it before?

When Keith reached the Knox house, Martha said her husband had gone out awhile ago. She thought he went to see if Mr. Gowney had returned from the west. He might be here any minute now.

Keith wasted a whole hour waiting for him, and then,

impatient at the delay, started out to try and find either Knox or Gowney.

"You say you think he has gone after Mr. Gowney?" he asked Martha, trying for the third time to fix her shifting eyes and make her commit herself.

"He *might* uv," said Martha, unwilling to be any more definite. "William doesn't tell me his business affairs, but I know he *was* trying to find him."

"And you are quite sure he hadn't found him earlier in the day, after he received my telegram?"

"I really couldn't say!" said Martha stiffly, as if she were offended. Martha congratulated herself in her heart that none of the statements she had made were actual lies. Martha had a terror of untruth, and sometimes quite ingeniously avoided it by an irrelevant remark that had little bearing on the subject, for she would never tell an out-and-out lie. But after Keith had taken himself away, saying that he would be back early in the morning, or call up, she waited until his footsteps had passed out of hearing and then she went to the foot of the attic stairs and called:

"William! He's gone! But you better not turn on the light. He might see it and come back." But William lying on an old mattress in the attic, covered with a horse blanket, a relic of former days, that he had rummaged out of an old trunk, was sound asleep and snoring peacefully. Martha had to creep up the stairs with a candle in her hand to rouse him. She was afraid to go to bed alone down in the second story, with all that money in the house, and William so sound asleep he wouldn't hear if a bomb went off beside him. Moreover she wanted the immediate pleasure of telling all that had passed between her caller and herself, and giving William more sound advice while her tongue was whetted for it. So she laboriously climbed up the steep attic stairs and shook William till he came to himself and followed her down.

But Keith Morrell was out under the far stars walking

toward his old home, sleepy and cross and wishing he hadn't come till morning. He was puzzling over why William Knox should be out all this time hunting Gowney, decided that was improbable, for the neighborhood where Gowney lived was not a very savory one if he judged by his brief excursion there with young Ransom Deane in search of the Gowney boy. And it did not seem to him that timid little William Knox was a man who would choose midnight for a visit to the haunts of possible semi-gangsters.

So Keith finally put away the thought of Knox and went toward his old home. He might just as well stay there for the night. It was too late to take the train to the city. He could hear the whistle now as it came around the curve, and he was too far from the station to make it in time. Besides, why waste time going back and forth to the city? There were plenty of comfortable couches and beds in his house. He could just drop down on the parlor couch and sleep. Then in the morning he would be on hand, and if there was any funny business going on about the old house he would be able to check up on it. Of course, there was a very nice boarding house in the town, and the Inn was a half a mile down the road, but why bother? He would go home.

His direction led past Emily Lynd's house. If there had been a light there he would have stopped to see her, late as it was, for he knew that she was wakeful and liked late guests to help her through the weary hours of the night. But the little white cottage with its wonderful old fanlight over the front door was dark as a pocket, so he walked on as silently as he could not to waken her.

He did not know that Emily Lynd had been lying in a dark room all the evening the better to watch the Morrell house and make sure if a light appeared there again, and that she had settled it with herself that she would call up the police the minute she saw that light again. But there had been no light so far, and only the distant muffled sound of a car a few minutes before. She was almost dropping off into a doze when Keith's quiet footsteps aroused her to alertness once more. But Keith's footsteps, quiet as they were, were not furtive enough for the tramp or gangster for whom she was watching. Her ears were attuned for gangsters. Long years of wakefulness had made her keen to judge people by their walk. She decided that the steps must belong to her neighbor Mr. Galloway who lived at the far end of the street and sometimes came home on the midnight train.

As Keith walked on past Miss Lynd's house intending to enter his own property by the little wicket gate at the side, he was suddenly surrounded by memories of other days, old friends and scenes like a panorama hedging his path. This was the way he used to take on his way home from school all his younger days. Here was the broad stone walk of the Whitman house where the boys used to stop to spin their tops and shoot their marbles when they were just in the Primary. Farther on in the road was the place he first learned to mount his bicycle, his mother and father standing at the fence to watch and applaud at his success. There at the corner was the spot in the hedge where his little dog Dash used to come out barking to meet him, and later, in high school days, limp down the path to the gate to wag his aged tail. This was the road where he rode his pony, too. And afterward when the pony was exchanged for a horse it was down this road he always rode for his morning constitutional when he was at home from college in summertime.

When he came to his own gate his breath caught in his throat, for it seemed to him, though the night was dark with scrappy clouds hiding most of the stars, that the little old gate stood out from the night and welcomed him, and that his mother must be there somewhere in the shadows waiting for him, as she used to do all through the years. Oh, how he suddenly missed his mother! He felt a return of that shrinking from the old house that had kept him away so long. Perhaps he had been wrong to come alone. The dreariness had been somewhat dispelled from his thoughts since he came with Daphne Deane in the brightness of the morning, but now it had returned full force. He cast a wistful eye across the lawn and over the street beyond, to the house where the Deanes lived. Perhaps he had a furtive hope that there would be a light there, and he could enlist Donald to come with him. It would be less forlorn. But the Deane house was dark and silent across that wide stretch of night, and he sighed as he put out his hand to open the little gate, half hesitating even then. But for shame! He was a man. What was this womanish dread that was upon him? He opened the gate and went up the grass-grown path of stepping stones, walking rapidly the familiar way toward the house.

If he had but known it, he was not alone. Quite near by there were a number of eyes that were not sleeping. Besides the eye of a loving God who was yearning over him, and preparing the way that he should walk in the days that should follow, there was Daphne Deane at her window, and Emily Lynd at hers, watching, listening, alert to any sound or spark of light. And there was always Mrs. Gassner whenever anything was going on in the neighborhood, no matter how silent and furtive. Ever since she had sighted that light from the coal hole in the Morrell cellar, she had been making a practice of taking an afternoon nap so that she would be fresh to keep vigil and sift this thing down to the bottom of the mystery. Mrs. Gassner loved a mystery, but better than all, her ambition was to be able to unravel it herself and give out the news of its solving to the world.

But Keith had not for a long time now been God-conscious, as he used to be when he was a lad, and he had never been conscious of the neighbors, except Emily Lynd, and he thought her asleep. There was Daphne Deane over there in that house in the darkness asleep, too, of course, and he had been schooling himself for the last few days to recognize the fact that she belonged to that new minister, and must not be reckoned on in his thoughts. He had enough complications without that.

And yet, perhaps all these were God's ministering angels that night in His great scheme of things; even Mrs. Gassner, though she might have been surprised if she had been told of it.

Daphne had been roused from her first sleep about midnight by the sound of that furtive motor, puffing under its breath, and the soft almost inaudible crunch of the stealthy car as it rolled to a stand in the Morrell drive.

She was at the window instantly and on the alert, her heart beating wildly as hearts will do when a mystery seems to be developing in the darkness. Silly! Of course it was nothing, and yet she had to wake up and watch. She wondered if father ought not to write to Keith Morrell and tell him about it. But no, of course, that would be foolish when it might be just a weary milkman taking a rest in between towns. Perhaps she ought to call Donald and let him listen, too. Though she hated to because he had to get up so early in the morning to get to his work.

Then she distinctly heard a low murmur of a voice. That couldn't be a mistake. Well, perhaps it was two milkmen talking.

But all at once a dim light flared, making a kind of dull glow for an instant, and while it lasted she distinctly saw an open doorway—the outside cellar door of the Morrell house and two dark figures carrying something bulky and heavy out of the door!

Her heart was in her mouth. Was somebody stealing things systematically, night by night, through the cellar door? Should she give an alarm at once, or stay here and watch? She might call Don, but that would waken mother, and perhaps the children.

There was utter blackness now where the light had been.

Maybe she had just thought she saw it. But no, there it was again, briefer, dimmer, but still the doorway with men and a bulky object between them. But—what was that? A quick sharp light like a single beam cutting the darkness back there in the cellar! Gone instantly like the rest, but then a dancing speck of light around at the end outside of the house, low-flashing, then sweeping in a wide circle, showing quick glimpses of shrubs and bushes, glancing across the dark hood of a huge truck, and darting away again as if someone were hunting for something! Suddenly a low sound of a curse rumbling on the night across the garden, but unmistakable! Something heavy dropped, a movement in the bushes, a stealthy closing of that cellar door, silence! Awful menacing silence! And yet with the return of the darkness, a tantalizing challenge that perhaps this was only illusion.

A moment later the sound of feet in the grass along the end of the house, hurrying feet, and three gun shots rang out in quick succession. And was that a moan? A cry for help?

"Don! *Come quick!* Wake up, Don!"

"I'm here!" said Donald from the doorway. "I heard! I'm going over! Someone is hurt!"

"Oh, Don! Not alone! Wait! I'm coming, too!"

"No! Don't think of it! Call the police, and get a bed ready if someone is hurt!"

He was gone.

There was utter darkness and silence now, when she turned her eyes back to the window, and then she heard the stealthy truck backing hurriedly out, sliding down the hill—! Silence!

She hurried to the telephone.

Emily Lynd had not slept a wink. She had lain there placidly, sometimes praying, sometimes just thinking, staring over at the familiar darkness. And then suddenly she saw the light, but not in the place where it had shone before. It was at the front door, flashing about like a will-o'-the-wisp, not in the least furtive, swinging about investigating the front porch like one who belonged there.

She stared at it in amazement. The mystery deepened. Then the light walked on across the porch and stood at the far end, pointing up and then down, and then sweeping around the lawn. She could dimly see a figure holding it high. But it stepped down and went out of sight and Emily Lynd reached out a trembling hand for the telephone. The time had come for her to act. The police might laugh at her afterward if they liked, for a silly old woman, but she could not stand this any longer. She got her call in a whole minute before Daphne reached her telephone, and Daphne was told the line was busy, so she went frantically back to her window to watch till the operator called her.

Meantime Mrs. Gassner over at her window was placidly eating a midnight lunch with which she had thoughtfully supplied herself before coming to her post of observation, a piece of apple pie, a hunk of cheese and a couple of doughnuts, with some cold coffee left over from dinner. But she did not take her eyes from the square of dark window before her, as she groped to the plate in her lap and fed her wide mouth generously.

Mrs. Gassner heard the truck, too. She had heard it before but had not connected it with the other light she had seen, as her window did not exactly face the back cellar door of the Morrell house, though it had a much better view of the coal hole than Daphne had. That coal hole had somehow escaped the notice of the intruders, whoever they were, perhaps because it was located in the alcove where the coal was kept and they hadn't seen it and covered it as they had the cellar windows. But there had as yet been no sharp light from the coal hole tonight as there had been other evenings, and Mrs. Gassner finished her pie in a leisurely way, and had about decided that it was folly to sit up longer, there would be no further doings tonight, when suddenly she saw the light flashing around from the end of the front porch and moving out to the lawn at the end of the house in her plain view. Her jaws paused in the manipulation of the last delicious bite of cheese to look in amazement. It had been a long time since anything so entirely satisfactory in the way of developments in a mystery had come her way to justify her vigils.

As the light continued to dance along the end of the house, coming nearer and nearer, she caught a glimpse of that dimmer light in the cellarway, vague and indistinct. But Mrs. Gassner had a good imagination and did not need much to go on. She reached out for her telephone and called William Knox's number.

And when Martha Knox excitedly came to answer, she shouted into the instrument:

"Is this Martha Knox? Well, this is Harriet Gassner, and there's queer doings going on at the Morrell house right now this minute, lights and queer noises, and I'm just letting you know that I ain't going to keep still any longer. I'm telephoning the police! I don't care whether you like it or not!" and she hung up.

Then she called the police:

"There's somebody breaking into the old Morrell house! Is this the police headquarters? Yes, I *said* there was someone breaking into the old Morrell house! What? Who am I? What does that matter? Oh, I see. Well, I'm not ashamed to tell my name. I am Mrs. Silas Gassner. No. *Mrs.*, I said. Silas is asleep! He's had a hard day and I didn't wake him. He doesn't wake easy. Besides, I wouldn't want him to go over there alone. I didn't think you'd like it. It's the business of the police, isn't it? What? Yes, I said there was somebody breaking in—What? Why I'm watching 'em right now!"—Mrs. Gassner would have made a splendid radio announcer for football games and prize fights.—"Yes, they've got a flashlight and some kind of a truck at the back door, and I think they're stealing all the furniture.

And there goes a shot! Goodness! You better come right now! I heard somebody groan! Maybe it's murder! There! I hear the truck backing out. They're getting away! You better hurry! It sounds as if they'd turned into the pike the other side of the Morrell house. You can catch them if you come around Maple Lane and head 'em off! What? Officer! *Officer!* I said!—*My word!* They've hung up! I wonder why! Now they won't be able to head them off. I'll have to call them again! Don't tell me men aren't hotheaded, even policemen! Operator! Operator! Give me that number again! I wasn't through speaking! You cut me off! Yes— you did! My word! Can't you attend to your work at this time of night when so few are telephoning, or were you asleep? Well, hurry up! What say? You can't get them? But I tell you I was just talking to them! My word! Such efficiency! And we pay to have telephones and police- men!" And then suddenly there flashed lights all about, springing up from everywhere, motor cycles, and police cars with long streams of fierce light pouring out columns of brightness into the night, surrounding the Morrell house on every side, tall stalwart state troopers from the nearby station scattering in every direction. It was almost more than she could handle and keep her head.

But over on Miss Lynd's side of the Morrell estate, two long bright columns of light streamed forth from a car that stood by the side entrance, and Emily Lynd almost too excited to look, suddenly saw a dark crouching figure dart from one clump of shrubbery to another and dash toward the long black truck without a light that was coasting down the gentle incline that passed Miss Lynd's house. The dark man moved stealthily, not knowing of course that the band of light from that car by the house made a brilliant back- ground and silhouetted him distinctly for an instant, just as he gave a spring to the running board of the truck and was drawn up by unseen hands while the truck slid on down the hill and rounded the curve out of sight.

"Did you see that, Delia?" Miss Lynd said to her nurse and companion, who in dressing gown and slippers had been watching from the other window.

"I certainly did!" said Delia. "That must have been the man who fired those shots. And he's got away!"

"He mustn't get away!" said Emily, reaching for her telephone.

"Is this the chief of police? Yes, this is Emily Lynd. Yes, the same one who called. Yes, your men are here, but there were shots fired and I saw a man run across the lawn and jump the fence in front of my house and get in a truck that was moving very quietly without lights past the house. He's getting away, but I should think you could head him off yet if you went at once. They're headed toward the pike. A long black truck. No, we couldn't see the license number. It was too dark."

The next morning the papers came out with a few of the facts concerning the shooting, and credit was given to Emily Lynd for first calling the police. The other calls were included under the phrase "and a few of the other neighbors also reported lights seen."

"Now isn't that the limit!" said Mrs. Gassner bitterly, sitting at her breakfast table beside her morning coffee, with the paper spread before her on the table. "Emily Lynd, a poor bedridden invalid! How could she see anything from away over there? To give her the credit of sending in the alarm, and never say a word about me, an able-bodied woman who knew what she was talking about. I've a notion to phone them and make them correct that in tomorrow morning's paper!"

17

DAPHNE, having sent in her report to the police, flew upstairs to prepare the guestroom for a possible patient. As she passed the window she heard Donald's special whistle for Ransom ring out. But Ranse had just passed her going down the stairs like a streak, pulling his sweater on, his tousled head bobbing in the doorway, then disappearing into the darkness. It seemed but an instant before he reappeared breathless, pausing at the door to shout:

"He wants the cot ta carry him over on. He says fer you ta phone the doctor quick!"

Then he disappeared again, the cot from the attic under his arm, bumping along on every step.

Daphne, quick and efficient, called the doctor, and then with swift fingers put clean sheets on the guest bed. She had it ready by the time the men came slowly up the steps carrying the cot with its burden.

Then her mother appeared, calm and collected.

"They'll want hot water," she said. "I wish your father were at home, but he'll be here in the morning. Go back to your bed, Beverly," she said to the little girl who appeared wide-eyed and shivering with excitement. "It's just somebody who has been hurt. They are bringing him here. There they come now. Get back to your room quick, dearie. And shut the door!"

Then to the men below she spoke, low-voiced:

"Right up here to the room at the head of the stairs, please." Silently they all worked, bringing water, old linen cloths. The doctor was there almost immediately, and down on his knees beside the injured man.

Daphne was not in the room when they brought in the patient. She had gone to the kitchen to start some coffee in the percolator. If the patient did not need it the doctor might, and it was just as well to have some ready.

She was standing there watching the percolator when Donald came down, his young face grave and troubled.

"You know who it is, don't you?" he asked, almost as if he were hesitant to tell her.

"No!" said Daphne looking up with sudden fear clutching at her heart. "Not—?"

"Yes," answered Donald sorrowfully, "Keith Morrell. He was out there in the grass at the end of the porch, his bag lying on its side beside him, and his flashlight in his hand. He must have come home and been trying to get into the house when they got him."

"He's not—?" Daphne looked up with every bit of color drained from her face, her eyes wide, her lips refusing to speak the terrible word.

"No, he's not dead—yet," said Donald gravely, "but they don't know whether they can save him or not. Doc thinks he has a bullet in his lung, right near the heart. Doc is doing all he can to save him. They've sent for McKenna, the surgeon. They'd take him to the hospital, but Doc thinks he couldn't stand the jolting. He's lost a lot of blood and he's pretty well smashed up. They must have hit him in the legs first and when he fell one of the fiends struck him on the head with a blackjack. He's got a nasty cut on his head, probably a fractured skull, too.

He's in pretty bad shape, and I guess by the looks of their faces there isn't much hope for him. I thought you'd want to know before you might have to go in there for something."

"Yes, thank you, Don," said Daphne, her lips white and stiff with the sudden shock. And then looking up at him with the horror of it all still in her eyes:

"Who—who—*did* it, Don? Do they know?"

"Well, they aren't sure yet, of course, but I heard one of the cops talking to another while we were waiting for the stretcher. He said they'd found part of a counterfeiting machine in the cellar, and they believe it belongs to the outfit the Federal government's been trying to trace for the last six months. An outfit that has been operating out west somewhere and suddenly disappeared from there when they almost had their fingers on them. It seems there's been a lot of counterfeit money passing around and they couldn't trace it. It's so good it's hard to tell, and these hot shots had covered their tracks so well that the police just couldn't catch them. It seems their stuff, great heavy machines, just disappeared in the night, as if they were wiped off the face of the earth."

"Oh, Don!" said Daphne, sudden comprehension in her eyes. "I've been hearing such strange noises over there almost every night lately—"

"Same here! Daffy, did you hear those, too? Shucks! I hoped you didn't. I didn't want you ta worry."

"Oh, Don, I almost told you about it once, but then I thought you might laugh at me for seeing and hearing things. We ought to have let the police know."

"You mean you heard that truck sliding into the drive over there about three A.M. and then slipping down the hill like a thief afterward? Sure I heard it, and a couple of times I got up and went out to investigate, but the trouble was, I was always too late. They were just slipping away when I arrived on the scene. I guess I should have reported it, but I couldn't find any definite evidence and I thought they'd take me for a fool."

"Oh, Don! You might have been shot, too!" said Daphne, sudden tears in her eyes. "But, did they catch the men? There were more than one, I'm sure, for just before the shot I saw a light in the open cellar door, and I distinctly saw two figures carrying something between them. That must have been a part of their machinery. Did they get away? I couldn't tell, for I had to call you when I heard the groan, and when I got back to the window the truck was slipping away in the dark."

"They got away," said Donald grimly, "but they didn't get all the machinery. There's a lot of it. Some of their counterfeit money, too, they said, but they haven't had time to see everything yet. What gets me is how they got all that stuff here and into that cellar without our getting onto it sooner."

"It can't have been there long," said Daphne, "because Keith Morrell went down to the cellar and looked all around the day he was here."

"He *did?*" said Donald. "Well, that's something the police should know."

"But how was it the police were there at all?" asked the girl, standing by the kitchen table to steady herself, trying to control the trembling that had seized her.

"Why, they said two or three phone calls came, I guess yours was one, and then Miss Lynd gave them information about a man jumping on a truck that went by her house."

"She did!" said Daphne. "Poor Miss Lynd! I'm afraid she'll be sick, staying awake at night so much, and all this excitement. But hark, there's somebody at the front door."

"That'll be the surgeon. I'll go." Don hurried away, and Daphne dropped down in a chair for a minute putting her head down on her arms on the kitchen table. She felt dizzy and sick. It seemed as if she could not face this thing that had happened. Keith Morrell shot, and perhaps dying, here in their house! She felt as if all the foundations of the earth were broken up.

She brushed the tears fiercely away, and got up. The coffee had begun to bubble in the percolator. She must attend to that, and try to forget what was going on upstairs.

She busied herself getting cups and arranging the table for the doctors when they should need it, and all the time her heart was heavy like lead. She must not, *must* not give way like this. It wasn't seemly. The young man who lay dying upstairs was nothing, absolutely nothing to her, and she should have no interest in him beyond the kindly interest one neighbor would have in another. Yet she could not get away from the bright memory of his face that day he spent with her, washing curtains, and rambling through his old home. She could not forget the touch of his hand over hers down in the sun-warmed earth of the garden.

Beverly stole down and came shivering to her arms. The little girl was frightened and could not go back to sleep. She had been startled from deep slumber, and was filled with terror over the fragments she had caught here and there.

"Who is it, sister? Is it a gangster that was shot? And did the police shoot him? And will he perhaps wake up and shoot us all?" she asked with wide eyes of horror.

Daphne gathered her into her arms, commanding a smile of comfort that she was far from feeling.

"No, dear. It was not a gangster that was shot. It was our friend Mr. Morrell. There were some bad men in his cellar. They had a machine there to make counterfeit money and try to cheat people, and when they heard him trying to get into his house they shot him and ran away. We think that was the way it happened. We don't know everything about it yet. But you needn't be afraid of any gangsters coming here. They ran away as fast as they could. They were afraid of the policemen."

"Do you mean it was our Mr. Morrell got shotted?" asked the little girl, curling down shuddering into her sister's arms.

"Yes," said Daphne sadly, "*our* Mr. Morrell." It somehow gave her a bit of comfort to say it that way.

"Will he die?"

"We don't know anything about it yet, dearie. We'll have to wait till the doctors are done examining him."

Then came Don's voice calling guardedly down the back stairs:

"Daphne, mother wants you up here quick! She wants you to get a roll of linen cloth for her."

"Run quick, and get into bed, dearie," Daphne whispered to the little girl, and then she went swiftly to do her mother's bidding, glad that she might be of a little service in this trying time.

Meantime through the night the dark truck had forgotten its stealthy ways and was speeding at a thunderous pace, turning sharp corners, trying to lose itself in a labyrinth of devious back roads. And three miles behind a posse of motorcycles was storming after it, sending scouts out at every by-road.

Back in Rosedale word had gone out everywhere, and all the main highways were watched. The radio was doing its part, too, to draw the net about the escaping criminals. Even in the black truck the word was being voiced, so that the men who drove it desperately were aware of every move against them, except insomuch as the directions to officers and scouting cars could be given in code.

"Car number forty-seven proceed to seventy-two; forty-nine, watch for black truck, no lights, no license plates—"

"Gem, you get out that third license plate, Califority, an' hitch her on the back," growled the thick-set man with a gun who sat alert beside the driver. "No, you can't have no light, and you can't stop. You gotta hang her on while we're goin'. Guess you druther do that little act than be a dead man, wouldn't ya? Don't be a baby! Kits, you put the tother plate on the front somehow.

On they went farther and farther from Rosedale, with yet more widening circles of followers hot upon their heels. The great piece of machine which they had managed to get away with in their hasty exit from the cellar refuge, kept rumbling and rattling grimly.

"There they come!" warned the man at the back, straightening up from his dangerous task. "Lights thick as berries! Be here in five minutes. Better duck somewhere quick."

"Drive in this woods, Bunny!" said the chief.

"'Thout any lights? You can't do that!"

"Sure you can. Climb a tree, anything, and make it snappy! Then we duck behind the press and shoot 'em up as they come. That'll give us a chance to get by the highway, an' then they can't catch us no matter how. We'll shift to Lonnie's truck an' go on like lords, with a truck load o' hay, see? Get over the border by daybreak inta Canada."

"We can't make it!"

"Who says can't?" and the cold steel of a gun touched the temple of the objector and brought forth a nervous laugh.

"All cars District 459 surround Gleason's woods!" came the order from the radio, turned as low as possible.

The chief started.

"We gotta get outta here! That's too many."

"We can't!" said the driver. "There's three motorcycles on the only road."

"We gotta give up the ship!"

"Go on foot? Get taken in cold blood? *Not me!*"

"Yes, *you! Start!*" and a cold steel rod touched the back of the man's neck.

"Remember! No squealing! Even if yer taken, keep mum! You'll get yours if you squeal!"

The sound of their hurried footsteps died away among the trees, but the forgotten radio went on:

"—all cars! Calling all cars—"

"There's the truck," pointed out one officer holding up his torch, "but the birds have flown. Get busy, men!"

That was a night not ever to be forgotten by those who lived through it. The anxious hours dragged by unnoticed as those in the Deane household waited, breathless, watching the faces of the doctors, and the nurse who soon arrived.

Daphne, unable to lie down and sleep when there was no longer anything she could do to help, made her mother go and rest, soothed her excited little sister until she slept, and then went and sat in a low window seat in the partly darkened upper hall and waited. Don, she knew, was sitting at the foot of the stairs in the hall, ready for orders if he should be needed. Ranse had curled up in the hammock on the porch, unwilling to admit his youth and need of sleep. Daphne as she sat there those endless hours was thinking. This was no ordinary accident of a stranger. This young man was a part of themselves, made so by their mother's pleasant stories. He had grown dear to them all without ever having been known to them. And even the hearts of the younger brother and sister were full of sorrow and anxiety on his account. There was something very lovely, even in their sorrow, about being allowed to minister to him in his need. Even if he were not to live, there would be a satisfaction in having had him here, and having been able to give him every possible chance for life.

Another doctor and an assistant were telephoned for, and arrived. Don brought them upstairs, and they went silently into the sick room. Later Daphne took them to her brother's room to change into their white garb. The surgeon was going to operate, they told Daphne, and she caught her breath in sudden fear. It was his only hope, they told her.

There followed a pitiless time of waiting, broken by the telephone. Mrs. Gassner wanted to know just what had happened. Daphne told her that she could not talk now, the doctors were there. She would give her news in the morning. She hung up indignantly. Mrs. Gassner, with her ferret eyes, wanting to know all the gossip even in the middle of the night!

Don came upstairs in answer to a call, with a powerful electric bulb the doctors wanted. When he came out of the room again he came over to Daphne.

"Better go to bed, sister," he said gently, as if he were older than she. "I'll call you if you're needed."

She shook her head.

"I couldn't," she said decidedly. "I'm all right here. How does he seem?"

"Just the same," said the boy. "Unconscious, I guess. He just lies there perfectly still, his eyes shut. Or, perhaps they've given him some dope. I don't know. They're going to operate right now."

"I know," said Daphne. "The young doctor told me. There wouldn't be anybody we ought to wire, would there? I wish father were here. Maybe mother knows of some relative, but I hate to waken her. She can't bear much excitement."

"No," said Don. "Don't waken her. We couldn't wait for any relative to be found anyway. The surgeon says the operation is his only hope. And anyway, nobody could love him more than we do."

"No," said Daphne slowly, "unless—"

"Unless what?" asked Don sharply, almost antagonistically.

"Unless there might be someone—someone who—is *engaged* to him or something."

Don uttered a low sound of protest.

"We don't know there is, and we don't have to worry about that!" he said almost fiercely. "He's ours tonight, anyway, and we'll do the best we can for him. You'd better go and pray, Daphne."

"I am!" said Daphne quietly lifting sweet eyes. "I'd like to think that you are praying, too, Don."

"Okay!" said Donald embarrassedly, "that goes without saying," and he left her and went noiselessly down the stairs.

Morning dawned at last, a strange gay morning outside with little birds splitting their throats and breaking the awful silence that had reigned in the waiting household all night. And you couldn't do a thing about it! Daphne softly closed the window up in the hall, they yelled so loud out in the apple tree almost at the window sill. It seemed somehow as if she ought to go out under the tree and explain to those birds that a loved one was hovering on the borders of death and wouldn't they please cancel their concert for that morning or at least go and sing in some other apple tree. But the little birds sang right on.

It was a lovely colorful morning with rags of coral glory tattered about the sky, and a golden brim to the world. The air was fresh as if it had been washed, and there had been no such thing as night and dread and crime stalking abroad.

Daphne went into her own room to put cold water on her forehead and eyes, and looking out across the Morrell garden a sudden horror shook her to think of all that had gone on in that sweet fragrant place. It did not seem possible that it had all happened. And yet there was the penetrative odor of ether filling the house, and there was that closed door, from which came only low monosyllables occasionally. Oh, would the suspense never end?

At last she heard the door open softly and a young interne came out smiling. He saw her hovering near and smiled importantly.

"Well, we did it," he announced in a low voice—"we" as if he had performed the operation. "We located the bullet and removed it, without having to go too near to the heart, and he's still living. So far so good!" He was very young. He could be forgiven for being so flippant about it. He almost looked as if he would like to whistle. Modern youth took things so easily. Daphne turned away sick with anxiety, but was nevertheless glad for this much news of the sick one.

Presently the nurse came out with basins and instruments and asked for more hot water. Quite suddenly there was a great deal to be done. But Daphne found that her mother was in the kitchen before her preparing a tempting breakfast for the doctors and nurses.

Things went more rapidly then, the doctors came down to the dining room and conversed in low grave tones, talking of the possibilities.

"He has a good background," one of them said, "at least two generations of good clean living. That's in his favor."

They did not give any further opinion, and Daphne gathered that Keith Morrell's life still hung in the balance, and the matter was gravely serious. "Oh, Father," she prayed in her heart as she went about the thronging duties of that weary morning, "if it be Thy will, save his life." But she did not ask the doctor, though her eyes sought reassurance every time she looked toward him.

After the doctors had gone away, her father came home from an educational conference in Chicago. It seemed as if things would be better then. Father was so strong to lean upon.

The family settled down into a new kind of routine. Beverly took her dolls out in the back yard as far from the guest room as possible, and played silently. Daphne overheard Ranse telling the boys that he couldn't come out and play ball today. They had serious sickness in the house and he had to stay home, he might be needed to run errands. He worked by himself on the porch, putting together a toy boat he had whittled out of wood.

Don of course had to go to his work. Daphne looked

after him compassionately. She knew how reluctant he was to leave, and how little sleep he had had. He would be asleep on his feet by afternoon.

The day wore on. Daphne got the cleaning woman to come and help so that her mother wouldn't be tempted to do too much. The children were eager to help, too. They picked and shelled peas and beans from the garden, they ran errands, dried the dishes, and set the table.

It seemed a strange house with that smell of antiseptics, and that unnatural quietness brooding over everything.

The nurse who remained after the operation was very kind. She made Daphne go and take a sleep. She saw to it that she was not disturbed, too. It was as if the whole household were her patients. She seemed to take them all under her wing and protect them and care for them.

Then, of all days the minister had to select this one to come and call.

"I heard that you had been having quite an excitement. It certainly is hard that you should have a thing like this thrust upon you. This young man is not your responsibility. I don't understand why he didn't insist on going to the hospital."

Daphne looked at him and tried to keep the contempt out of her eyes as she answered:

"Well, in the first place, being unconscious he wasn't consulted, doesn't even know yet where he is. In the second place, the doctor didn't dare take him to the hospital; he said he probably wouldn't live to get there."

"Oh, I doubt that," said the minister in a superior tone. "That sounds like a fish story to me. All doctors that are truly eminent recommend the hospital rather than a private home. It sounds to me as if that doctor was lazy, didn't want to bother getting an ambulance, and took advantage of your house as being convenient."

Daphne's eyes were flashing, but she tried to steady her voice as she answered.

"We had three of the most eminent doctors in the city in consultation and they all agreed it would have been fatal to have moved him any farther. Doctor Fisher, Doctor McKenna, and Doctor Rowan. I suppose being a stranger in this section you do not recognize their pre-eminence. But even if they had not felt that way, there was another reason for our bringing him here. We wanted him. He is our friend. We have known his family for years, and we are very glad that he was so near and that we might take care of him."

"That certainly is most kind of you, but of course I suppose the young man will want to be removed to a hospital as soon as he is able to go. It really isn't right that you should have such a burden thrust upon you. You are not strong enough for nursing. It seems quite inconsiderate of everybody to think of it."

Daphne was angry enough to throw things, but she suddenly grinned.

"I don't think anybody has thought of it," she said. "We have two nurses, a day nurse and a night nurse. Though I would be only too glad to share such service if the case were not too serious at present to trust in inexperienced hands."

"Oh, really? Is he still so seriously ill as to require two nurses? I didn't realize. Do you think he would like to have me go up and pray with him?"

Daphne gave him a swift startled look.

"He is still unconscious," she said. "It might not do him any harm of course, but I'm sure the doctors and nurse would not allow anyone to go in there."

"Oh, well, then of course I won't bother. After all, it was really you I came to see. I have my new car at last and I thought you would be glad to get away from all this smell of antiseptics and gloom that is hanging over your home, and take a ride with me. It is a lovely day and you need to get out away from all this."

Daphne looked at him gravely.

"You don't understand," she said with dignity. "We are very anxious about our friend. I would not go away for anything just now. We do not know from hour to hour whether he will live or not."

"Oh, he'll probably pull through. Healthy young men don't die from a shot or two. And besides, you can't keep him alive by staying here and brooding over gloomy things, you know. Nobody would expect you to do so. You'd better come out and have a short ride at least. Besides, I want to consult you about that class of young girls and what we can give them in the line of a social and recreational character. We really are in need of more gatherings of a lighter character in our church. Come, I know you can help me."

Daphne's eyes grew distant as she heard him.

"You'll have to excuse me," she said coldly. "I have no time nor thought for such things now."

And then to her relief she heard the nurse calling softly down the stairs.

"Miss Daphne, could you come here just a minute and get me something I need?" And Drew Addison took himself away, promising to drop in later in the week.

18

IT took three days for the news of the shooting to reach New York, and another day and a half for it to drift down, in somewhat garbled form, to the shore mansion where Anne Casper lived. And perhaps it would never have got to either place if the men who perpetrated the dastardly deed had not been captured, and proved to be three of the most sought for public enemies.

And because they had been for sometime successfully evading the law and getting unbelievable sums of counterfeit money into circulation, and because their whole outfit of presses and money had been discovered and confiscated, even to the heavy press that they had managed to get out of the cellar and into the truck before they left, the affair had taken on the character of national interest. It made the front page headlines in many a prominent paper, and drew the attention of people everywhere, even in the social realms.

Keith Morrell, though known to a number of New York's social lights, had been but a quiet member of the group that surrounded Anne Casper, one of many who basked in her smiles, or her frowns. But now his name had suddenly jumped into prominence and he became a hero. Actually a martyr to "those horrid unprincipled gangsters," suffering in the good cause of apprehending and bringing to justice men who were defrauding society. Some who would never have hesitated to accept and spend counterfeit money if any came their way and they could get away with it without going to jail, held up their hands in horror at the wholesale production of it.

And so the news came to Anne Casper. After studying over the paper for some time she gathered herself together and decided to go and investigate the truth of this account. She wrote a note to her father before she left:

> Dear Daddy:
>
> Keith Morrell has got himself into some kind of a jam and I'm going down to see what it's all about. If he's really hurt, and it has taken him down enough to make him tractable, I may bring him back with me. If I do, please be prepared to forget old scores and let's try him again.
>
> Hastily,
> Anne

Then she dressed herself smartly and took the noon train.

The Deanes had a good many callers that morning. People had been getting curious as the days went by quietly, without any definite bulletins concerning the young man who lay at death's door.

Mrs. Gassner was the first one to call. She had decided to go to the source of information and get her news firsthand. So she came over with a cup to borrow some sugar. She had run out of sugar while she was mixing up a cake, she said. It was remarkable how many times Mrs. Gassner ran out of sugar. It was such a respectable device for getting into a neighbor's home. So unanswerable.

"You folks are having a real hard time, aren't you?" she

said to Mrs. Deane who had answered the knock at the kitchen door, and had taken the cup to fill with sugar.

"Oh, it is always hard to have someone you are fond of suffer," evaded Mrs. Deane pleasantly.

"Oh, yes? I s'pose you were fond of him, seeing as he lived so near when he was a little kid. But I don't seem to remember his being over to your house very much. His ma was kind of snooty, wasn't she? She never called on me, I know."

"Why, I always thought she was very pleasant," said Mrs. Deane. "I admired her very much. She led a busy life. She was a writer, you know, and that kept her busy. She wasn't a society woman and she hadn't time to go out much."

"Oh, she was a writer, was she? Poetry? I never could be bothered reading poetry. It always seemed to me they tried so hard to say a common thing all decorated up with words to confuse you."

"Why, yes, she wrote some poetry, but more prose, I believe. I read some lovely things of hers in the magazines sometimes. She wrote delightfully."

"H'm!" said the caller. "I never heard anything about her in the woman's club."

"Well, I guess she wasn't much of a club woman, either. She didn't have time for that. She was just a quiet home body who loved her home and her work. I liked her."

Mrs. Deane didn't say that she had never spoken a word to Mrs. Morrell in her life, but only admired her from a distance. She didn't feel that it was wrong to suppress that fact. She had really loved her neighbor well, though she had known her only from afar. Being sure of the sweet strong woman her neighbor had been, Mrs. Deane wanted to let Mrs. Gassner see her as she saw her.

"Well, her son's pretty fortunate to get took care of this way," went on Mrs. Gassner. "I guess she'd be surprised if she was to come back to earth and know her son was laying over here in your house. How is he? Any better today?"

"There's been no change yet," answered Mrs. Deane gravely. "The doctor says it may be a little while before he can tell just how it will come out. There was a concussion, you know, and that sometimes is very serious."

"Does he know how sick he is? What does he say about how it happened?"

"Oh, he hasn't been conscious at all, you know," said Mrs. Deane.

"Not yet? Why that's bad. Don't look as if he might be going ta live, does it?"

"The doctor says it is too soon to tell the outcome," said Mrs. Deane sadly.

"H'm! I guess your daughter Daphne feels pretty bad about it, don't she? Wasn't they pretty thick?"

"Oh, no, they were not intimate," said Daphne's mother quickly. "They went to school together, but that's all—just old schoolmates. But we all feel very anxious."

"Oh, then Daphne wasn't engaged to him, was she? I heard say they were, but I wasn't sure, the new minister comes here so much."

"Why, the minister goes everywhere, doesn't he? Being a minister he has to. You know Daphne is the organist and choir leader, and of course he has to consult with her about the services. Is this sugar enough, Mrs. Gassner? I could let you have one of these pound packages if you need more?"

"Oh, no, a cup's enough. I got some ordered, but he didn't bring up the things in time, and I wanted to get the cake in the oven. I better be going. I just thought I'd run over and get the true lay of the land, so many ask me, you know, me living next door and all. But you say there isn't nothing to it, do you?"

"Why, I don't know that I said anything about it, Mrs. Gassner. I think such things ought not to be discussed. Young people do hate it so. They want to manage their own affairs. Here, let me give you a tumbler of my quince jelly. It came out so pretty this year I like to look at it."

"Thanks a lot! It does look good. Well, I'll be running in again to see how the patient gets along. I'm sure I hope he lives after all the trouble you've had with him. Well, good-bye!" And Mrs. Gassner took herself home.

And William Knox came.

He came because Martha told him he had to, that it wasn't decent not to. He told her that if the young man should die and there should be any trouble about his letting Gowney have permission to take possession of the house, it was just as well that he shouldn't appear to be mixed up in the affair. But Martha said the young man might *not* die, and then if *he* found out that William hadn't even been decent enough to call and enquire how he was, he might think it very strange. And now that all this trouble had come out about Gowney and that counterfeit money affair, she said it was just as well that William should keep in with young Morrell, at least as long as he was alive.

So William came with frightened eyes and a fat roll of money concealed in his trousers pocket, in case he should find it necessary to hand it over.

But he seemed rather relieved than otherwise to find the young man still in a serious condition and not able to see him even for a minute, and he took himself away like one who has had a sudden reprieve.

Emily Lynd, thoughtful always, forebore to telephone, and sent her nurse Delia over for a whispered word with Daphne at the back door, to find out just how the young man really was, and tell briefly what she had seen and heard the night of the shooting.

She was scarcely gone when Evelyn Avery arrived, noisily, at the front door.

"Hello!" she greeted Daphne casually. "I just ran in to see Keith a few minutes and cheer him up. Hard lines having to lie still, and I thought he might like to see some of his friends. Brought over a pack of cards if he feels like playing, and some candy and magazines to pass the time away. Shall I run right up? Which is his room?"

Daphne drew her out on the veranda, and closed the door behind her, speaking in a hushed voice.

"Mr. Morrell is in a very serious condition," she said with dignity. "He would not be able to see you. He has not been conscious at all so far yet."

"For heaven's sake!" said the girl quite taken aback. "What doctor have you got? I should think a doctor could always bring anybody around if they were alive at all."

Daphne named the imposing array of eminent physicians.

"Well, I suppose they're all right," reluctantly admitted the young woman. "But I should think you ought to have a nurse, as serious as that is."

"We have two of them," said Daphne quietly.

"Well, how soon do they think he'll be up and around?" asked Evelyn after an annoyed pause.

"They do not know whether he will ever be up and around. It is a question of whether he can possibly live or not."

"Why, I understood he was only shot in the ankle. I don't see how that could possibly be so serious. Are you sure you know what you are talking about?"

Daphne gave her a steady look, and then said gently:

"He was shot three times. One bullet entered the lung near the heart. They operated and took that out, but he lost a great deal of blood. In addition he was struck on the head with a blackjack, and has a serious concussion. The doctor has said that there is only a slight chance that he can pull through, and he may die at any minute. If you want to know anything more than that, you had better ask the doctor yourself. I have told you all I know, and we ought not to be talking here so near his window. The nurse is trying to keep it very quiet."

"Oh, my goodness!" said the caller turning swiftly toward the steps, "I'd better get away. I never can bear to be around where there's talk of dying. It makes me actually sick. If he rallies you might tell him I called!" and Evelyn hurried down the steps to her car and was soon out of sight.

There came a bevy of reporters almost at once, but Daphne made short work of them, for the doctor had told her what to say.

And then came Anne Casper.

She arrived in a taxi which she left throbbing at the gate.

Daphne, weary-eyed and sad, came to the door again, and the two girls eyed one another hostilely. Daphne was very tired, and this seemed but another Evelyn Avery. A little more expensively dressed perhaps, but even more beautifully insolent than Evelyn.

Did that moment's pause as she stared at Daphne show that Anne recognized the beauty of the girl before her, and was measuring swords, wondering who she was and what she was doing here?

Then she lifted her haughty chin naughtily.

"Is this the gardener's cottage?" she asked loftily.

"Oh, no" said Daphne amusedly, "this is where Mr. Deane lives. I don't know any gardener living around here."

"Well, but I understood this was the place. A young woman in a car just directed me. She said she had just come from here, and that I would find the gardener's daughter here. Aren't you the gardener's daughter?"

So, this was the way Evelyn Avery had taken her revenge! It was so like her it was almost funny. A whimsical little twinkle came into Daphne's eyes.

"Sorry," she laughed softly, "but my father happens to be a professor in the university, chair of English. However, who is it you want to find? I might be able to direct you."

"I want to find Mr. Keith Morrell," said Anne Casper coldly. "I understood he had had an accident and had been brought to some house in this neighborhood. It is unaccountable that he should not have been taken to a hospital. I cannot understand it. Do you know where he is?"

Daphne's eyes were suddenly shadowed. Who was this insolent creature?

"Yes," she answered quietly, "he is here."

"Well, take me to him!" commanded Anne Casper.

"I'm sorry," said Daphne. "It's against the doctor's orders. Nobody but the nurse is allowed in the room."

"Indeed! Well, *I'm* somebody who *will* be allowed, you'll find out. I've come to take him to the hospital, and I'm keeping the taxi waiting while he gets ready. Won't you hurry?" Anne Casper stepped within the hall and glared up the stairs.

"Come this way," said Daphne quickly leading her down the hall to the dining room and closing the door behind them. "We must speak very quietly. They want no noise. I brought you in here to explain. Mr. Morrell is in a serious condition. It would be quite impossible to move him anywhere. That was why he was brought here, because the doctors were afraid he might die on the way. He has lost a great deal of blood and he is unconscious. There are symptoms of delirium, and his life is hanging in the balance. We have been told that no one must go near him, and that the house must be kept very quiet."

"All this is quite irrelevant," said Anne with a sweep of her jeweled hand. "I came here to take charge. I must see Mr. Morrell and I intend to see him at once! Stand aside, won't you! If you won't show me where he is, I'll find him for myself."

"No!" said Daphne, placing herself firmly in front of the door, "you cannot see him now. It might make all the difference between life and death for him."

Anne Casper was white with anger.

"I guess you don't understand who I am!" she said furiously.

"Does that matter now while his life hangs in the balance?" said Daphne wearily. She felt as if she would like to break down and cry. Suddenly all the reserve strength seemed to have gone out of her.

"Matter?" said Anne, growing angrier momentarily. "It certainly does. I am Mr. Morrell's fiancée! Now, do you understand? I have a right to see him and to take him away from here to a hospital where he would stand some chance of getting well under proper professional care."

Daphne was very white and her head was reeling with a sudden faintness that came over her, but by sheer force of will she controlled herself and answered steadily:

"If you are his fiancée I am sure you will want to do what will be best for him, and will be reasonable. You can sit down here and wait till the doctor comes. He was to be here about five o'clock, and you can talk with him. I was sent here to keep people away from him, and I'm going to do it until he gets here."

"The very idea!" said Anne Casper furiously. "If you think for a minute you are going to control me, or hinder me going to Mr. Morrell when I like, you are sadly mistaken. Get out of my way!" and Anne Casper caught Daphne's wrist with a jerk, digging her long sharp fingernails into the firm flesh, and looking like a small storm of fury.

"That'll be about all of that!" said Donald's cool voice as he appeared at the side door. "We'll just go out this way!"

Then the broad football shoulders stooped and he picked up Anne Casper as if she had been a doll and carried her outside, setting her down in the kitchen garden among the carrots and spinach, far enough from the house that her voice could not be heard.

"Don't you dare to lay your hands on me!" she raved, stamping her foot, and then stopping to stare at the good-looking young giant who stood grinning at her. "You insolent creature! I'll have you arrested."

"You dared to lay your hands on my sister!" said Don pointedly. "Think that over. And while you're thinking, just remember you're not to make any noise around here or I'll lay some more hands on you. In fact, I'll turn you over my knee and spank you if you don't shut right up. And I don't care whose fiancée you are. If you're worth anything at all, you'll realize that it's more important that Keith Morrell gets a break to live, than that you should have your own way."

"Donald!" said Daphne, coming out and laying a gentle hand on her brother's arm, "you're forgetting yourself! You mustn't speak that way to a lady."

"Maybe I am forgetting myself, Daffy," said Donald vexedly, "but she's no lady!"

"That's no reason why you shouldn't be a gentleman!"

"That's all I care to hear from either of you!" burst forth the visitor, having recovered from her amazement. "I'm going down to the city and bring a doctor and an ambulance. We'll see who's master here!" And she flounced away toward the taxi.

"Hop to it!" called Donald after her, before Daphne could put her hand over his mouth. "I hope you get to ride in one yourself some day! It'll do you good!"

"Donald!" said Daphne, "why did you do that? If she's really Keith Morrell's fiancée and he ever gets to know it, how terrible you will feel. How we will all feel!"

"If she's his fiancée I'll eat my hat!" said Donald fiercely. "In fact, if she's his fiancée, if he's gone and tied himself to a piece of selfishness like that, I don't know as I care what he thinks of me. But he's not like that, Daphne. You know he's not."

Daphne looked him sadly in the eyes.

"Perhaps not," she said wistfully, "but Donald, you know you didn't do right."

"Well, no, I don't suppose I did, not what you call right, but I'm still glad I did it! She had it coming to her."

"But Mother and Father would have been so ashamed of you."

"Would they? I wonder! Dad might not have done it in the same language, but if he'd seen and heard what I did, I'm not so sure but he'd have secretly rejoiced. However, I'm sorry. Of course I knew I would be," and he gave his sister a sheepish grin and then lifted her up and carried her in to the couch.

"Now, you lie there, sweetie, and shut your eyes for a few minutes. You're all in and need a wink of sleep."

He tucked her up on the couch with a light shawl that lay there, and tiptoed out of the room.

19.

THE doctor arrived ten minutes ahead of Anne Casper and her procession. She was still riding in her taxi, followed by her doctor in his own car and the big white noisy ambulance clanging its bell importantly in the rear, bringing all Rosedale in excitement to its front windows. There hadn't been so much excitement in Rosedale in many a day.

"Now," said Donald looking out of the window as they drew up before the house, "we'll see the fur fly! I'd better warn Doc so he'll know what he's up against. He's upstairs, isn't he?"

"I've already told him about it," said Daphne, coming to look out of the window. "She's brought the ambulance all right. I wonder if she will really take him after the doctor talks to her."

"Oh, she's got her own doctor. Great Caesar's ghost! Will ya look who she's got! His majesty Doctor Morgan himself! Now, how do you suppose she managed that? He's not a man who usually goes for money, I hear."

"She has probably represented that Keith is dying and he is the only hope of saving his life," said Daphne bitterly.

"Has Father come back from the university yet? I wonder if he couldn't do something?"

"I guess you'd better go to your room and pray, little sister," advised Don with sudden gravity.

Daphne prayed, but she had to go and let the strangers in. She was thankful to see the doctor in charge coming down the stairs as she walked down the hall to the front door, and to have him stand looming behind her, a grave and imposing figure with brows drawn down.

She could barely control her voice to introduce him: "Miss Casper, this is Doctor McKenna who is in charge of the case," she said, and saw contempt in Anne Casper's eyes.

"Well, he won't be very long," Anne said haughtily. "This is Doctor Morgan. Show him to the patient right away, please." The please was an outward touch of courtesy for the doctor, that was not included in the tone of voice used.

But suddenly the look on Anne Casper's face changed as she saw the look on the two doctors' faces.

"Why, hello, Dick, have they brought you here? Say, this is great!" said Doctor McKenna heartily. "I haven't seen you out of the operating room in a year of Sundays. I certainly am glad to greet you."

And the great Doctor Morgan fairly beamed.

"Pat McKenna, as I live!" he exclaimed shaking the other's big hand eagerly. "Say, how did you get here? You're not the inefficient country doctor I was led to expect, are you? Because if you are, I start back at once. I've three very sick patients to see yet tonight before dinner and nobody wants any better doctor than you are."

Doctor McKenna grinned.

"Not on your life!" he said. "You don't go back till you've given your opinion on this case. I tried hard to get you three days ago but they said you were out of town."

"I was. They took me up to Hoover's Island to see a man

who had to be operated on right away. I got back sooner than I expected. But I couldn't think of stopping now. I've got all sorts of important cases waiting."

"Really, Doctor Morgan," began Anne Casper freezingly, "I brought you here to take charge of this case, and get the patient to the hospital at once. I don't see why you waste time gossiping with this other doctor. He can be dismissed now. I want you to take entire charge."

Doctor McKenna suddenly looked sharply at Anne:

"You're supposed to be the fiancée of the patient, I believe? Well, I've only this to say. If you want to kill him, you'll attempt to move him now. I'll be only too glad to turn the case over at once to my old friend and colleague Doctor Morgan, but when he hears just what condition the patient is in, I am quite sure he will agree with me that it would be sure death to move him."

He turned to Doctor Morgan and said a few words in technical terms that neither Daphne nor Anne understood, and Doctor Morgan turned to Anne:

"He is quite right," he said. "It would be nothing short of criminal to move the patient."

"But you have not seen him!" gasped Anne angrily. "I brought you here to take full charge, and you have nothing but the word of this other man to judge by. I insist that you take charge."

"The word of Doctor McKenna is not to be doubted," said Doctor Morgan decidedly. "Besides, my dear little lady, I could not think of taking over a case of so eminent a doctor as Patrick McKenna. It is not professional etiquette anyway. As you represented the matter to me, the man in charge was inexperienced and *wanted* me to come. Now I must withdraw entirely from the matter and hasten back to my work. Don't be worried. You have the best doctor I know on the job, and if anybody can save the life of your friend he will."

"Indeed, I do not wish him to have anything to do with

the matter," said Anne stamping her foot childishly. "They told me at the hospital that you were a great doctor, but I don't think much of you if you would let a man die for the sake of professional etiquette. If you don't take charge at once I shall tell the men from the ambulance to carry Mr. Morrell to the hospital and find some other doctor when we get there."

"Well, the men wouldn't do it," grinned Doctor Morgan. "I should tell them not to. They know me."

"*I'm* paying them!" said Anne haughtily.

"Yes, but you see *I'm* bossing them. Now, come, little lady, sit down and let me tell you a thing or two."

"I shall not sit down!"

"Oh, very well, stand then," he said in perfect good nature. "You see it's this way. You couldn't have a better physician to care for your friend if you were to search the world over. What he says goes, and you might as well understand it now. You'll save yourself a lot of trouble and mortification."

"Look here, Dick, I want you to go up and see the patient and satisfy the lady," spoke Doctor McKenna. "Besides, I'd like your advice."

"Very well, I'll go. No, you stay here, Miss Casper. I'll come down in a few minutes and tell you just what I think."

"I'm going with you. I have a right."

"I'm not so sure of that. Not if it makes the patient worse." Doctor Morgan looked at his friend.

"Let her come," said Doctor McKenna. "It may open her eyes. That is, if she knows how to keep her mouth shut and not make a fuss."

Anne Casper flashed her brilliant eyes at him in contempt and followed the doctors up the stairs. Daphne watched them go with a sinking heart. Would that heartless self-willed girl gain her point after all, and perhaps kill Keith? Well, perhaps he would be just as well off as married to her. How could he ever have cared for a girl like that? Then she resolutely put such thoughts away from her. Perhaps this determined girl really loved him and wanted to help him. Perhaps she was only blind and foolish, not knowing what wonderful doctors these were, and how wise and skillful.

So Anne Casper had her way and entered that quiet room where Keith Morrell lay turning his head restlessly and moaning in a rising delirium. But in the doorway she stood riveted to the spot, staring at the man she thought she wanted. Was that the handsome Keith Morell, that white-faced man with the bloody bandages covering his head, and with cuts and bruises about his eyes? Across one cheek was an ugly cut strapped up with adhesive. Perhaps he would be scarred. Horrible! They had cut his hair away, his wonderful dark hair. How ghastly! And there was blood on his scalp. Blood always made her ill.

She watched him in horror for a long minute, saw his fingers restlessly picking at the bed covers, heard his low moaning, and suddenly turned away and leaned against the door frame.

"Take me away!" she commanded. "I—never could stand—the sight of blood!" Her childish complaining voice made the sick man moan the more.

Doctor McKenna signed to the nurse and she came and led Anne downstairs. Daphne, sitting on guard below with her troubled thoughts heard her talking to the nurse.

"I'm *very* sensitive," she explained loftily. "I never could bear to see anybody suffer! It makes me quite ill!"

The nurse established her on the couch in the living room, gave her a glass of water, though she said she preferred wine and looked her contempt when Daphne told her they hadn't any wine in the house.

Then the nurse went back upstairs, but Daphne did not stay with Anne Casper. She went into the kitchen and busied herself about getting supper for those who could eat it. Till she heard a call from the living room, "Where *are* you? Isn't there *any*one about?" and she went back to see what the unpleasant guest wanted now. She found her standing by the front window looking out across the road and down through the Morrell garden toward the old house.

"Isn't the Morrell house near here somewhere?" she asked when Daphne came in, never turning her head to look at her.

"Yes," said Daphne, with difficulty controlling her voice. "That is it right across there."

"Heavens! Not that shabby old barracks! You don't mean it? Why it's hideously ugly and old-fashioned. It hasn't a bit of smartness about it. I should think he would want to sell it as quickly as he could. I can't imagine anyone wanting to keep that!"

"It is almost two hundred years old," said Daphne with all her love and reverence for the old house in her voice.

"It certainly looks it," laughed the other girl contemptuously. "It ought to have been pulled down long ago."

Daphne wanted to cry out against this iconoclast, and was glad to hear the doctors coming downstairs. She escaped to the kitchen without reply, and found tears in her eyes when she got there. This girl seemed to have torn down all the beautiful things in connection with the old Morrell house and the dear lives that had been lived there. She had ruthlessly tried to destroy with a word something that was precious. It was as if the fairy story that had been going on so many beautiful young years, had suddenly ended in a hideous nightmare.

She never knew just what Doctor Morgan said to the petulant little heiress that made her decide at last to go home and not return until she was sent for, but she went. A few minutes later as Daphne came into the living room bearing a tray with coffee and sandwiches for Doctor Morgan who would have no time now to get his dinner, she heard him saying to Doctor McKenna:

"So that's his fiancée, is it? Poor fellow! He might better die than come back to that!"

The tone he said it in not only expressed contempt for Anne Casper, but also implied a grave doubt as to whether the young man would ever come back, and Daphne went back to the kitchen with a heavy heart.

But Daphne had not long to indulge in anxiety, for there came a knock at the back door. It was just turned dusk, and Mrs. Gassner stood there. She hadn't even stopped for her excuse of a cup of sugar. She was breathless with haste.

"I just stepped over to find out what has happened," she said as she came puffing into the kitchen. "He isn't dead yet, is he? I couldn't make out whether they took him away in that ambulance or not, it wasn't turned the right way for me to see. Those syringa bushes hid the entrance where it was standing. And I just couldn't wait to know. You know a lot of people will phone me, hesitating to disturb you. They'll think I'm the next door neighbor and ought to know."

Daphne realized that she was under scrutiny, and that whatever this ferret-eyed woman saw or heard would be reported verbatim, and highly illuminated. So she tried her best to look calm and casual.

"Of course," she said. "It's kind of you, and we appreciate your wanting to help." She gave a little fleeting smile. "Of course everybody is anxious to know about Mr. Morrell. They all loved his mother and father so much. But there isn't much change since morning I'm afraid. The doctor thinks it may be several days more before we can hope for any, that is, if he lives that long. We'll just have to be patient."

Mrs. Gassner looked disappointed. Almost any change would have been good news to her.

"But that ambulance. Did they take him away to a hospital?"

"No," said Daphne coolly, "when it got out here the doctor didn't think it was wise to move him."

"Oh, my goodness!" said Mrs. Gassner appalled. "Now who will have to pay for that? You won't, will you? I've heard ambulances cost a lot. Who ordered it, anyway? You folks or the doctor? I should think the one who ordered it would be responsible."

"I really don't know," said Daphne coldly. "Certainly we did not send for it. It doesn't matter, does it, a little thing like that? The thing that concerns us is to have Mr. Morrell get well."

"Well, I s'pose you could look at it that way, too, of course. But say, who was that girl? What did she have to do with it? She wasn't another nurse, was she? She seemed too well dressed for that."

"One of his friends, probably. I really didn't enquire whether she was a nurse or not. I've been too busy."

"Well, she didn't come from around here, did she? I don't think I ever saw her before. Did she come from New York?"

"I didn't ask."

At last Mrs. Gassner took her leave, realizing that she was pretty well baffled and would be obliged to draw on her imagination for most of her information. And Daphne plunged into hasty preparation of the evening meal. It was to be a very simple affair, eaten in the kitchen, to keep the house as quiet as possible. Broiled steak and roasted potatoes, peas that the children had shelled. It didn't take long to prepare, but Daphne's heart was heavy as she went about setting the kitchen table. The days stretched long ahead filled with anxiety. Where would they end? In death and sorrow after all? And would that unspeakable girl return? She seemed the one drop too much in the bitter cup of the days. In fact, her existence seemed to take the joy out of a good many things that had been dear to them all. She seemed to have taken away their right to call Keith Morrell their friend.

It was just after the evening meal was concluded that there came another caller. Daphne, as she went on weary feet to the door, glanced out and was glad that it would be too dark for Mrs. Gassner to keep tab on this one anyway. But she reckoned without her host for the taxi which took the visitor away hadn't reached the corner before Mrs. Gassner telephoned.

"Is that you, Daphne? Say, I heard a car drive up. That wasn't the undertaker, was it? I've been so worried I had to call up."

"No," giggled Daphne hysterically, "it was Mr. Sawyer of New York, the head of the firm where Mr. Morrell is employed. He merely called to enquire how he was."

"Good night! Let me answer that old hag next time she calls," said Donald. "I'll tell her where to get off! Does she think you haven't anything to do but sit around and answer her nosey questions?"

Daphne turned from the instrument and wiped the tears from her eyes, still laughing nervously.

"Donald, dear, if this keeps on I'm afraid your kindly disposition is going to be utterly ruined," she said.

"I'll say it is!" muttered Donald, frowning. "Such a lot of old hens, so curious they can't wait a minute for things to happen."

But night settled down at last, and Daphne, too weary to think, lay down upon her bed and prayed:

"Oh, Father, don't let him die!" She opened her eyes and looked across to her window from which she could just glimpse Emily Lynd's light shining, and she knew that the dear old saint would be praying, too, for the child of her beloved friend.

The papers were giving daily bulletins now of Keith Morrell's condition. It had become an affair of wide interest. If Keith Morrell died, Gowney and his associates would be indicted for murder. A Federal case! Public menace Gowney tried for murder! Newspapermen were hot on the case. There was scarcely an hour of the day when reporters did not call at the house or on the telephone. The Deanes had to have the telephone bell muffled, and the instrument put in the kitchen, for every time it was used in the lower hall the patient grew restless and moaned.

It came to be necessary for the doctor to write a brief line of a daily bulletin each time he came, and leave it on the telephone stand. Daphne had learned to save herself by sending Ranse or Beverly to the telephone to give the doctor's word and no more.

But among others who made friendly telephone calls of enquiry each day was a Mr. Dinsmore. He said he was a friend of Keith's father, and wanted to come out as soon as there was a chance he might see the invalid, and Daphne always answered him gently and went more into detail about the invalid than when others called. She told the children always to call her when he was on the telephone. He seemed a kindly, fatherly man.

Then one morning there was a change. The fever had abated somewhat, the wound was draining nicely, the cerebral condition seemed decidedly better, and the patient had dropped into what seemed like a normal sleep for the first time since the shooting.

Doctor McKenna came and went several times that day, and toward evening he brought Doctor Morgan out with him for a few minutes. When they went away they seemed almost cheerful.

"We may have some good news for you now in a day or so, if the cerebral symptoms don't return," he told Daphne, and wrote on the telephone pad that the condition of the patient was slightly more hopeful. Daphne went about as if walking on air. Her heart almost felt like singing, though it had to be a silent song, for the doctor had cautioned special quiet during the next few hours. It was possible that full consciousness might return at any time, and there must be nothing to startle or weary the sick man.

That evening just as Daphne was about to retire the nurse came through the hall elated. The patient had opened his eyes and asked for a drink of water. He had taken several spoonfuls, and then dropped off to sleep like a baby.

"He'll be better in the morning, I'm sure," said the nurse. "I know the signs."

And Daphne went to sleep, her heart full of thanksgiving.

ONE morning after the reports in the papers had for three days in succession announced improvement in the patient, whom now the whole town had come to consider their own personal property, William Knox entered the police headquarters and requested an interview with the chief. The interview was granted and they sat down, William fearsomely on the edge of a straight wooden chair, and the big police head in a swivel chair behind his desk. William resembled a poor little whipped puppy requesting life of a big mastiff.

"I've come to see you about a personal matter," said William, lowering his voice and looking about him as if he expected to see spies in every corner ready to fly to Martha with the matter. "It is strictly confidential."

"Go ahead, Knox," said the mastiff, "this room is sound proof. Nobody to hear you. Personal, you say?"

"Well, not altogether personal, either," said Knox, looking down at his old hat which he was fingering nervously. "It has to do somewhat remotely with this case of Gowney and Morrell."

"You don't say!" said the chief. "Well, let's hear! Why didn't you come around sooner?"

"Well, I figured that what I knew I should tell directly to Mr. Morrell himself. It had to do with the sale of the house to Gowney. You see, Mr. Morrell wanted to sell, and Gowney had agreed to buy, but the price wasn't just settled. And then Mr. Morrell came down and changed his mind about selling. After he had gone back to New York, Gowney came around hotfoot and offered a lot more. He offered so much I hadn't an idea Morrell wouldn't take it. I thought he'd just jump at the chance. So to make sure Gowney wouldn't get away before I could get in touch with Morrell, I let him give me a retainer. Then I tried to get in touch with Morrell and couldn't—found he'd gone to Boston. It was three days before I contacted him and then I had to write a letter, and right away I got a telegram he wouldn't sell at any price. So I wired back it was already sold, and he wired for me to cancel it, and return the retainer that he wouldn't sell it for *nothing*. So I went everywhere trying to find that skunk Gowney, and his folks said he'd gone away to a funeral. And then all of a sudden come this here shooting and I didn't know what to do. I'm up a tree. I figured I'd go tell Morrell, but they won't let me see him, and I can't keep all this money in the house, not with folks like Gowney around town, and so I come to ask your advice. Who belongs to that money? Should I go give it to Gowney, or should I wait till Morrell's well and give it to him, or should I put it in the bank or what?"

The chief had watched the sad worried little man step by step, his own face like a mask, with no expression on it at all. And now as Knox came to an embarrassed stop and looked up frightened, he said:

"Got that money with ya now?"

"Yes," said William, like a little dog owning to a bone that the big dog wanted.

"Lets see it." He reached a burly hand out and William with difficulty extracted the unwonted roll of bills from his trousers pocket and handed them forth in a trembling hand, with an if-I-perish-I-perish expression on his face.

"All that?" the chief gave him a dagger of a searching glance. But the little man had told everything and his eyes were no longer shifty. At least he had told practically everything. He had fixed up that story so that there was no mention of that money having been a personal retainer for himself which gave possession immediately. But that, he told his conscience, was all right. He might not have kept that money anyway, even if all had gone as planned. He hadn't ever really settled that with his conscience as yet.

"Yes, all that!" he said with a sigh of relinquishment. Martha didn't know yet. What would Martha say when she found he'd come to the police? But she couldn't do anything about it now it was done, except yammer, and she might as well yammer about one thing as another. Anyway, his conscience was clear at last. He told himself he was an honest man at heart, and he wanted everybody to know it.

The big policeman fingered over the money slowly, lifting some of it up to the light and looking at it, bill by bill. At last he rolled it up firmly and held it in his hand.

"Well, William, I'll just tell ya, it's a lucky thing you turned that money in ta me ur you'd a ben in real trouble, and I don't mean mebbe!"

"Oh!" said William, wide-eyed and fairly shaking with anxiety. "I *would?* How?"

"It's a luckier thing, too, you didn't try passing none of it!"

"Oh?" said William, wetting his lips and trying to think how to ask another question. But all he could manage was a feeble "Why?"

"Because," went on the chief, "this here is *counterfeit* money. This money is wanted by the Federal government."

"Counterfeit money?" said William in weak amazement. "Let me look at it again. I never saw any counterfeit money."

"You've seen this here!" said the chief laying it on the table beside him, yet keeping his big paw over the half of it.

William reached out a hesitating finger and touched the money.

"Why, it looks just like real money. I never suspected it. I don't see how you know."

"That's why it's counterfeit. It's so good most folks couldn't tell it from good money. What would they wantta make counterfeit money for if they couldn't fool folks and pass it out?"

"Well, that's so! I never thought of that before. Well, I am all beat out about that. And I had all that worry about it and I needn't to've worried about it at all. If anybody had uv stole it they wouldn't uv got nothing."

"Well, you're lucky, you are, that you didn't try to pass any of it. You'd have got tied up in this here case that may turn out to be a murder case yet, fer all we know. Young Morrell ain't any too well yet, I'm told."

"Gosh! I'm glad I came to you," said William naively. "Gosh, what I gotta do now with it?"

"I'll take care of it. You leave it with me."

"But what'll I do if Mr. Morrell gets well and I have to give him evidence that I had that money, ur thought I had it, which amounts to the same thing?"

"Here, I'll give ya a receipt. Now don't you go blabbing to everybody about this. Keep it under yer hat till the time comes. You'll probably be called upon ta testify in the case when it comes up, but until then keep quiet. Don't tell anybody. Not *anybody*!"

"Gosh! I wouldn't like ta have ta testify," said William Knox. "I've always been a peace-abiding man, and I don't liketa get in the public eye. It might injure my business."

"Oh, that won't injure your business, just give you a little pep in the eyes of folks, make 'em think you're up and coming."

William looked troubled and wriggled on his chair.

"But I've heard these gangsters always get their revenge on anybody that tells on 'em. I wouldn't liketa be shot after testifying. What would become of my wife?"

"Oh, you needn't worry about that. You aren't important enough for that. They only risk their necks on big shots. You're all right. Good-bye, and don't say nothing to nobody!"

William went away blinking, wondering what he was going to say to Martha. He couldn't tell her a lie when she asked, and she would ask, he was sure. He never seemed to get a lie straight. It always had LIE written across the face of it, written in his timid eyes, and all over him. And what else could he tell Martha if he mustn't tell her the truth? He wondered miserably whether that chief was married, and whether he had a wife like Martha who always ferreted out everything.

The days went by and at last it was an assured fact that Keith Morrell was going to get well. It was going to be a slow process, days, perhaps weeks, before he would be able to be out and about again, but he was not going to die. Not now anyway.

As the daily bulletins showed Morrell's progress there began to be talk about the Gowney trial, and a hint that more of his counterfeit money had been found. Every time that William Knox read anything like this in the paper he managed to lose the paper somehow before he got home, and Martha began to tell him he was getting old, couldn't keep a paper till he got home. He'd better have it delivered at the house instead of the office.

These were busy days for Daphne now, though happy ones. Just to pass the door of the guest room and get a glimpse of Keith's quiet face against the pillow was enough to make her heart glad. She had been in to see him several times, just on some errand, to take a tray or bring a letter to the nurse, and always there had been a feeble flicker of a smile to greet her. His lips would sometimes form the word "Hello!" feebly. It was enough for her just to serve him quietly afar, and feel he was friendly again.

No one had spoken to him as yet of what he had been through, nor had he asked. He seemed content just to lie there and be cared for. Whether he remembered anything about the shooting or not no one knew. The doctor said in view of the cerebral conditions that had lasted so long it was better not to let him think about those things. So they came and went and smiled at him, and he smiled back. Or if he seemed too tired to smile with his lips his eyes always seemed to smile anyway.

One day while he was sleeping the nurse received a telephone call on business, and she asked Daphne to sit with the patient while she ran down to the bank to straighten out a little matter. The patient was asleep and would likely stay so until her return. So Daphne caught up her Bible from the bedside table in her room, and went in to sit by the window and study a little while.

It was very quiet in the room, a meadowlark was singing off in the distance, and the soft white curtains were blowing in the breeze. There was a peace about the room, and a peace in Daphne's heart, as she read. Keith Morrell was getting well and she felt that her prayers were being answered. Her heart was full of great thanksgiving and trust. She would not let herself think about anything in the future. The Lord had helped in this great crisis, and He would help in whatever came afterward, of either joy or sorrow. She had opened her Bible to the thirty-fourth psalm, a favorite one with her, and as she read on it seemed to voice the gladness in her own heart.

Now and then she would glance up and see that her patient was still quietly asleep, and so she sat, a little smile upon her lips as she let her heart rest down hard upon the words of the Book.

Suddenly she looked up and saw that Keith's eyes were

open and he was looking straight at her, and when their eyes met he smiled. It reminded her of the day they had first met on the ball ground and he had smiled as if he knew her, and her heart thrilled. He was back from the borderland with friendly eyes and a smile. Life had sunshine again and was greatly worth living. No need to question what it all meant. God was good. God was leading in His own way.

Then he spoke, slowly, his voice weak and not so buoyant as in health:

"What are you reading?" he asked wistfully.

"My Bible," she said shyly.

"Read it to me," he said. "I'd like to see—what—makes—you look so—happy."

She looked up and smiled, a soft color blooming in her cheeks.

"It's a psalm," she said. "It seemed just to voice my own feelings. We are all so glad you are getting well—"

He smiled again.

"That's nice!"

"But you mustn't talk," she said. "The nurse will scold me if I let you. I'll read."

"'I will bless the Lord at all times, His praise shall continually be in my mouth.'"

His eyes kindled as she read.

When she came to the words: "This poor man cried and the Lord heard him, and saved him out of all his troubles," he lifted his hand feebly and let it drop again on the counterpane.

"That's me!" he said with a smile.

A flood of joy came into her eyes, and then she read on to the end of the psalm. After she finished he was very still, his eyes closed. She thought he had fallen asleep again, but presently he spoke.

"I—used to belong—to the Lord—!" he said slowly. "I took Him for my Saviour! I've always—believed—on Him.

But—I—got—way off—in—the—world."

It was very still there for a minute. Then he went on.

"I've—been—trying—to come back! I—think—He sent—me—here!"

"Of course He did!" said Daphne with a lilt in her voice. "I'm so glad! I thought you belonged to Him!"

He smiled and closed his eyes.

"You are tired," she said quickly. "You mustn't talk another word. It's time for your orange juice," and she sprang to get it.

He swallowed the orange juice obediently, and then lifted his hand with an effort and laid it on hers as she held the glass.

"You're—something like—an angel—yourself—you know! Angel—of—the Lord!"

Daphne, too much moved to say much, simply laid her other hand on his and patted it softly.

"Thank you," she said, "that's beautiful! Now, you go to sleep, or I shall get scolded."

His eyes followed her as she smoothed the covers and went across the room to draw down the shades. Then she curled up in a big chair and closed her own eyes, trying to contain the beautiful gladness that swelled over her whole being. Of course, she told herself, it was just because she had been so tired and anxious and overwrought that she was such a silly as to feel almost like crying with gladness.

That was just the day before Anne Casper came again, came in a big limousine with a liveried chauffeur and the smartest costume she owned.

21

"OH, so you're here yet, are you?" Anne Casper greeted Daphne as she came to the door. Daphne was white to the lips at the sudden apparition, her great happiness shattering in fragments at her feet.

"Well, I've brought Doctor Morgan's permit, so I suppose you'll allow me to come," she said with fine sarcasm, and followed Daphne up the stairs, in spite of her request that she would wait until the nurse said it was all right to come.

Daphne, her heart in a strange tumult that she did not understand, went slowly up the stairs, and tapped ceremoniously on the partly closed door, holding out the doctor's permit.

Then they both heard Keith's voice, a bit imperious, eager, in the tone of a convalescent:

"Is that Daphne? Tell her to come in. I want her to read to me again."

Anne darted a sharp glance at her and Daphne's cheeks flushed, but she kept her poise and did not look at the other girl.

Then the nurse's voice:

"It's someone else you'll want to see, Mr. Morrell. Miss Casper has come to see you," and she swung the door wide open.

"What the dickens—!" said Keith in quite a cross tone, and turned his head toward the door just as Anne stepped smiling triumphantly into the room.

Keith studied her for a minute, with his brows drawn down in an ungracious scowl. Then he said in a merely casual tone, as if he had seen her only the day before:

"Hello, Anne! How're you?"

"I'm fine," said Anne smilingly, turning her glance to see if Daphne had gone. Daphne had, but not far. She heard every word that was said, although she hadn't meant to. The door of the nurse's room in which she had taken refuge was blocked open by a little table, and she couldn't get it shut without making a lot of fuss, so she just stood there out of sight with scarlet cheeks and trembling limbs.

Keith continued to stare at his visitor.

"Nice of you to come and see me," he added as if he had had a hard time thinking it up. Then, after an instant he pointed to a chair.

"You can sit down there and talk to the nurse if you want to. I'm not allowed to talk," and he dropped back on his pillow and closed his eyes.

Anne looked startled, and then rallied:

"This isn't the first time I've been to see you, Keith!" she said with her very sweetest smile. "They wouldn't let me stay the last time I came."

"No? Well, I don't remember. But it doesn't matter. I'm not very sociable nowadays. I'm getting rested and I can't be bothered. You'll excuse me if I go to sleep, won't you? I find I'm rather tired again."

He turned over on his pillow, his face away from her and closed his eyes. Anne stared at him in bewilderment, and then she went and stood over at the other side of the bed looking down at him.

"But Keith, listen. I've come to take you away out of this horrid little stuffy room into a nice great big beautiful room by the sea."

"This is a *nice* room!" he said suddenly, opening his eyes and looking around. "What's the matter with this room? I like it better than any room I ever saw. It has nice curtains that blow in the breeze, and there's a bird I know out there that sings to me every morning."

"But Keith, you're coming home with me to our beautiful place by the sea, and we'll have the grandest times together while you get all rested and strong again. I've brought the limousine and you can lie down in the back seat and go to sleep all the way, and you won't know where you are till you wake up in another bed and hear the waves down on the beach."

"No!" said Keith quite crossly. "*No!* I never want to see the sea again! I never want to hear its awful beat. I'm fed up with the sea! Don't mention it to me again. Go away, Anne! You don't understand. I'm very tired and I've got to go to sleep. Good-bye. Where's Daphne, nurse? I want her to read to me and put me to sleep."

"I think you had better go out now," said the nurse a bit alarmed at the turn things had taken. "He hasn't had a caller before, and you know he's had these cerebral symptoms. The doctor said we must be very careful and not excite him or they might return."

"Why, the very idea!" said Anne indignantly. "Go out when I've just come? I should say not. Go out yourself and let me talk to him. I know how to bring him to reason."

"What is all this about?" asked Doctor McKenna appearing in the doorway. His voice was gravely apprehensive.

"I've come to take my fiancé down to the shore to get well," said Anne, "I have Doctor Morgan's permission to come here today. The nurse has it, if you insist on looking at it, and I've come to take Mr. Morrell away. He's been dragging along too many weeks already, and I'm going to take him where he will get well right away. Nurse, won't you call my man to come and lift Mr. Morrell?"

Suddenly with a strength born of his exasperation, Keith lifted himself right up from the pillow.

"Look here, Doctor, I'm *not going* to any shore! I don't *want* to, and I *won't*. And she's *not* my fiancée either, and never was, and she knows it! I wish you'd go away, Anne, and stay where you belong. I've got to get some sleep right away!" And he dropped back on the pillow again white and limp.

Anne stood there petrified with rage, unable to believe her senses.

"Keith!" she said, "Keith darling! You don't know what you're saying!"

"No, I guess I don't!" murmured the boy opening tired eyes, "but I guess you know what I mean, all right."

"Keith, if I go away now, you'll be sorry, for I'll never come back again." Her voice was angry.

"Go as far as you like and see if I care!" said Keith, reverting to a phrase of his high school days, and fainted dead away.

The doctor and nurse were immediately too busy to see what became of the visitor, and she walked downstairs and away to her great car in a towering rage. He should suffer for this. He would see. She would ruin him. She would drive him out of his precious position and see that he never succeeded in getting another. She would show him what he had lost. She would marry the elderly millionaire and take every occasion to bring him to scorn. She would ruin him with the social set. He and his Daphne indeed! Who was *she*? He would soon tire of her, and then he would come crawling back and she wouldn't receive him. Not she. When he tired of this little simple Daphne and wanted *her*, she would show him that "hell hath no fury like a woman scorned." Even if he was sick yet and didn't know what he was saying, she would never forgive what he had done to her in the presence of that insolent doctor and nurse, and that little pussy-faced Daphne! Never, *never,* as long as she lived! She had never really loved him anyway. She just wanted to conquer him and carry him around as a trophy, a handsome trophy that she could afford if she wanted. But now, well, now he would see!

Daphne, standing trembling in the nurse's little hall bedroom in the shadows, her heart quivering with joy and fear and sudden knowledge of herself, heard the low exclamation of the doctor and the swift steps of the nurse as they went to the bedside, knew that there were more serious things to consider now than her personal joys or fears, and turned to see what she could do to help.

Then it was all to do over again, the anxious days and nights of nursing and waiting, the bulletins to the papers: "Young Mr. Keith Morrell who was shot while attempting to enter his own house, by the criminal and counterfeiter Gowney, at present in jail awaiting trial, has had a relapse, and is in serious condition. It may be that even yet Gowney may be indicted for murder."

Anne read the paragraph on the second page of a New York paper, wide-eyed with horror, and cast about in her mind how soon she could slip off to Europe in case anything happened to Keith. Those contemptible doctors might even dare to charge her with having brought about this relapse. She wished she had never heard of Keith Morrell. She was done with him forever. He was the first man who had ever stirred her to step down from her small throne and offer favor, and how she hated him now! She could never forget that look in his eyes when he took her hands down from about his neck and told her he did not love her. Well, if he died now it was nothing more than he deserved. Though somehow it didn't seem to give her the satisfaction she desired to have him punished by death. She would rather have had him live and be tormented by her petty annoyances. There was no point in showing to a dead man how easily she could have his job taken away from him and send him adrift upon the world without a reputation. Uneasily she watched the papers from day to day for more news. But New York had gone on its way and was no longer concerned about a young man who might die, and Anne Casper had no contacts with local papers.

Doctor Patrick McKenna, anxious and disappointed, called up Doctor Morgan that first night:

"Say, what's the idea, Dick, butting in on my case after you declined to take it over? You've made a pretty kettle of fish for me to fry, and now you'd better come out post haste and help me."

"What do you mean, Pat?" came the puzzled reply. "How did I butt in on your case? What case?"

"I mean why did you send that blamed little fool of a Casper girl back here to heckle her so-called fiancé before he was by any means out of the woods?"

"Why, I never sent her out, Pat. Where'd you get that idea?"

"Oh, yes, you did. Don't try to excuse yourself that way. She brought your note along with her. We have it right here. It says that you authorized her to see the young man, and she came with a limousine to take him away to the shore. She's some tartar, she is! She would have carried him off right under the nose of the nurse and the household, if I hadn't appeared on the scene while he was telling her where to get off. He told her plenty, too, while he was at it, and then he fell back in a dead faint and it took me the best part of an hour to bring him back. He's in a raging fever now and going up at jumps every hour. Oh, you did plenty, and you'd better get on the job and help me out. This means a Federal murder case, incidentally too, if he should die, and he looks to me mightily like he was headed that way now."

"Well, I'll come of course, but I tell you, Pat, I never

gave that girl a letter. I haven't laid eyes on her since I left Rosedale that night, and I haven't written her either. I never gave another thought to the little scatterbrain. But I'll come. I'll start at once. Better look at that letter again, and you'll surely see it isn't my handwriting. It may be a clever imitation, but I never wrote it myself. You know I wouldn't do a thing like that without asking you, Pat! What's the matter with you?"

"Well, I thought it was something like that," said Doctor McKenna with satisfaction, as he hung up the receiver.

And after that the two famous physicians worked together, night and day, so that there were scarcely two hours during the most anxious time, when one or the other of them was not there. There came a day when both of them stayed and watched momentarily, and thought they were losing the fight. When the nurse never took time to eat, and Daphne and her mother prayed as they went about what work had to be done, and Donald prayed while he worked, and even the children slipped into their rooms now and then with grave sweet young faces and knelt by their beds for a moment with God.

And the prayers prevailed. Keith rallied almost miraculously. The doctors looked at one another in relief and wonder.

"It's this praying household," said Doctor McKenna solemnly to the other, although he had always been supposed to be a scoffer. "They've prayed him through, I guess. I couldn't have done it, I'm sure of that. Not even with your help."

"Yes," said Doctor Morgan thoughtfully. "I guess that must be it. I thought he was gone once and when I came downstairs, there was that mother down on her knees beside the dining room couch praying, and when I went back upstairs I caught a glimpse of the girl kneeling over in the back bedroom. And when I went into the sickroom I'm blamed if he hadn't rallied again. That's a great girl, that

Daphne. Why the dickens couldn't the man see how much more she's worth than that poor little fool from New York?"

"Well, if he doesn't see it yet, Dick, he's not worth bringing back, even by prayer," said the red-haired Doctor Pat.

Keith improved rapidly after he really began to come back to life. It seemed as if he had crossed some hindrance and put it behind him at last, and was going to recover soon.

The sun began to shine again in the Deane household. Don even whistled on his way to work and joy and peace came on all the faces. Daphne felt every hour as if she could shout for joy and even the nurse grew brightly happy.

Neighbors began to drop in again with eager interest to know about the invalid, and the daily bulletins in the papers ceased. The last one had announced definitely that Keith Morrell was recovering rapidly.

Even the invalid seemed to be happier, though still very weak. He lay placidly and watched his world revolve about him, well content just to lie still and smile at them. How much thinking he did on various subjects during that time he never let them know, but it was obvious that he was happy, happier than he had been before.

One day when Daphne had been reading to him, she was about to slip away thinking her patient was asleep, but he opened his eyes and smiled.

"That's good," he said, "and now, read my psalm! The first one you read me, you know."

So she read, her heart full of thanksgiving that he had asked for the Bible.

He lay with closed eyes listening, to the end, and then he opened his eyes as she finished and looked at her with a question.

"Do you suppose He will take me back again?" he asked almost shyly. "After all my indifference through the years?"

"Take you back?" said Daphne, a lilt of joy in her voice. "Why, He has never let you go! If you took Jesus as your Saviour long ago, you were born again, a child of God. You can't be *unborn*, you know."

"But you can be disinherited!" said Keith sadly.

"Earthly parents sometimes do that," said Daphne quickly, "but never our Heavenly Father. He has said: 'Him that cometh to me I will *in no wise* cast out.' You may have been willful and disobedient, and wandered far away out of *fellowship* with Him, but He has had His eye upon you all this time, and has been guiding all your circumstances so that you would finally realize that you were wrong, and come back to Him of your own free will."

He lay thinking about that for a long time. At last he looked up with a radiant smile.

"That is wonderful!" he said.

They talked for a little longer and then the nurse came and told him it was time for his nap. She said after he awoke that that was the most natural sleep he had had yet, and she believed he was going to get well by leaps and bounds now. She prophesied that he would be sitting up before the end of the week.

And so he was, to the great joy of the family, and the utter satisfaction of his two doctors, who still came together to see him, as often as they could manage to get away from their other patients.

The first caller Keith had after he was able to sit up was Mr. Sawyer of the New York firm.

"You've been mighty good and patient," said Keith, answering the kindly smile of his chief with one of gratitude. "I ought to have written you long ago to get somebody else in my place. I was thinking about it just last night, but I haven't felt able to write yet, and I didn't exactly want to dictate such a letter."

"That's all right, son, don't write. Just wait till you're

fully able to return and you'll find your desk and your work waiting for you. We fully realize that you're going to be a valuable asset to our firm some day, and we're willing to wait for you till you are quite well. You've done good work so far, even in the few months you've been with us, and I prophesy great things for your future."

Keith studied the kindly, but world-hardened face of the man before him awhile, and then answered with a smile:

"I thank you a lot for saying that. I'll think it over and write you." And the great man went away wondering what the boy had in mind, speaking in that indefinite way.

The next day came Mr. Dinsmore.

Daphne liked him at once. She felt that his visit would do the invalid a great deal of good.

"Well, well, son," said the genial elderly man, who seemed to Daphne much like the first visitor, only with something more vital in his eyes. "I certainly am glad to see you looking so well after your siege."

Half an hour later as Daphne was passing through the hall she heard a scrap of their conversation:

"Well, what are you going to do now, son? Going back to your job in New York? I was half hoping you might be lingering here, but I suppose since you are well fixed there I shouldn't be wishing to keep you here."

"I don't know," Keith answered. "I've been thinking a lot about it the last few days. Mr. Sawyer was here yesterday. He was very kind. They are willing to wait for me, and I believe there is a future there, but I'm not sure I want it."

"Oh?"

"You see," went on Keith, "I have a longing for home. I don't belong up there in that atmosphere. I have a foolish feeling that I have left my house empty long enough to be the victim of gangsters and circumstances, and I'd like to get back. Perhaps I am foolish. Perhaps I am losing my nerve or something, but I've had a sneaking desire to come back and try to find a job around here. Do you think I am crazy?"

"No, I don't think you are crazy," said the older man with a deep note of satisfaction. "Perhaps I'm too prejudiced to advise you wisely in the matter, for I've been praying for months that God would send me the right one to take the place in our business of our junior partner who went abroad six months ago and got himself called to a very flattering position there. And boy, there's no one in the world I'd rather have than the son of my dearest friend George Morrell. If you'll stay here and take hold I can offer you a junior partnership, with any prospect ahead you are willing to take."

Daphne's unwilling feet carried her out of hearing then, but her heart was in another tumult of joy and wonder. Keith wanted to stay here! With all those flattering words of that nice Mr. Sawyer in his ears he *wanted* to stay here! He was really considering it. Then he did love the old house after all. He wasn't willing to go away into the world!

But the happy light in her eyes didn't last long, for even before Mr. Dinsmore had gone out of the house the afternoon mail arrived and there was one for Keith with a shore postmark. The high smart handwriting gave her instant dread. Was this from that insufferable girl, and would it upset Keith again? Ought she perhaps to show it to the doctor or consult the nurse before giving it to him? But she couldn't do that. He was sitting up and seeing people. He seemed to be calm and fully able to cope with his own problems. She had no right. It wasn't her business to withhold his mail.

So after Mr. Dinsmore had gone she took it to him. She hated to do so lest it might take away that happy look in his face that seemed to be left from his recent visit with Mr. Dinsmore.

He looked in surprise at the letter, scowled as he noted the handwriting, tore it open impatiently as she turned away, and read it with a frown.

> Dear Keith, [he read,]
>
> I've seen by the paper that you are fully recovered now, and as there seems to be such a hostile group surrounding you I shall not venture to come to see you again.
>
> This is just to say that I am glad you are better at last, and you will be welcome here to rest and recuperate as long as you please. If you will let me know where to come for you I'll be glad to meet you, and I am willing to give you one more chance.
>
> Yours as ever,
> Anne Casper

"Daphne!" he called almost impatiently, and then as she appeared in the doorway, "I wonder if you could get me some writing paper and a pen? I've got to write a letter at once."

"I'll be glad to," said Daphne, her heart sinking, "but—do you think you ought? You don't want to put yourself back now that you are doing so well."

Her voice had a frightened quake in it.

"I shan't be but a minute," he said quickly. "This must go at once!"

She brought the writing materials and he wrote, as if he did not have to pause to consider what he said.

> Dear Anne:
>
> The nurse tells me I was very rude to you, and I apologize. It is kind of you to offer a resting place, and I thank you for your invitation, though it is quite impossible for me to accept.
>
> You and I are not of the same world and I should

have known it long ago. I am saying definitely and finally goodby, and good wishes.

Keith Morrell

He called to Ranse who happened to be passing the door and asked him to post the letter at once, air-mail and special delivery. After that he called to the nurse that he was hungry, and ate a better supper than he had yet managed since his illness. He seemed to be almost festive as Daphne came in later with another piece of toast he had demanded. But Daphne only smiled half-heartedly. She had seen the address on that letter he wrote as it lay on the kitchen table while Ranse obeyed his mother's command to wash his face and hands and comb his hair before going to the post office, and her heart was full of foreboding. If he was making up with that girl again he was only bringing more trouble to himself, for she never would live in the dear old house. She would pull it down and build a modern one, if he married her. She could not forget the look on Anne's face as she said it ought to have been pulled down long ago.

But the days went by and no Anne made her appearance on the scene.

For as soon as Anne received that letter she went in a rage to her father down in his office.

"Dad," she said imperiously, "the time has come when you must fulfill your promise about putting Keith Morrell out of a job. He has utterly refused all overtures and I want his blood to the last drop."

"All right, girlie," said her father, "it's your funeral, not mine. But don't make any mistakes. You can't undo a thing like this."

"I don't wish to undo it," she answered, her voice stiff with anger.

So he called the number and asked for Mr. Sawyer, senior.

"Mr. Sawyer," he said in his most commanding tone, "I am about to donate a handsome building to my alma mater and have been thinking of you with regard to the plans and contract. There is however one condition attached to this contract. I cannot go into details until I am assured that it will be fulfilled."

"Well, certainly, Mr. Casper, I am sure if it is anything within our power, we'll be glad to do what you want."

"I don't imagine it's a very difficult thing to do," said Casper in his haughtiest tone. "You have a young man, Morrell by name, working for you, I believe. I want him dismissed from your service at once. You are at liberty to let him know that it was done at my request."

There was a silence and then Mr. Sawyer spoke. His tone had lost its genial softness, and was hard and cold.

"I am sorry, Mr. Casper, we would like to take your contract, but your condition happens to be one that we cannot undertake to fulfill."

"What? You can't fulfill it? Man, this building will make you famous as a firm, that is, I should say will add to your honors in that line already achieved. It is to cost in the hundreds of thousands—"

"That would make no difference, Mr. Casper. It is quite impossible to do what you have asked, because the young man has already resigned from our employ, and though we have prized him highly and were intending to advance his position, he firmly refuses to reconsider. So as he is no longer with us, we couldn't possibly dismiss him, even if we were willing to do so, which *we would not be!*"

Mr. Casper hung up the telephone and stared at his daughter.

"Well, Anne, I guess you're a fool yourself this time. I shouldn't wonder if this young man is worth more than all your addlepated followers put together, even if they have the money. He's resigned and gone out of our world, and you might as well learn a lesson and then forget him."

22

THERE came a day when Keith Morrell was to be allowed to take a walk. He had already been out on the front porch several times, swathed in blankets at first, and then as he grew more accustomed to the outside world, just wearing a light overcoat. Mrs. Gassner had looked her fill from her pantry window and watched his progress from day to day, counting exactly how many times it was Daphne and how many less times it was the nurse, who brought his mid-morning orange juice, or bowl of soup. She had remarked upon it as significant to a number of callers, too.

"I should think he ought to be getting back to his job, that is if he still has one," she climaxed. "If you ask me, I'd say that Daphne is hanging onto him, and I can't think what she's about. Doesn't she know that Evelyn Avery is getting thick with the minister? She'll lose him next, and then where'll she be when this Morrell goes back to New York? He's got a girl up there, I'm morally sure, and she's been down here twice, in spite of all they say to the contrary over at Deanes'. They're so awful close-mouthed you can't get anything definite, but I'm not blind nor deaf, and if that girl didn't have something to do with that big white ambulance coming here for half an hour and then going away, I'm much mistaken."

The caller would be duly interested, and Mrs. Gassner would go on:

"But say, had you heard that the minister has had a call to a big city church and that he's considering it? And did you know he's taken that Avery girl twice to those symphunnies up in the city? Queer, isn't it, that he thinks she'd do for a minister's wife, her with her cigarettes and her wild parties, and drink. Pretty minister's wife she'd make."

"Yes," said one caller, "but I'm not so sure she wouldn't fit him better than Daphne Deane. I heard he went up to New York with Evelyn and took her to the theater!"

"Oh, you don't say! A minister! Ain't that turrible? Not that I mind going to a movie once in a while myself when Silas is away. But a minister! It's somehow different."

"Yes, I think so myself. It doesn't seem *dignified*, does it? But everything is changing today, and maybe in New York they wouldn't mind a minister's wife smoking and drinking."

"Oh, but I did hear that it wasn't a church he was called to, it was some queer kind of community center or maybe it was a new kind of school. That wouldn't be so bad."

"No, not quite," sighed the visitor.

And so Mrs. Gassner was on hand early and saw Keith Morrell start out on his walk, accompanied by Daphne.

"Of course, she would!" sniffed the Gassner contemptuously. "But where in the world are they going? Over to the Morrell place, as I live. You'd think he wouldn't ever want to see it again after his awful experience with those gangsters!"

But Keith and Daphne, utterly unconscious of her espionage, walked on into the plesant fall sunshine, round the path to the back door, across the grass to the little back gate in the white picket fence that Don had made to get through with the lawn mower when he cut the grass, over the grass and down the garden path until a friendly lilac bush hid them from sharp eyes, and then they walked more and more slowly.

"You are sure you aren't getting too tired?" asked Daphne turning anxious eyes toward Keith. "I'm afraid you are trying to go too far the first time."

He turned beaming eyes on her face and caught her hand in a quick warm clasp. "I don't feel as if I should ever be tired again. I'm so thankful to God for all He's done for me, and to you. If it hadn't been for you, I might never have come back to God. You've been wonderful taking care of me and all, but bringing me back to Him was the best thing you ever did."

Daphne's face was flooded with quick sweet color.

"No, don't say that," she protested. "God would never have let you get away from Him finally. He would have used somebody else to help. You were His, you know."

"I believe that now," he said, smiling down into her face and still holding her hand close in his, his very soul in his eyes, "but I'm mighty glad it was you God sent to help me."

"Why, I didn't do anything at all hardly, just prayed," she said earnestly.

"Ah, but how you prayed!" he said. "I didn't know what it meant to have prayers like that before. I felt those prayers, even through my sickness and pain. I've been thinking I owe a great deal to that stupid agent of mine. If he hadn't gone off to the city when he knew I was coming and he ought to have stayed at home, I would never have gone to that grandstand to wait, and seen you. And if I had never seen you—!" He paused and looked down at her again, and suddenly drew her arm within his, bringing her close to his side.

"But first," he said, holding her close as they walked

long, "there is something I've got to tell you. I've got to make it all clear about Anne Casper!" Daphne had thrilled at his touch, and walked in a daze of joy these few steps, and then the mention of that other girl's name suddenly brought her to her senses. With quick dignity she spoke, trying to make her fingers in that clasp recognize that she was only helping an invalid to take a walk, and he was trying to thank her for waiting on him while he was sick, reading to him and bringing him toast, and he hadn't meant anything personal at all by all this he had been saying. She even tried to draw her fingers away from his, casually, as if it were nothing, this thrilling handclasp, but he wouldn't let her.

"Oh," she said rather breathlessly, "don't feel you must explain anything to me. I understand of course. Don't let's talk about anything exciting. Let's have this a peaceful pleasant walk for you."

"Yes, but you don't understand," said he earnestly, "and I can't possibly have a peaceful pleasant walk until I have told you everything."

"Well, then let's go over and sit on the end of the piazza in the sunshine where you can rest, and get it over with."

She tried to laugh as if it were nothing, but her voice was strained and she had to take a deep breath to keep from trembling.

"All right!" He dropped down on the porch, too excited to realize that it was a relief to sit down again. "Now, in the first place that girl said she was my fiancée, and she never was, and never will be. It is true that I asked her once to marry me, but she turned me down absolutely when I refused to enter into a crooked game of finance that her father was carrying on. It was then I began to see what she was. I had met her with some friends whom I knew in Europe, and there was a glamour about her. She can be awfully attractive at times when she chooses to be. Oh, I was a fool of course to think—well

I don't think I ever did really get convinced that I cared for her. She put on a line I wasn't used to, and seemed— well—better than she was. But there never was much intimacy between us, she kept all her men friends at arm's length, and when I finally asked her to marry me it was more to bring the matter to a climax and find out whether there was anything to it for me or not, or whether I was just a bit light-headed with her intermittent attentions. But when she answered by her ultimatum I went away. It was then I came down here the first time and saw you——" His eyes were down. He was not looking at her. He had an almost shamed look.

"You see," he went on, "I was trying my best to think I was broken-hearted about her that day. It was the nearest I had ever come to falling in love, and I rather wanted to think it was real, and that she would come around pretty soon and be the sweet ideal I had visioned. Two days here with you were a sudden jolt in my life. I realized that I had been getting very far away from the things my mother had taught me. I realized that your home life here was sweet and sacred and the kind of thing I would want in my home, and that Anne Casper would probably never have any of those ideals. Seeing you had made a big difference. I couldn't get away from the look in your lovely face. I didn't understand my feeling. I thought it was because you looked like my mother. But then——"

He was still for a long minute and Daphne was trying to school herself to be a good adviser and friend to a man whose idol had turned to clay. But suddenly he turned and looked straight in her face:

"Daphne, are you engaged to the minister?" he asked her point blank.

And Daphne, her nerves already taut with the strain of the weeks, and the present situation, suddenly burst into laughter:

"Engaged to the minister? Me? Engaged? No, I'm not engaged to anybody—but thank heaven, not to the minister! What put that into your head?"

Keith looked a bit sheepish and the lines of his face were relieved.

"Well, I heard that next door neighbor of yours shouting it out to somebody who was deaf, the night I ran for the train. But I'm glad. It's troubled me a lot, and I couldn't go on till I knew that. You see——" suddenly he paused and then went ahead, his words fairly falling over one another:

"Oh, Daphne, I love you. I think I've loved you ever since I first saw you there on the grandstand, and I can't stop loving you even if you hate and despise me for having ever thought I could look at a girl like Anne Casper!"

"Oh!" said Daphne, suddenly hiding her happy eyes on his shoulder. "Oh, as if I could ever hate and despise you——"

"But wait, you haven't heard it all."

"I don't need to. If you say it's all right and that you love me, that is enough for me."

He drew her in a close embrace, lifting her chin and looking into her eyes. "But I want you to know it all. I went back to the city and wasn't going to see her again, but she sent me a charming letter ignoring all that was past and inviting me to dinner at her summer home at the shore. Thinking maybe she had changed I felt perhaps I ought to go. I might be making a mistake. I was a fool of course but I went. And there I found she had got her father to offer to take me into a great financial hoax that would have pauperized thousands of poor ignorant victims and made me rich, and when she found I couldn't be coaxed by her father's schemes, she made me walk out on the beach and she put on the tenderness act. She strung herself around my neck like the clinging vine and begged me for her sake— well I don't remember all she said—I don't want to—but suddenly I knew she wasn't the girl for me, and I took her hands down from my neck and told her so. Then she turned spitfire, slapped me in the face, and ran away into her father's house. There! That's all I know of her till she came here. I walked the beach that night as far as I could go, and took the early morning bus home, and I hadn't laid eyes on her till she appeared by my bed that day I had the relapse. Now, you know it all. Could you love me after a thing like that?"

"Love you?" said Daphne lifting a radiant face. "Love you? Why I think I've loved you always."

Then his lips came down to hers, and he held her in that close sweet embrace, and they sat there a long time in the sunshine together, heart to heart, tearing away the distance of the years, forgetting that there was anyone but their two selves in the world.

"Well," said Mrs. Gassner annoyedly when Silas came in earlier than usual, "I think it's about time somebody went after those two. They've been over to that old Morrell place all the afternoon and it's getting chilly. A sick man, too, out so long. That Daphne Deane hasn't any sense at all. If they don't come in pretty soon, I think maybe you ought to run over there and see if any more gangsters have got in that cellar and shot them both."

And about that time William Knox came slipping into his own house from his office, and sat down with the evening paper.

Martha bustled out from the kitchen.

"Well, you've come at last, William. I've been worrying myself sick all the afternoon about that money. I went to look in the safe and I found it wasn't there. William, that money is gone! All that money! And now they say that young Morrell is getting well and you'll probably have to tell him all about it, and if it's gone what will you do? We never could pay it back."

William lifted his erstwhile quailing old eyes and looked at her with dignity over his spectacles.

"Martha," he said in a tone he had not dared use for years, "I have attended to that money and I don't want to hear anything more about it."

"But William," said Martha aghast, "what'll we do if it can't be found?"

"Martha, that money is perfectly safe, and I don't want to hear another word about it."

"But William, suppose you were to die," she said tearfully, "what would I do about it? I wouldn't know where it was."

"You wouldn't need to know. That money is in better hands than ours."

She was still for a moment in horrible apprehension, then she began to reproach:

"Oh, William, have you given that money up? You didn't need to tell anybody. We could have kept it and nobody would have known. It would have made us comfortable in our old age, and—"

"Martha," said William giving her another severe look over his spectacles, "that money was counterfeit money. I knew it the minute I laid eyes on it, but I didn't want to tell you. Now if you say a word about it we'll both be clapped into jail when it comes time for that trial! Now, you stop talking about it, and don't mention it to anyone in the world."

Martha was blank with amazement and fear for a moment and then she turned and walked back to the kitchen, saying meekly over her shoulders as she went:

"Yes, William."

She hadn't spoken as meekly as that to him since they'd been married forty years ago.

But the two young people who had found a great love walked slowly back across the dear old garden, arms about one another, never realizing that Mrs. Gassner was looking out her kitchen window scandalized.

They went into the house, and the nurse who had just

come in from a trip to town, getting ready to leave next day, said:

"Well, I think you made a day of it. Aren't you tired to death, Mr. Morrell?"

And Daphne's mother appearing from the dining room said with a smile, "Why, you dear children, I was just coming after you. But how well you both look I believe it has done you good."

"Yes, mother," said Keith suddenly stooping down and astonishing her with a kiss on her forehead, "it has. I've a great appetite and I'm coming to the table tonight myself. I feel wonderful!"

The mother looked from one to the other, noticed that Daphne's hand was still in Keith's clasp, and comprehension swept into her eyes. Then Daphne, laughing, came and kissed her also, and the mother said with a breathless happy look:

"Why, you dear children! Where's Father? You must go and tell him right away. He'll be so glad!"

About the Author

Grace Livingston Hill is well-known as one of the most prolific writers of romantic fiction. Her personal life was fraught with joys and sorrows not unlike those experienced by many of her fictional heroines.

Born in Wellsville, New York, Grace nearly died during the first hours of life. But her loving parents and friends turned to God in prayer. She survived miraculously, thus her thankful father named her Grace.

Grace was always close to her father, a Presbyterian minister, and her mother, a published writer. It was from them that she learned the art of storytelling. When Grace was twelve, a close aunt surprised her with a hardbound, illustrated copy of one of Grace's stories. This was the beginning of Grace's journey into being a published author.

In 1892 Grace married Fred Hill, a young minister, and they soon had two lovely young daughters. Then came 1901, a difficult year for Grace—the year when, within months of each other, both her father and husband died. Suddenly Grace had to find a new place to live (her home was owned by the church where her husband had been pastor). It was a struggle for Grace to raise her young daughters alone, but through everything she kept writing. In 1902 she produced *The Angel of His Presence, The Story of a Whim,* and *An Unwilling Guest.* In 1903 her two books *According to the Pattern* and *Because of Stephen* were published.

It wasn't long before Grace was a well-known author, but she wanted to go beyond just entertaining her readers. She soon included the message of God's salvation through Jesus Christ in each of her books. For Grace, the most important thing she did was not write books but share the message of salvation, a message she felt God wanted her to share through the abilities he had given her.

In all, Grace Livingston Hill wrote more than one hundred books, all of which have sold thousands of copies and have touched the lives of readers around the world with their message of "enduring love" and the true way to lasting happiness: a relationship with God through his Son, Jesus Christ.

In an interview shortly before her death, Grace's devotion to her Lord still shone clear. She commented that whatever she had accomplished had been God's doing. She was only his servant, one who had tried to follow his teaching in all her thoughts and writing.